DIALOGUES

DIALOGUES

A Novel of Suspense

STEPHEN SPIGNESI

BANTAM BOOKS

DIALOGUES
A Bantam Book

PUBLISHING HISTORY
Bantam hardcover edition published May 2005
Bantam trade paperback edition published July 2006
Bantam mass market edition/September 2008

Published by
Bantam Dell
A Division of Random House, Inc.
New York, New York

This is a work of fiction. Names, characters, places, and incidents either are the product of the author's imagination or are used fictitiously. Any resemblance to actual persons, living or dead, events, or locales is entirely coincidental.

Excerpt from "The Baby's Room" reprinted by permission of the publishers and the Trustees of Amherst College from *The Poems of Emily Dickinson,* Thomas H. Johnson, ed., Cambridge, MA. The Belknap Press of Harvard University Press copyright © 1951, 1955, 1979, 1983 by the President and Fellows of Harvard College.

Bantam Books and the rooster colophon are registered trademarks of Random House, Inc.

ISBN 978-0-553-59199-6

Printed in the United States of America
Published simultaneously in Canada

www.bantamdell.com

OPM 10 9 8 7 6 5 4 3 2 1

To my trinity of the female spirit . . .

My wife, Pam
My mother, Lee
My sister, Janet

Lights for me in dark places

DIALOGUES

PROLOGUE

Euthanasia Day

Friday, October 11, 2002

8:00 A.M.

Today is Friday. Euthanasia day at the Waterbridge Animal Shelter.

The shelter stands at the corner of two New Haven streets in a century-old house. The house is tall, gabled, and has large windows with many panes. It is weathered and has a wraparound porch in need of painting. Many families have walked its halls and slept in its rooms since it was built.

A pretty young woman with dark brown hair moves through the rooms of the shelter. Her face is expressionless. Not empty or blank, though—it is more . . . *neutral*.

The linoleum in the house is cracked and worn. It is a hideous brown and green pattern, a style that was very popular in the fifties. She sometimes thinks what a pity it is that the house's beautiful hardwood floors were covered by the atrocious linoleum . . . but animals are messy.

The young woman wears a light-blue smock with a name badge attached to it: Tory. The smock is spotless. In one pocket of the smock is a box of Tic Tacs, the orange ones—not many people like the orange ones—and a small spiral notebook. Around her neck is a set of small bud headphones, worn like a choker. In the other pocket of her smock is a pink iPod. She always brings it to work but rarely gets a chance to listen to anything on it.

Tory is known to be pleasant and agreeable, both with her coworkers and visitors to the shelter, but sometimes she seems a little distant. She only *really* smiles for the animals.

Tory knows that certain of her duties are terrible, but she takes some comfort in knowing that they are also merciful. Her face sometimes shows this conflict. It is a state of uneasy surrender. She is resigned to what she must do, but it is difficult, and lately, with each day that passes, it becomes more so. She is not a Stephen King fan by a long shot, but she sometimes thinks about a line she heard in the movie *Pet Sematary:* "Sometimes dead is better."

This is a new job for Tory. After college, she took a job with a pharmaceutical company as a sales representative. The job had nothing to do with what she studied in college—American literature—but it paid well, and it came with benefits. She traveled around New England, visiting doctors and introducing new medicines to them, and she also worked with large hospitals, handling their drug needs. Her psychology minor often came in handy when dealing with doctors and hospital buyers, as well as with their staffs. One of the company's biggest sellers was the generic form of Pavulon, pancuronium bromide, which is used to paralyze patients before surgery.

Tory did well with the drug company and managed to put aside a fair amount of money. She lived at home with her mother, Viviana, who would only accept a small contribution to the household expenses each month from Tory, insisting that she save as much as possible. That money came in handy when Tory's position was eliminated after the company launched a secure, interactive Web site for ordering pharmaceuticals.

She was out of work almost a year—a year she spent writing, and reading, and trying to decide what she wanted to do with the rest of her life. She completed a few things she was happy with—a novella, a short story—but she couldn't stop herself from wondering if she would ever fulfill her college writing professor's hope for her. "Don't tell me a story, Tory," Mr. Mundàne used to say to her, always giving the "story/Tory" rhyme a sly little grin. "Show me life. I know you can do it." *She* still wasn't sure she knew precisely how to do it, but some of her writings were things she would not have been embarrassed to show Gabriel Mundàne.

Then, one day during that solitary time, she saw an *Animal World* documentary on cable that truly touched her, and she suddenly knew she wanted to work with animals. In fact, it felt like what people who have had a calling say it feels like. She applied at Waterbridge the following day. When she was offered training to become a euthanasia technician, she accepted, and has been working as one ever since.

This morning it happens to be raining. Heavily. Tory mostly ignores the rain, but every now and then she walks to a window, stares out at the gray sky, and watches the sheets of water pour off the house's clogged gutters.

It is cold today. The song may have lamented rainy days and Mondays, but Tory always felt that a cold and rainy Friday, especially one in October, was much sadder.

Today is Friday. Euthanasia day. The gas chamber is in the back of the building on the ground floor. It holds a few animals at a time, and Tory is the euthanasia technician who operates it.

Tory knows the black Lab will go today. And probably the terrier. The black-and-white kitten too.

Rainy Fridays are the worst, she thinks to herself as she prepares the coffee. Marcy should be here any minute. Jake'll probably be late.

Tory has already checked on and fed the animals. For some, the food she gave them would be their last meal.

Shelter workers who must deal with the unavoidable reality of euthanizing sick, unwanted, or violent animals usually adopt one of three modes of coping. Some become withdrawn and robotic and completely distance themselves from the animals. Some become sadistic. Tory has heard stories about these kinds of workers, and her loathing for them runs deep.

Then there are workers like Tory, who believe whole-

4

heartedly that they are working for a greater good, that a merciful and humane death is better than . . . well, better than any alternative other than the impossible one of finding a home for every animal.

The Waterbridge Shelter uses carbon monoxide to euthanize animals. Tory Troy is a state-certified animal euthanasia technician, and she knows it is only a matter of time before the shelter switches to lethal injection, which some say is more humane. Waterbridge is state- and city-funded, though, and change takes time. So, for the foreseeable future, Tory euthanizes the animals in a gas chamber.

Tory hears voices but continues to stare out the window at the pouring rain. The voices belong to Marcy and Jake. They arrived together, Tory thinks. Imagine that. Jake is on time.

She steps away from the window and calls out, "I'm in here, guys. . . ."

3:30 P.M.

The gas chamber is silent. Tory knows that the lethal carbon monoxide has done its job. Now comes the removal, the disposal, and the cleaning of the chamber.

Tory pulls on heavy yellow rubber gloves, dons a face mask, and steels herself for the task before her. This is getting harder, she thinks. Much harder.

Jake doesn't leave his office when Tory is emptying

the chamber, and none of the front-office staff comes anywhere near the back of the building.

This part of her job sometimes summons to Tory's mind a quote from a favorite poem of hers, Tagore's "Stray Birds": "This life is the crossing of a sea, where we meet in the same narrow ship. In death we reach the shore and go to our different worlds." She takes comfort in the image of all the euthanized animals finding their way ashore and spending the rest of eternity happy and content. Sometimes she scolds herself for being such a sentimentalist, but this does not stop the thought; her mind automatically makes the leap to such a comforting ideal.

Tory pauses a moment, her gloved hands hanging by her side, her silent headphones embracing her neck. She feels something welling up inside her, but she can't identify the feeling. Is it sadness? Anger? Panic? Fear? She doesn't know, but she does know she has never felt like this. Yes, there have been moments when she has felt *all* of those emotions, in brief flashes stabbing at her consciousness . . . but today is different.

And then, a sudden kaleidoscope of images and sounds flood her mind . . . the dogs and cats that have passed through the shelter over the past many months . . . the inside of the death chamber . . . the families walking through the kennel area, the children looking for the absolutely perfect pet . . . the pleading expressions in the eyes of the caged animals as they mentally beg these strangers to take them home—and away from this place . . . the workday chatter of the office staff, oblivious

6

to the reality of what is happening at the back of the building . . . the image of Tory herself sitting on the couch in her mother's living room on any Friday night over the past few months, hugging a pillow, her legs curled beneath her, utterly unable to eat a thing until, at the earliest, Saturday night . . . the looming shadows the old house throws when the sun hits it a certain way . . . and then, once again, the animals . . . the animals . . .

Tory reaches out and grabs the door handle of the gas chamber.

She closes her eyes a moment and takes a breath. Then she opens her eyes . . . and then she opens the door.

my kat henry
by victoria troy

i have a kat. his name is henry. he ~~is~~ has blak furr and his nose is wite. i love my kat henry very much. sometimes he sleeps on my pilow at night. he purrs ~~becau~~ when I pet him. sometimes he wakes me up when he purrs. ~~Two~~ Ate days ago my dady made henry cry. he stepped ~~in~~ on his tail. i cried too when daddy stepped on my kat's tail. so i pet henry and made him feel beter. he rubed his nose on me and he likes to eat treets.

the end

1

Tory Troy
Dr. Baraku Bexley

"I've been thinking about suicide lately. A lot."

"How often is 'a lot'?"

"At least once a day, although sometimes I may go a couple of days without thinking about it."

"When you say you've been thinking about it, what does that mean? Are you imagining ways of doing it? Are you thinking about where you would do it?"

"No, I know how I'll do it."

"Yes?"

"Pills."

"What kind of pills?"

"Painkillers. I've got hidden away on the outside eighty-seven hydrocodone tablets. You know: the generic of Vicodin. I got them from a friend who had a prescription for a hundred and only used thirteen. She had some kind of really bad disk problem in her back, but they fixed it and she didn't need the pills anymore. So she gave them to me. I figure I could take the whole batch in three or four swallows and within a few hours I'd be dead."

"What if you don't die?"

"Oh, I'll die."

"How can you be so sure?"

"I did my homework."

"What does that mean?"

"I looked up hydrocodone on the Internet. The lethal dose, depending on tolerance, could be anywhere from around fifty or sixty milligrams up. If I take all eighty-seven, I'll be getting over six hundred fifty milligrams, which should be plenty for someone my size. I'm only a hundred nine pounds. Some kid who weighed eighty-nine pounds died from taking only ten pills. I'd say eighty-seven ought to do the trick."

"Yes, I suppose it would."

"Plus I forgot to tell you—I'm going to down them with tequila."

"You're talking like this is a done deal."

"No, of course not. I'd have to get out of here first, right? And in all probability, that's somewhat unlikely. It's just that you asked how I would do it, so I told you."

"Could you tell me why you think about killing yourself so much?"

"Not really."

"Are you depressed?"

"What does that mean?"

"Are you filled with a sense of the utter meaninglessness of life? Do the routine activities of life like eating, working, reading, watching movies, having sex, and other normal events hold no interest for you? Do you spend a lot of time sleeping?"

"No to all of the above. I don't think life is meaningless. I love to eat, I don't normally mind going to work, I read constantly, I'm at Blockbuster at least twice a week, and if I'm not in a relationship in which I'm having regular sex, I masturbate a lot. As for sleeping all the time, I wish. My life is—was—so busy I can barely squeeze in six hours a night."

"Suicide is usually looked to as a last resort solution—what someone will consider when their life becomes unbearable, unlivable. You sound like you're engaged with your own life and relatively content."

"I am. At least I was . . . until I got locked up, that is."

"So I'll ask again. Why have you been thinking about taking your own life?"

"Don't you want to know where I would do it?"

"Excuse me?"

"You asked me if I've been thinking about where I would do it."

"Yes, you're right. I did. So, have you?"

"Yes."

"And where would that be?"

"I don't know."

"Are you toying with me?"

"No, not at all. I'm telling you the truth when I say that I have been thinking about where to do it. I just haven't decided yet."

"What's holding up your decision?"

"Lots of things. Like who will find me. What kind of mess I'll make. I know I'll . . . make a mess when I die, and I don't want whoever finds me to have to clean it up. For a while, I was thinking about walking into the ocean. Maybe down at Fort Hale Park. But then I risk the chance of no one finding my body. And I want to be cremated, so they'll need that."

"This conversation is leading me to a conclusion I do not want to make."

"Oh? And what's that?"

"I think you have already decided to kill yourself and that all these assurances to me that you're not going to do it are your way of deflecting me from further inquiry or action. I think you know that I am obligated to act if I feel that you are a serious danger to yourself, and you are thus trying to convince me that this is all just an intellectual exercise rather than your true plan."

"I'm not going to kill myself. But I do think about it. What are you going to do? Ha-ha, have me committed? Last time I looked this was still America and I was free to say and think anything I fucking want to."

"That may be true in most situations. But this is not a typical situation. If it was, you would not be sitting there, would you? I would not have *voluntarily* come to you to discuss these things, right? So the normal rules do not apply, and if I think you're on the verge of suicide, I have to put it in my report and act."

"Court-ordered bullshit. I'm already on a suicide watch, for Christ's sake."

"Perhaps. Shall we move on?"

"Okay with me."

"Tell me why you're here."

"You know why I'm here. I'm incarcerated . . . is *institutionalized* a better word? . . . and the court is making me talk to you."

"I want you to tell me what you did and why you did it."

"You know what I did. As for why I did it, you'll have to figure that out yourself. Isn't that what they're paying you for?"

"In a sense."

"Well, then . . ."

"Let's put aside the reason you are here and talk about some other things that are—were—going on in your life."

"Fine with me."

"Can you tell me about your job?"

"Sure. But isn't all that in my records?"

"Yes, but I'd like to hear it from you. What is it you do?"

"I'm a certified animal euthanasia technician. I make $451.92 a week. That's a whopping twenty-three five a year."

"And what is a certified animal euthanasia technician?"

"Every Friday afternoon, I euthanize all the cats and dogs in the animal shelter that have not been adopted by then."

"How do you euthanize these animals?"

13

"We use a gas chamber."

"What is your role in this process?"

"Process. You guys are funny. Only shrinks would describe mass execution as a process. Did you all get that from Auschwitz? I understand the Nazis were big fans of euphemisms."

"Please do not trivialize or make fun of the Holocaust. I lost my grandfather at Auschwitz."

"Sorry."

"So, what is your role in this process, please?"

"I take the animals from their cages and place them in the gas chamber."

"Don't they try and run away?"

"They all have choke chains around their necks, even the cats, and the room has steel rings embedded in the floor every three feet in a grid. We start in the far left corner and hook one animal to each ring. We can do around a dozen animals at a time, although usually it's only five or six."

"What happens after they're all hooked to the floor?"

"I close the door and bolt it with a sliding bar. The room is airtight once the door is closed. Ironically, the animals would probably all suffocate to death if we just left them in there. The air would run out after a while. But that would be traumatic and painful. And take a long time. So we try to get it over with as quickly as possible."

"What happens after you bolt the door?"

"I sign a form."

"What kind of form?"

"It's a form that lists the animals I put inside the gas

chamber—you know, *one brown terrier, one black-and-white cat . . .*"

"And then what happens?"

"I hand the clipboard to my supervisor, Jake. He double-checks everything and then he signs it. A copy of this form has to go to the state every week."

"What does Jake do after he signs the form?"

"Well, usually, he goes back to his office and finishes eating his lunch. He likes a late lunch."

"You know what I'm asking."

"We both walk over to a computer panel on the wall outside the gas chamber. We then go through a specific procedure that I had to learn cold before I could get my certification."

"Go on."

"Jake does all the talking. 'Nine animals confirmed for euthanasia. Door seal confirmed. Quantity of lethal agent confirmed for nine animals. Initiating.' Then I push a button. But I forgot something."

"And what is that?"

"Before we start the procedure, he puts on a CD."

"He plays music? For the animals?"

"No, they can't hear it. He plays it for us, although he really plays it for himself."

"What does he play?"

"The White Album."

"The Beatles?"

"Yeah."

"What track?"

" 'Helter Skelter.' "

"I see. What happens after you push the button?"

"A thermometer lights up."

"Excuse me?"

"A gauge that looks like a thermometer lights up on the main panel and a red light starts to rise to the top of the tube."

"I understand."

"On the side of this tube are numbers from one to ten. Supposedly, once the red hits the two, all the animals are asleep. I've never looked to see if that was true, though. There's no window in the door. Once it hits five, they're not supposed to be breathing anymore, and when it gets to ten, their hearts have stopped. That's about a six percent CO concentration. Fatal."

"What happens after it gets to ten?"

"Nothing. Jake goes back to his desk and I go do whatever else I have to do."

"What about the animals?"

"A timer starts as soon as the gauge hits ten. A bell rings after fifteen minutes. Then we can get them out."

"Who opens the door?"

"Me. I'm the tech."

"Could you talk about that, please?"

"No."

"Why not?"

"Because I don't want to."

"I think it would help your situation if I wrote in my report that you were cooperative. Plus I do believe it will also help you personally to talk about it."

"What do you want to know?"

16

"Take me through what happens after the timer bell rings."

"The first thing I do is go into the rear storeroom and get the disposal cart."

"And what is that?"

"It's a big folding cart on wheels. It holds a thick rubber bag that is stretched open. The bag has a heavy zipper running across its top."

"The animals go in this bag?"

"Their bodies do. Yeah."

"Do they all fit?"

"The bag holds the equivalent in weight of about a dozen cats or six dogs. Sometimes we need two bags."

"Go on."

"I wheel the cart over to the gas chamber and place it on the right side of the door. Then I put on thick rubber gloves and a mask and then I unbolt the door and open it."

"Doesn't gas get out into the room?"

"There's a reverse exhaust system that sucks out all the gas and then runs it through an afterburner that renders it nontoxic. It's an OSHA thing. By the time I open the door, the air inside the room is perfectly safe. In fact, I'm pretty sure the door won't open until the gas is completely cleared. And there are CO detectors throughout the building too."

"Why the gloves and mask, then?"

"It's a mess inside the room. The animals' bowels and bladders let go when they die."

"I see. What about the smell?"

"The exhaust system gets rid of some of it, but it's still pretty rank."

"What do you do next?"

"I start with the animal closest to the door. I unhook the choke chain, pick it up, and carry it outside to the disposal cart. Everything goes in the bag. The collar, the choke chain. Everything. They're all made of copper or tin, so they melt in the crematorium."

"What do you think about as you're emptying out the gas chamber?"

"Anything but the animals."

"How so?"

"I don't think about the animals and I don't look at their faces."

"Could you talk about that?"

"I knew these animals. Even though we only had them for a week or so, I got to know every one of them. They each had a personality too. And they were all so trusting. They were always happy to see me. And they were incredibly grateful for any attention I gave them."

"This is difficult for you to talk about."

"You bet your ass it's difficult. These animals were my friends. And I had to kill them. What bothered me the most was that they came with me willingly, just happy to be with me. And then I locked them in a room and fucking killed them. I completely betrayed their trust in me."

"Why did you take this job in the first place?"

"I thought I could do some good."

"How so?"

"You know . . . helping find homes for animals . . . helping kids pick out a pet . . . that kind of stuff."

"But you knew you'd be involved in euthanizing them too, didn't you?"

"By the end of the job interview I did, yes . . . but that's not why I applied at the shelter."

"Why don't you tell me about that?"

"I applied at the shelter for an office job. I wanted to man the front desk and take in the animals people found or couldn't take care of anymore. Like I said—to help. A lot of animals came from elderly people."

"What do you mean?"

"A lot of elderly people have pets, and when the old person dies, no one in the family wants to take their animal. So they bring it to us."

"What do they tell you when they bring in these animals?"

"Usually that there's no one to take care of it and they want us to find it a good home."

"What do you tell them?"

"That we'll try."

"And do you?"

"Absolutely. People come to the shelter every day looking for a cat or dog. And we always take our time with them and make sure that they are comfortable with the animal they pick out. We don't like anyone to walk out without a pet."

"So why all the killing . . . euthanizing?"

"Because we don't have the money or the space to keep animals longer than a week. They come in all the time and there's just no way we could keep them all until they were placed with families."

"You keep them a week?"

"Yeah, but it's not a calendar week. It's seven whole days. We start counting on the day after they arrive, and they are euthanized on the first Friday after the seven days are up."

"So theoretically, some animals can stay alive longer than seven days."

"You know, you're pretty quick for a shrink. Yes. That's true. Weekend animals get almost two weeks."

"You're open on Sundays?"

"Just for drop-offs. Tommy works one day a week for us. He spends Sundays at the shelter and takes in any animals that people bring by."

"So Saturday and Sunday animals are pretty lucky."

"Sure. We start counting on Monday, and seven days from Monday is the following Sunday, which means they get to live until the next Friday. Almost two weeks. Thursday's animals are the unluckiest."

"How so?"

"We start counting on Friday, which means that the seventh day is a Thursday, which means that they get whacked the very next day."

"So, getting back to your duties. What happens after you empty the room and the bag is full?"

"I zip it up and then go get the hose."

"The hose?"

"Yeah. I get a heavy black hose from the storeroom and hook it up to a faucet on the outside wall of the chamber. Then I open up the sealed drain in the middle of the floor, and then I hose down the floor and walls until they're clean."

"Then what happens?"

"I put everything away, close off the room, lock the panel with a password that only Jake and I know, and then call the crematorium."

"What do you do after you make the call?"

"I have coffee."

"Coffee?"

"Yeah. By then, it's usually near four, and I like a cup of coffee in the afternoon. By the time I finish, Evelyn is there with the truck."

"What happens then?"

"She backs up to a loading dock at the rear of the building and I open the overhead door. She then wheels a portable lift to the edge of the loading dock, and I wheel out the disposal cart. She attaches a heavy hook to a steel ring on the bag and then turns on the lift to carry the bag into the box of the truck."

"I'm just curious. What does it say on the side of the truck?"

"Nothing. The whole truck is painted dark blue and there is no lettering anywhere on it."

"I see. Go on."

"There's not much more to it. She puts the bag on top of the other bags she's already picked up and then she's gone."

"What do you do then?"

"I go feed the animals that have come in that afternoon."

"What's that like?"

"It's kind of uplifting, to tell the truth. The newcomers are either frightened or all worked up, and feeding them and giving them water always calms them down. They're all just so goddamned happy to be getting even the slightest bit of human attention."

"Do you ever play with them?"

"Sometimes. Although I'm not supposed to."

"Why's that?"

"Well, Jake'd say it's because I'm not getting paid to play with the animals and that I've got other work to do. But Jake can be an asshole, and, to tell you the truth, I believe I *am* getting paid to play with the animals. I'm not talking about spending hours with them tossing a ball or wrestling with them. But I believe that part of my job is to make sure that the animals that come into the shelter are cared for, and I think playing with them and giving them attention is part of taking care of them."

"You make a good point. Do you ever get into trouble for thinking like this?"

"Sure. Jake gets pissed as hell if he comes into the kennel and sees me fooling around with a dog or playing with one of the cats. But screw him."

"You mentioned . . . Tommy? What's he like?"

"I have no idea. I've only met him briefly a couple of times. I told you, he only works Sundays. I'm never there on a Sunday."

"Who else did you work with?"

"There's Jake, of course. He's in charge of the place. And in the office are Marcy, Ann, Philip, and Teresa. And then there's Renaldo, who's the janitor."

"Do you like these people?"

"I suppose. Marcy, mostly. She and I get along."

"Do you not get along with the others?"

"No . . . I do . . . but they bother me sometimes."

"Why?"

"Because none of them seems to realize how they earn their money."

"That might be a little unfair, don't you think?"

"Why do you say that?"

"It seems somewhat self-righteous."

"I disagree."

"Do you really believe that you are the only one at the shelter who fully understands that part of your job is to dispose of unwanted animals?"

"I didn't say that."

"Forgive me if I misunderstood you. Perhaps you could explain more clearly what you meant?"

"I know they all understand what we have to do. How could they not? It's just that it doesn't seem to bother them very much. I don't understand that. They all say they love animals, and yet they work in a place that kills cats and dogs every week."

"But you work there too."

"Yeah, I know."

"That really doesn't seem to make all that much sense. It's inconsistent. If the underlying function of the place bothered you so much, why didn't you just quit? Before it got to this."

"I have a cousin who was an ROTC officer. He served during the Cuban Missile Crisis. He once told me that he went into the navy knowing it meant he'd be training as a professional killer. He knew what ROTC meant. But when he had to strap on a .45 and get ready to board a Russian ship, the idea of *being* a professional killer hit him hard. Maybe that's the kind of thing that went through my mind . . . I don't know. He's a pacifist now. He always says, 'The Pacific made me a pacifist.' "

"Isn't it possible that you are just as unfeeling and hypocritical as you judge all the rest of them to be?"

"No, I'm not."

"But you work there too."

"How many times are you going to tell me that I work there too?"

"I am simply trying to understand you. You say you are empathetic toward the animals and that it bothers you to have to euthanize them, and yet you continue to work in the very position that requires hands-on participation in their killing. You are not working in the office like Philip and Marcy. You are not simply sweeping up and washing the floors like Renaldo. You are, in a sense, flipping the switch."

"You do not have to remind me."

"Well, then please try to explain to me why you did not just quit."

"I don't know."

"My job is to determine your state of mind and to make a recommendation to the court. You really should try to be more helpful in communicating your true feelings and thoughts to me. It could be a matter of life and death for you."

"Is that supposed to scare me?"

"No. Not at all. But once I sign my report, it's all over. So let's try to get through this as evenly as possible. And you should also know that I will be speaking with others about you as well."

"Others? Who?"

"I'll not say right now."

"My mother?"

"Probably."

"No."

"Ms. Troy—"

"I won't allow it."

"You don't have a say in the matter. But I can assure you that any and all interviews I do will be with the intent of delivering as honest an assessment of your current state of mind as possible."

"Do you think I'm crazy?"

"Tory, listen. I do not want to write a report that will leave the judge no other choice than to recommend . . . well, let's just say, I would like to arrive at conclusions that work in your favor."

"My favor? That means you have to say I'm crazy, right?"

"No. Simply not mentally competent to stand trial. If I find that you *are* fit to stand trial, then the jury will determine if you were sane when you . . . when the precipitating incidents occurred."

"All right. What do you want to know?"

"Why don't we begin with how you decided you wanted to work at the animal shelter."

2

Dr. Baraku Bexley
District Attorney Brawley Loren

"Can you give us a preliminary report?"

"No. I am nowhere near ready to show you anything."

"Doctor, I hope I do not have to remind you that you are on the taxpayers' nickel, and that every day that goes by without you filing a report is another day that justice goes unserved?"

"No, District Attorney. You do not have to remind me that I am being paid by the commonwealth. I am made aware of that every time I cash my biweekly check and see the state crest above my name. But please listen carefully. I hope I do not have to remind *you* that I am first and foremost a doctor and that it is my obligation to treat this young lady as a *patient*, not a suspect."

"She *is* a suspect."

"That is not my concern. I was commissioned by the court to examine this woman and determine if she is mentally competent to stand trial. My conclusion will affect everything that happens from the moment I sign my name to the report, and it will also impact greatly the future of this young woman."

"Yes, Doctor. This is not the first time we have dealt with a court-ordered psychiatric examination."

"You needn't sound so smug."

"Well, I apologize if I come off as a little irritated. I hope you will forgive my tone and any future insults to your dignity."

"Now you give me sarcasm."

"Doctor, please listen to me carefully. This young lady—your 'patient'—has been charged with six capital murders. Six premeditated Murder One charges. Now, I fully understand that there is a good chance that if you declare that she is mentally incompetent, she will avoid trial and spend the rest of her life in a mental hospital, enjoying three meals a day, complete health and dental care, and cable TV. I think they even get HBO. This upsets me, sir. Six bodies are lying in the morgue due to the actions—sorry—the *alleged* actions of this girl. And you may be the one person who will prevent justice from being served. Thus my sarcasm and impatience with you and your 'profession.' "

"I will not rush my examination, nor will I make any statements that I do not fully believe. I know what you want, District Attorney. Regardless of what I believe to be the truth, you want me to state that she is fully competent and that she is capable of understanding the charges against her and participating in her own defense. You will then be able to prosecute her to the fullest extent of the law and work diligently toward guaranteeing her a lethal injection. But what if a jury later decides that she was insane at the time of the murders, sir?"

"I don't really care, Doctor. We've got enough evidence to convict her, and convict her is what I want to do. Whether she was nuts or not does not bring those poor people back to life, now, does it?"

"No, it does not. But unless you can rewrite the law on your own, she may not be legally responsible for the crimes if she was not mentally competent. And, again, it is my job to make the determination whether or not she is able to understand this and stand trial."

"I don't like the way this is heading. I can try to get you pulled off this case, you know."

"Go right ahead. You'll be assuring the defense of grounds for an appeal and everything will have to start all over again. And what makes you think the next doctor the court assigns to this case will make you happy? And also, by the way, what makes you so sure I'm going to issue a report that will state she is incompetent?"

"I've just got a feeling about you. You come off like an anti-death-penalty liberal. It's just a vibe I'm picking up off you, but I feel like you are going to look for any possible hook, no matter how weak or improbable, to hang an *incompetent* label on her."

" 'An anti-death-penalty liberal,' you say? Why, thank you, Counselor. I'm flattered. I've always loved being prejudged. Why don't you simply wait for my report, though, before coming to a conclusion about me? Is that too much to ask?"

"No, Doctor, it is not. And I do not have a choice in the matter, now, do I? I will tell you this, though. If you come back with a determination of mental incompetence, I will go to the judge and demand a second examination, no matter how much it costs or how long it takes."

"That's fine with me, Mr. Loren. You certainly don't mind spending those taxpayers' nickels when it's for something you want, eh?"

"We're finished, Doctor."

"Always a pleasure, Counselor."

3

Dr. Baraku Bexley
Mrs. Viviana Troy

"How long have you and Tory's father been divorced?"

"About fifteen years. Is she going to be put to death, Doctor?"

"I think it's much too early to be thinking along those lines, ma'am. Why don't you just answer my questions and we'll leave that for later, okay?"

"Yes, I suppose. It's just that I love her and worry about her so much."

"I understand. How could you not worry? You're her mother."

"Yes."

"So you and her father divorced fifteen years ago, correct? Could you tell me why you two split up?"

"He drank. And he hit me. And he cheated."

"I see. All three, eh? When did this behavior toward you begin?"

"When we were dating."

"And yet you married him anyway?"

"I loved him."

"Did your daughter witness any of his physical violence toward you?"

"Oh, yes. Her father and I were together until she was in her early teens, so she saw everything."

"Did he ever physically abuse your daughter?"

"Do I have to answer that?"

"No, of course not. You are not under oath or on trial. And this is not a deposition either."

"Why do you want to know that?"

"Mrs. Troy, I am a doctor who has been given the assignment of determining if your daughter is mentally fit to stand trial. What I can tell you is that the more I know about your daughter, the more accurate will be my determination, which will be best for everyone in the long run."

"I understand. Then, yes. The answer to your question is yes, my husband did abuse our daughter."

"Physically?"

"Yes."

"How?"

"With his belt. And his fists. And . . ."

"Go on."

"His cigars."

"He burned her with the ends of his cigars?"

"Yes."

"Did you ever tell anyone about your husband's abuse of you and your daughter?"

"No."

"Why not?"

"I was afraid we would end up on the street with no money and nowhere to live."

"How did your daughter react when her father abused her?"

"She fought back."

"I see. Did your husband ever sexually abuse your daughter?"

"Yes."

"How?"

"With his hands."

"Did you know about this when it was occurring?"

"Yes."

"Did your daughter fight back when he molested her?"

"Not at first, but as she got older, she did."

"How?"

"She would lock herself in her room when she knew he was going to come to her. Sometimes she would fight with him. And eventually, she stabbed him in the eye with her nail file."

"What happened?"

"I took him to the emergency room. But he lost the eye."

"All right. Let's move on to the years after you and your husband divorced. What was your daughter like after your husband was out of the house?"

"She was like a completely different girl."

"How so?"

"She was happier. She smiled more. She ate better."

"You do know what your daughter is charged with, yes?"

"Yes."

"Six counts of premeditated murder."

"Yes."

"And you do understand that she faces the death penalty if she is determined fit to stand trial and a jury finds her guilty?"

"Yes."

"Well then, ma'am, let me ask you this. Is there anything you think I should know that might help your daughter?"

"She always loved animals."

"I see."

"She always loved animals."

4

Tory Troy
Dr. Baraku Bexley

"Last time we met, you were telling me about your decision to apply for a job at the animal shelter."

"Did you talk to my mother?"

"Yes."

"What did she tell you?"

"I can't talk about it."

"Why not?"

"Because it's unethical and inappropriate."

"Even though she told you stuff about me?"

"*Precisely* because she told me 'stuff' about you, Tory. Now, can we move on, please? What made you decide to apply for the job at the animal shelter?"

"*Animal World.*"

"The cable channel?"

"Yes."

"How did *Animal World* spur you to apply for a job at an animal shelter?"

"Can't you figure that part out?"

"I'd like to hear it from you, please."

"It was because of a documentary. About leopards."

"Go on."

"The documentary showed a bunch of assholes with cameras and guns and trucks invading a wildlife area where families—leaps—of leopards lived. That's what a group of leopards is called. Did you know that? A leap of leopards. Isn't that funny?"

"Yes, Tory. It's hilarious. Please continue."

"I remember it was raining out when I was watching the show. I was home alone and I had just microwaved some macaroni and cheese. I like it with ketchup, if you can believe it. But it makes sense when you think about it. What is ketchup but pureed tomatoes, right? You wouldn't think it odd if I cut up some fresh tomato and mixed it in, or even if I bought a can of those Contadina diced tomatoes my mother likes to use and mixed those into the mac and cheese, right?"

"Tory . . ."

"Sorry. So, like I said, I had just eaten and I was alone watching *Animal World*. I was in the living room. I think. I may have been lying in bed. I'm not sure."

"You can't remember where you were in your house when you were watching a TV show that had such an enormous impact on you?"

"Crazy, right? Oh. I probably shouldn't say that. No, I really can't remember. Let's say I was in the living room, because that's probably where I would have flopped after I ate."

"Okay. You were in the living room."

"Yes. The show started at eight."

"What do you remember about the show?"

"I remember everything about it."

"How did it begin?"

"Sunrise on the veld."

"The veld?"

"It's an open grazing area in Africa."

"I always thought it was veldt."

"It's either."

"All right. Go on."

"They showed this beautiful expanse of grass waving in the wind, and then the camera moved to show leopards walking across the veld."

"What do you recall about these animals?"

"They were so incredibly beautiful my heart almost stopped beating. That's what I recall about them. Their coats were gorgeous, their limbs were muscular and perfectly shaped. Their eyes were clear, and focused, and serious. They were in complete control of their environment. They did not need us, that's for sure."

"What does that mean?"

"That means that mankind is completely irrelevant to these magnificent creatures. Every human on earth could die tomorrow from some weird exotic virus and those spectacular animals wouldn't miss a beat."

"How did this realization make you feel?"

"Embarrassed."

"How so?"

"Even though I was tens of thousands of miles away from Africa, and I was watching something that had probably been taped months earlier, I felt like an intruder. I felt like we did not belong there and that I was seeing something I had no business seeing."

"All this went through your mind during the introduction?"

"Yes."

"How did you feel when the camera crew and all the others involved in the show appeared?"

"Horrified. I had just experienced some kind of epiphany, Dr. Bexley . . . of insight, I guess you could call it . . . and then there they were . . . these guys in khakis and sunglasses, driving jeeps and trucks that you just knew were belching out exhaust smoke . . . barreling through the grass like they goddamned owned it. It was disgusting."

"So what did you do?"

"I sat there hugging a pillow to my chest and sobbing."

"Did you watch the entire program?"

"No. I couldn't."

"How much of it did you watch?"

"I turned it off after I saw a mother leopard start growling and hissing when a cameraman got too close to her cub. That was it. But I'll tell you this, Dr. B. As I changed the channel with the remote, I said a prayer that mama would bite somebody's something off."

"You prayed that someone would get hurt?"

"Yes, I did. And I'm not ashamed to say it."

"Why would you wish such a tragedy upon someone you don't know and who never did a thing to hurt you?"

"Because he and all his cohorts upset me. They shouldn't have been bothering that mother leopard, and they deserved to be punished for it."

"Very well."

"Boy, you sure are making a lot of notes. I must have struck a nerve."

"Just routine note-taking, Tory. The same type of recording I do in all my interviews."

"Yeah, right."

"Let's continue, please. Is there anything else about the *Animal World* documentary that you remember affecting you in any way?"

"No, the leopard stuff was what really bothered me. *Baraku*. Is that an African name?"

"It's probably Bantu, but I'm not positive of that."

"Bantu?"

"The official language of Tanzania."

"Is that where your people come from?"

"Yes, my father emigrated to the United States. Can we get back to the night of the documentary, please?"

"How old were you when he came here?"

"I was born here. The documentary?"

"Oh, all right."

"You turned off the documentary after it made you cry. What led to you then deciding to apply for a job at the animal shelter?"

"I just decided that I wanted to help animals."

"How long after that night did you apply?"

"The next morning."

"You went to the animal shelter the very next morning to apply for a job?"

"Yes. As soon as they opened."

"Can you tell me about that?"

"There's nothing really to tell. It's only a few miles from my house over the Q-Bridge. I've known about it a long time. I just walked in and went to the front desk. I told a girl that I now know was Marcy that I was looking for a job, and the next thing I know I was sitting in Jake's office."

"Tell me about that interview."

"I sat in a chair in front of his desk and looked around. Jake wasn't there yet. On the walls were posters of animals and stuff about procedures and government stuff. He had that stupid cat poster too."

"Which one is that?"

"The one showing a cat hanging from a tree branch with 'Hang in there' written on it?"

"Yes, I've seen that."

"Well, I sat there and I notice he's got a CD player on the cabinet behind his desk. Propped up against it is the Beatles' *White Album*. Remember what I told you earlier about that?"

"Yes, Jake played 'Helter Skelter' as the animals were dying."

"Right. The sick fuck. As I was debating about whether or not to get up and look through his CDs, the

40

door opened and in walked Jake. In *ran* Jake, I should say."

"How so?"

"Type A type. Rushing around, always nervous. Made me crazy."

"What did he say?"

"Nothing at first. He just sat down at his desk and picked up my application and started to read it. Then he looks up and says, 'You're Victoria Troy.' It wasn't even a question, it was a statement. So I nodded, and then said, 'Tory.'"

"How were you feeling during this?"

"A little edgy, I suppose. I got the sense that I was interrupting him, that he didn't really want to have to spend time with me right then."

"Do you think you were projecting somewhat? From what you've told me, he didn't seem to suggest impatience with you, just a sense of being distracted and busy."

"I suppose. It's just that he didn't even say hello when he walked in the room, and that kind of threw me a little."

"I understand. Go on."

"Well, after he finished reading my application, he says to me, 'We don't have any openings for office staff.' Just like that. Blunt. Cold. So I got up, figuring the interview was over, and he said, 'We do have something else, though, if you're interested.' I sat back down again and said, 'I am.'"

"What was going through your mind?"

"Actually, I thought he was going to offer me a janitor's job, or maybe a job cleaning cages."

"Were you surprised when he told you what the job actually consisted of?"

"*Surprised* is too tame to describe how I felt."

"How so?"

"At first, I didn't believe him. I didn't really have much knowledge about the whole animal shelter mojo, you know? I thought he was making stuff up to goof on me."

"Why would he do such a thing?"

"He wouldn't. Which is why I'm a bit of an idiot."

"Tell me what he said and what happened after that."

"He started right off. 'The job is animal euthanasia technician.' I was speechless."

"Why?"

"Because I immediately understood what he was talking about. He was talking about a job putting animals to death."

"Yes."

"You know what I felt like? I felt like I did when I realized how intrusive the *Animal World* crew was in the African veld. Thoughts started rushing through my mind, and the loudest one was a sense of horror."

"You said you were horrified when watching the documentary. How did the feelings you experienced sitting across from Jake compare with the ones you had when watching the documentary?"

"They were actually very similar. It was surreal. Here I was, a grown human person, sitting across from another grown human person who had his own desk, and papers, and clipboards, and pens . . . and we were talking about a job as a killer. I would get paid for killing living creatures."

"It does sound like you had a very strong visceral reaction to the title *euthanasia technician* and that you were quite repulsed."

"You got it, Doc."

"Well, then, Tory, I must ask the question. Why didn't you simply get up, say 'no thanks,' and walk out the door?"

"Because I couldn't."

"Why not?"

"Because I had to know."

"What the job entailed?"

"Yes."

"Why?"

"Why do people like to read about atrocities? Why do we say 'Ooh, that's terrible' when we look at pictures of concentration camp torture victims, but we don't look away?"

"You had to know?"

"Yes. I had to know."

"Very well. Go on."

"So after I sat there for a minute or so without saying anything, Jake finally says to me, 'Did you understand what I said?' I nodded and said, 'You're talking about killing the animals.' He said, 'We use the term *euthanize*, but yes.'"

"Then what happened?"

"He asked me if I was interested and I nodded."

"How did he respond?"

"He said, 'Good,' and then he stood up and said, 'Come with me.' "

"What was going through your mind?"

"I was wondering if he was going to make me kill an animal. You know—like a test?"

"Now, Tory. Obviously that would never be legally allowed. Did you really think he was going to ask you to euthanize an animal?"

"No, I guess not. Deep down I knew he couldn't make me do that, and I also knew that I would have refused if he had asked me to."

"And yet you went through the training and took the job."

"Yes, I did."

"So where did Jake take you?"

"To the death chamber."

5

Dr. Baraku Bexley
Gabriel Mundàne

"Thank you for seeing me, Mr. Mundane."

"It's *Mun-daah-ne*—there's an accent grave over the *a*."

"My sincerest apologies."

"Oh, no problem. I'm simply correcting you."

"Thank you. People are sensitive about the pronunciation of their name."

"I suppose. But with me, it's more of a technical thing . . . a literary thing, rather than a matter of family pride."

"Can you tell me how long you taught Tory Troy?"

"I had her for a course in her senior year—a two-semester course. Creative Writing. It lasted the full school year."

"I see. What do you remember about her?"

"Oh, I remember quite a lot about her, Doctor. She

was an excellent student, and we got to know each other fairly well."

"Why's that?"

"Mainly because she always turned in far more work than was required for the course. I always left the door open for my students to write more than I asked for if they felt so inspired. I promised to read whatever they wrote and comment on it too. Not very many students, I'm sorry to say, took me up on the offer. But Tory was different. She seemed to write constantly, and she kept me busy."

"Do you know why I am here?"

"Yes. Tory is in trouble. I've seen the papers."

"She has been charged with six counts of premeditated murder, and I have been assigned the task of determining if she is mentally fit to stand trial."

"You're going to decide if she's crazy or not?"

"No. I am going to decide if she is mentally competent to understand the charges against her and participate in her own defense. If I say she is fit, then it will be up to a jury to decide if she was insane at the time of the alleged murders."

"I see. Seems like a no-brainer, though."

"And why is that?"

"Well, wouldn't you have to be crazy to kill six people the way she is supposed to have done it?"

"That remains to be seen. Can you tell me if there was anything in Tory's behavior, or in her writing, that had to do with animals, or euthanasia?"

"Both."

"Excuse me?"

"Both. She wrote a short story for my class about an animal—a pigeon—being euthanized."

"Would you happen to have a copy of that story?"

"Yes, I do. I never throw away my students' work. You never know who will be the next Salinger—or the next Stephen King. And when Tory made the news, I looked up her record."

"Indeed. The story?"

"Of course. It's in this file cabinet. Please bear with me while I look for it."

"Take your time."

"No . . . nope . . . no . . . ah, here it is. 'Skyline Pigeon.' "

"May I make a copy for my files?"

"Of course. There are some other works in here you are free to copy as well. There's a novella titled *The Baby's Room* that I especially like."

"Thank you very much for your help, Mr. Mundàne."

"You are very welcome. And please give Tory my best wishes and tell her she will be in my prayers. I always liked Tory. In fact, we spent a few lunch hours together talking about books and writing."

"I will do so. And thanks again."

6

Dr. Baraku Bexley
Medical Log: Tory Troy

I include here in my files the complete text of a short story written by Tory Troy titled "Skyline Pigeon." It is my belief that the subject matter of the story may prove relevant to my final determination in this case.

"Skyline Pigeon"

by Victoria Troy

Turn me loose from your hands
Let me fly to distant lands.
"Skyline Pigeon"
ELTON JOHN

It had been a bad week for Caleb. In fact, it had been a
bad *year* up until now, and the forthcoming Labor Day
weekend did not look to be much better.

Caleb locked the back door of his mother's house
and trudged slowly down the walk leading to his car
parked in the driveway. It had rained last night, the
grass was wet, and the sidewalk had that stained look
it gets when it's been soaked and the sun hasn't dried
it yet.

Mom was still asleep and Caleb wanted to get an
early start on his errands before she woke up. He had
prepared the fixings for her breakfast and left everything ready to go, but he knew that she would be upset
that he wasn't there to make her breakfast and serve it
to her when she got out of bed. Too bad, Mom, Caleb
thought. If he waited till she got up and finished eating

before heading out ("No dirty dishes in the sink in *my* house," Mom whispered in his head), he'd be in the car most of the day, and he really wanted to get to bed early tonight. Caleb was physically exhausted and looked it.

Caleb's mother had been sick since Christmas with acute leukemia, and none of the treatments had done much good. Mom had gotten weaker and weaker through the spring and summer, and the doctors were now saying that she probably wouldn't make it to see another Christmas.

Since Caleb was the oldest of three brothers, and the only one of them not married, the bulk of Mom's care had become his responsibility.

Caleb didn't work and lived quite comfortably off the enormous Internet profits he had banked before the dot-com crash in early 2000. This fact served to make his brothers perfectly comfortable letting him know quite clearly that they were busy, and that they expected him to take care of Mom, because, after all, you're home, and what are we supposed to do, leave work? Some of us have to earn a living, you know. And who will take care of our kids if we're taking care of Mom? Sorry, Caleb, you're the only one for the job.

Caleb didn't argue with them and even went so far as to move back into his old room at the house so he could be there for his mother, take her to her appointments, cook for her, and generally do whatever else she needed him to do.

Caleb was wealthy enough to afford round-the-clock

care for his mother, but his siblings wouldn't hear of it. Let strangers take care of Mom when you're home all day? No way, Jose. Out of the question.

So Caleb packed up some clothes, his CDs and CD player, his computer, a few books, a portable color TV, his VCR, and he moved back home—a forty-two-year-old pilgrim returning to the village where he had been born. He stopped by his apartment every day to get the mail, but he slept at his mother's house and spent most of his day taking care of Mom.

Mom was still functional and mobile and had all her wits about her and Caleb didn't really have to worry about leaving her alone, but the chemo and the radiation and the painkillers and the emphysema all made her very weak. She couldn't go shopping, she couldn't climb the stairs to do the laundry, and she definitely couldn't mow the lawn anymore or even take out the trash. She could still get to the bathroom on her own, thank God, and she could still bathe herself (even if it took eons to do it), but Caleb did almost everything else.

This past week had been exceptionally trying. Here it was, Friday morning, and Caleb was utterly drained.

He ran through the week in his mind.

Monday had been Mom's oncologist appointment, and then he had gone grocery shopping, come home, vacuumed the whole house, and then paid his mother's bills.

Tuesday morning had been a three-hour bone-strengthening IV treatment at the clinic in Guilford, followed that afternoon by trips to the bank, the dry cleaner, and Wal-Mart.

Wednesday was a chemo treatment, which did not go so well. Mom threw up in the car on the way home and, after getting her settled in bed with some ginger ale, matzo crackers, and her remote, Caleb had to wash the front seat upholstery of his brand-new Accord, and then go through the car wash.

After that was a trip to, first, Rite Aid, because they were the only ones who carried the Kleen-Rite lint-remover rolls Mom liked, and then a stop at CVS to pick up Mom's blood-pressure pills and pain medication, because CVS was cheaper and Mom liked the pharmacist better.

Thursday Mom felt better enough to make her weekly trip to the beauty parlor (Caleb drove her and picked her up) and then he made an afternoon trip to Stop & Shop and the hardware store for an air conditioner filter and some weed killer.

In addition to all these duties, Caleb also had to make Mom's breakfast, lunch, and dinner every day. Was breakfast a simple bagel and a cup of coffee? Of course not. Mom insisted on half a grapefruit, two poached eggs, two slices of whole-wheat toast—with real butter only—and two cups of Sanka every morning. Caleb had to be sure he always had four fresh grapefruits in the refrigerator for the week, and he had to time his purchases so that the seventh half a grapefruit wasn't spoiled or too ripe. Oh, Mom would eat it if it was a little overripe, but she would be pissed about it and Caleb would eventually pay for it.

Lunch, which had to be eaten precisely at noon every day during the twelve o'clock news, was always either a boiled ham or bologna sandwich on white bread, or a small dish of tuna salad, made fresh, or an American cheese–egg-white omelet with diced tomatoes. No matter what her lunch "main course" was, it always had to be accompanied by a handful of Wise's lightly salted potato chips and a glass of Canada Dry ginger ale.

Dinner was a nightmare for Caleb, since Mom would not eat anything from a restaurant (except pizza) and insisted on everything being fresh. Caleb had often mused over the irony of someone who refused to eat processed foods because the chemicals might cause blood cancer.

Monday Mom had wanted pasta. Tuesday was baked chicken. Wednesday was stuffed peppers. Thursday was broiled scrod.

And now here we were on Friday and Caleb was already fretting over what kind of fish he would buy for tonight, considering that Mom had insisted on scrod last night and would be especially picky about what kind of fish they would have tonight. Caleb's family were all practicing Catholics, and even though the Church had eliminated the "no meat on Fridays" rule decades ago, Mom still ate only fish on Fridays, out of respect for Jesus. "If Jesus could die on the cross for us and sacrifice His own life, not to mention a wife and kids too," Mom would proclaim to anyone who would listen (and even to some who wouldn't), "then I think I can skip eating meat one lousy day a week out of gratitude to the son of God."

Caleb remembered once sarcastically wisecracking to his mother that he was sure Jesus was delighted that she ate one of His fish instead of one of His cows on Fridays. For this witticism, he had been rewarded by getting a whole glass of Canada Dry ginger ale thrown at him from across the kitchen. After that, Caleb kept his theological musings to himself. Although Mom was weak and somewhat frail, he'd bet she could still throw a glass of Canada Dry ginger ale across the kitchen if she wanted to.

Caleb stuck his key in the car door lock and paused a moment. He looked around the neighborhood where he had grown up and saw that, except for cosmetic changes, everything had pretty much stayed the same.

Caleb turned the key and opened the door. What would happen when Mom died? he wondered. There had not been any new people in the neighborhood for as long as Caleb could remember. Would his brothers want to sell the house? Would they expect him to buy it and live in it? Would they consider leasing the house to a family?

Caleb didn't want to think about the future. If it were up to him, they could *give* the house away. He certainly did not want to live in it, and he was sure his siblings would think about the money they could get if they sold it.

Caleb got in the Accord and closed the door quietly so as not to wake Mom, whose bedroom window was only a few feet away from the driveway. Just as he was getting ready to turn the ignition, he suddenly realized he had forgotten The List.

The List was the piece of long, lined yellow paper on which Mom wrote down all the things she needed and all the errands she wanted Caleb to do. Mom made a new List every day of the week.

Shaking his head in frustration, yet not really surprised that he would be forgetful, Caleb removed the key from the ignition, got out of the car, and began walking into the backyard.

The path he had to walk led him past the west side of the garage. Perhaps it was because he had to look to the right of the gate to work the latch that he now noticed the gray ball in the grass next to the garage. This gray ball had to have been there when he left the house, but it had completely eluded his gaze.

Caleb stopped. He bent down a little and saw that the gray ball was a pigeon. He bent a little closer and saw that the bird had a gaping wound in its side and he could see its chest heaving rapidly as it panted in a feeble effort to get air into lungs that were probably crushed. The bird was obviously in a great deal of pain and was also in shock. To Caleb it looked as if the bird had either fallen from a great height and gouged itself on a gutter or a fence, or it had been bitten by some kind of animal. Caleb was betting on the latter and was even fairly certain it was a dog that had done the damage to this poor creature. Specifically, a husky with one brown eye and one blue eye named Kilo that belonged to the Beahms three houses over. Caleb had often seen the dog chasing pigeons all over the neighborhood, and it looked like Kilo finally caught one—at least long enough to inflict this terrible wound before the bird escaped and flew off as far as it could before tumbling to the ground and landing here, next to Caleb's mother's garage.

Inexplicably, a scene from the old *Andy Griffith Show* popped into Caleb's mind. It was the episode called "Opie the Birdman," and it told the story of three tiny songbirds that Opie raised by himself after accidentally killing their mother with his slingshot. At the end of the show, Sheriff Andy, Opie's dad, convinced his son that the time had come to let the birds fly away, to open the cage and set them free. After Opie frees the third bird, he says, "Cage sure looks awful empty, don't it, Paw?" Andy nods in agreement, but then says, "But don't the trees seem nice and full?"

This whole scene played itself out in Caleb's consciousness in a millisecond, and it occurred to him that this pigeon might never visit a tree again, might never coast silhouetted against the skyline—unless he did something to help.

In less than a heartbeat, Caleb decided to try to save the life of this gravely injured pigeon. This is probably a waste of time, he thought, but he simply could not stand there and watch this poor thing suffer without trying to do something to help.

Caleb and his family had all had pets when they were growing up and, like every family that owns cats and dogs, they had established a relationship with a veterinarian, specifically Dr. Wilborne at the Westwoods Animal Hospital. Caleb didn't even think twice about his decision. He would bring his injured friend to Dr. Wilborne, and Dr. W would fix him up so Caleb could set him free to fly again and fill the trees wherever he chose to roam.

The cost didn't matter, and bizarrely, another sitcom, *Seinfeld,* popped into his head, specifically the episode where a vet has to fly in "really tiny instruments" to operate on a squirrel George accidentally drove over with his car. George was more worried about the cost of the operation than about the squirrel, much to his girlfriend's disgust, but he okayed the operation and paid anyway.

Caleb planned on telling Dr. Wilborne that money was no object. Caleb wanted to save this pigeon and he would do whatever it took to do it.

Caleb ran into the garage and found a cardboard box filled with Styrofoam peanuts. He remembered that his mother had ordered a cheese tray from the Wisconsin Cheese Factory to give as a Christmas gift to Echo, the nurse who gave her her chemo treatments, and UPS had delivered it in this box. Caleb was glad he had not cut it up and put it in a trash bag or crushed it flat. This box would be perfect. Its sides were high enough so that the bird would feel secure and, yet, it couldn't climb out if it panicked.

Caleb carried the box outside, set it down next to the injured bird, who was still panting and whose wound was still oozing blood.

Being very careful not to hurt it further, Caleb gently slid his hand under the pigeon's body and cradled its small form in his palm. He picked it up—it felt warm—and the bird flapped its wings weakly in fear, but then calmed down when Caleb placed it inside the cardboard box. Caleb picked up the box and carried it to the car. He placed it on the back seat and strapped the box to the seat with the safety belt.

He then got in, started the car, and slowly backed out of the driveway. "Don't worry," he said softly to the dying pigeon. "It's only a ten-minute ride to the vet's and then you'll be good as new."

Caleb glanced repeatedly into the box as he drove, and he could see that the bird was getting weaker. Caleb drove faster, and his mother and her errands and his brothers and the grapefruit halves and the Wise's lightly salted potato chips and what kind of fish he could serve on a Friday after a fish Thursday were all tiny sparks of distraction that floated through his mind and were ignored, like the specks of dust that build up on your eyeglass lenses and that after a while you don't even see.

Caleb pulled into the fire lane in front of the veterinary hospital eight minutes after he pulled out of his mother's driveway. He turned off the car, got out, and opened the back door. The bird was still breathing, but there was blood on the bottom of the box and its eyes looked glassy.

He carried the box into the hospital and walked right up to the counter with it.

"Hi. My family has been coming to Dr. Wilborne for years and I found this injured bird in my yard and I need him to take a look at him." He said all this in one breath and before he finished speaking, the veterinary technician manning the front desk had stood up and looked inside the box at the pigeon. She then picked up the phone, pressed two keys, and said, "Dr. W, I need you in Exam six stat."

She hung up the phone and picked up the box. "Have a seat and I'll bring it to Dr. W immediately."

Caleb nodded and said, "Listen. You tell him money is no object. I'll pay whatever it costs."

The tech looked down at the pigeon and replied, "Well, I can't imagine it will be too expensive, but I'll tell him what you said."

Caleb watched as the tech carried the bloodstained cardboard box into the back where she would meet Dr. W in Exam 6 "stat," and then he sat down on an orange plastic chair. Never any fabric on a vet's waiting room furniture, Caleb thought to himself. Ticks and fleas and animal hair can't stick to plastic.

Caleb looked at his watch. It was already past ten and he hadn't done anything yet that his mother had written on The List. He should have already been to the bank and been on his way to the grocery store, but here he was, in the waiting room of Westwoods Animal Hospital, waiting for word about an injured pigeon that he had found in his mother's yard and that he had driven here in a cardboard box.

He wondered if he would be home in time to make his mother's lunch. He knew she could fix herself something if she wanted to, but she had become very dependent on him. He also knew deep down that she hated being so helpless and that she would definitely prefer to do everything herself, but she couldn't, so Caleb did.

Caleb's mom had always been fiercely independent. Even when his dad was alive, Mom had set her own agenda. Dad's death diminished her and now her illness was making her a prisoner in her own house, with her own son as the warden. Caleb knew that this was killing his mom as much as the leukemia, but there wasn't much anyone could do about it.

Ten-thirty. What was going on back there? Maybe they've got him in surgery already and they just haven't had a chance to come out and tell me, he thought.

Caleb hoped his mom had made herself breakfast. He decided he would not be able to stay here much longer, and that he would have to come back to pick up the pigeon after it had recovered. He already knew where he would set it free. There was a grove of trees by a lake near his mother's house where he and his brothers had once gone to summer camp. He would wait until his bird was completely healed (the pigeon was now "his" bird) and then take it there and let it fly up into the trees. Caleb smiled at the thought that he would be doing his part toward making the trees in that sunny grove "nice and full."

Suddenly, the door in the waiting room that led to the exam rooms opened and Dr. Wilborne strode into the room. "Caleb!" he boomed with his hand extended. "Good to see you, boy! How's Mom?"

Caleb shook Dr. Wilborne's hand and smiled. "She's good, Doc. You know her. She's not gonna let anything keep her down."

"That's terrific. You give her my love, hear?"

"I will." Caleb nodded. "So how's my bird, Doc?"

Dr. Wilborne grew a puzzled look on his face. "*Your* bird? Was the pigeon a pet?"

"No, no, it was just a bird I found in our yard. But I figured I'd bring it in and have you fix it up. How's it doing?"

"I'm sorry, Caleb, but I put it down as soon as Vicki brought it back to me. It was mortally injured and there was nothing I could have done to save it. Euthanizing injured wildlife and pigeons is a regular part of our business, Caleb. We don't even charge for it. People are always bringing in raccoons and squirrels and birds that have been hit by cars. Once I had to go down to Route Nine and put a deer to sleep that had had three legs broken by a tractor-trailer. One little girl even brought in a skunk once." Dr. W smiled. "I put that one to sleep out back in the woods. They release their bodily fluids when we give them the needle, you know. Luckily, I didn't get sprayed. I didn't want to chance the hospital getting blasted, though."

Dr. Wilborne paused and put his hand on Caleb's shoulder.

"So we put your pigeon to sleep, Caleb, and it went very peacefully."

Caleb just stood there. His fantasy about setting the healed bird free withered and floated away like dust.

But I guess he is free, Caleb then thought to himself. It's just another kind of freedom, I guess.

"Thanks, Doc. I appreciate it. Can't I give you something for your time and the, uh, materials?"

"No way. This is our way of giving a little something back. If we can put an injured wild animal out of its misery, then that's payment enough."

Caleb nodded and shook Dr. Wilborne's hand again. "Well, then, thanks again. And I'll tell my mother you were asking for her."

"Good. You do that. And my best to Alan and Paul, okay?"

Caleb nodded and turned to leave. Then he stopped and turned back to Dr. Wilborne. "Just out of curiosity, Doc. What do you do with the . . . you know, the remains?"

"We'll cremate it."

"Oh, okay."

Caleb walked out of the building and got into his car. Just as he turned the key in the ignition, though, the floodgates opened and he began sobbing like someone who had just lost his best friend. It took Caleb several minutes to compose himself before he could drive. When he was calm enough, he headed home. He figured he'd better stop home first to check on his mother and explain what happened. She would probably be worried and he didn't want her to get upset. Stress was no good for her immune system, the doctors had told them.

Caleb drove slower on his way home than he did on his way to the vet's, and it was about fifteen minutes before he turned the corner to his street.

Caleb's heart dropped. There was an ambulance in his mother's driveway and his brother Alan's car was parked behind it.

Caleb sped down the street and screeched to a halt in front of the house. He jumped out of the car and ran into the house. Alan was standing in the kitchen with two EMTs. When Alan saw Caleb, his eyes widened and a furious look exploded on his face.

"Where the hell have you been?" Alan shouted.

Caleb didn't take the bait. Staying calm, he said, "What happened?"

"Mom had a stroke and fell and hit her head on the bathtub. She pushed the emergency button she wears around her neck but we think it took her too long. By the time the ambulance got here . . ." Alan's voice was now trembling and his eyes were watery. "By the time the ambulance got here . . . it was too late." Alan paused and looked behind Caleb. Or maybe he was looking through Caleb.

"Mom's dead, Caleb."

Caleb's legs buckled and he collapsed. Luckily, the two EMTs caught him before he hit the floor. They carried him to a chair and sat him down, his face pale and his forehead covered in sweat.

"I was only gone for a couple of hours. I had to . . ." Caleb stopped. He knew he couldn't tell Alan about the pigeon.

"I had errands."

Alan did not ask Caleb about the errands, and Caleb just sat there at his mother's kitchen table with his head down.

"I had errands," he whispered.

It was late in the afternoon by the time everyone left and Caleb was alone in the house. The coroner had taken away his mother's body, and Caleb and his brothers had met with the funeral director to arrange Mom's funeral and burial.

No one had come right out and blamed Caleb for his mother's death but he knew what they were thinking. If he had been home, maybe they would have been able to save her. But he had been out on his errands, and they knew that he left her alone for a few hours every day, and the truth was that this was just something that happened. The fact that he was at the vet's trying to save the life of a wild pigeon instead of at the bank or the grocery store or the drugstore meant nothing. Absolutely nothing.

Caleb got up and walked over to the kitchen sink,

where he poured himself a glass of water. As he drank, he realized this water was the first thing he had put in his stomach all day. Rather than restore him, it made him queasy.

Caleb went out into the backyard and stood by the rear fence with his hands in his pockets, looking up at the darkening sky. Caleb had always liked dusk, that in-between time when the light was so strange and beautiful. Mom is gone, he thought to himself. So is my pigeon. He realized that he had suffered through two deaths in one day, although he knew that he would be ridiculed (and probably castigated) if he even spoke about the death of a lousy pigeon in the same breath as the death of his mother.

But it was true, and Caleb keenly felt both losses, felt them in his heart, and felt them in the deepest recesses of his soul.

Caleb sighed and decided to go inside and try to eat something. Just as he was turning to leave, though, he felt the slightest wisp of a breeze flutter across his face. He looked back at the fence and there on the peeling crossboard sat a tiny spotted gray chick. The chick's head was cocked and it looked straight at him. Caleb didn't move, and the bird sat there, fearless, and stared at him with what appeared to be great interest.

Then the oddest thing happened.

The chick flew off the fence board (it was more like a short hop actually) and landed on Caleb's right shoulder, where it sat for a moment and looked directly into

Caleb's eyes. Apparently satisfied, the chick then let out a little chirp and flew off into the trees.

Caleb looked up, and in the deepening twilight he could just make out the tiny round body of the chick, perched on a branch so thin, it was still bouncing slowly from the bird's landing.

The little pigeon was the only bird Caleb could see, and yet it occurred to him that he had never seen these trees look so full. As if able to read Caleb's thoughts, and needing to express his complete agreement with him, the chick suddenly let out a series of whistles and chirps that Caleb knew, in his heart, were manifestly triumphant.

Caleb smiled and went back into the house, where he drank water and thought about Canada Dry ginger ale and lists written on long sheets of yellow paper.

7

Tory Troy
Dr. Baraku Bexley

"I read your short story."

"What? What do you mean?"

"I read 'Skyline Pigeon.' "

"Oh, really? And how did you get your hands on that, if you don't mind my asking?"

"I met with Mr. Mundàne."

"How'd you find him?"

"What do you mean?"

"How did you know he had been my teacher?"

"Tory, haven't you noticed the large briefcase I carry around with me all the time? Inside that briefcase is my *Tory Troy* file. It is quite exhaustive."

"What does that mean?"

"It means that I have copies of all your school transcripts, your work and earnings history, all your residences—all three of them—utility bills, bank statements, medical records . . . essentially, I have your entire life in my briefcase. I even have a copy of the detention you received in seventh grade for giving your teacher the finger. As well as the speeding ticket you received when you were sixteen and you took your mother's car without permission. Not to mention every prescription you've ever filled, and every long-distance phone call you've ever made."

"You're kidding, right? It can't be legal for you to have all that stuff, can it?"

"Not only is it legal, it's required. If I don't review all your records carefully and something surfaces at your trial—if you even go to trial, of course—and you get off on a technicality, *I* will be the one who will get in trouble, not you."

"It just seems so invasive."

"It is. Intentionally."

"So you read my story."

"Yes."

"Well?"

"Do you want my literary review, or my thoughts on how it factors into my work on your case?"

"Both. Start with what you thought of the writing."

"Competent."

"Competent? That's it?"

"Actually it's more than competent. It's modestly accomplished."

"Jesus. 'Modestly accomplished.' Dr. B, you are a cornucopia of tact and thoughtfulness."

"Are you insulted?"

"Not really. You're probably right. What else? How about the characters?"

"I think the Caleb character is you."

"Oh, you do, do you? Why's that?"

"What do *you* think? Why *would* I feel that way?"

"Probably because in the story Caleb brings an injured bird to the vet and then gets upset when it has to be put to sleep. Euthanized."

"Are you Caleb?"

"No. The incident in the story actually happened to a friend of mine, and after he told me about it, I wrote the story."

"It happened to a friend."

"Yes."

"And he told you about it."

"You sound suspicious. Don't you believe me?"

"Of course I believe you. Why don't we move on to a discussion of the people you work with at the animal shelter. We've already discussed Jake and we can come back to him later. What can you tell me about . . . Marcy?"

"What do you want to know?"

"Anything that comes to mind about her."

"She liked cashews."

"Go on."

"Every afternoon around three, she would take out a little Ziploc bag filled with salted cashews. Whole ones. She never bought the pieces."

"She told you that?"

"No, I asked her."

"I see. What else can you tell me about her?"

"She's single, but she's been dating some guy named Mike who seems like a real creep. She still lives with her mother. Like me. She told me her mother caught her, uh, pleasuring herself one day. Marcy said she had never been more embarrassed in her life. It took her a week before she could even look her mother in the face again."

"How did this incident come up in the conversation?"

"Oh, you know . . . girl talk. We were sitting in the office one afternoon and there was nobody else around and she told me."

"Go on."

"More about Marcy? Well, I know she collected PEZ dispensers. She has a pretty big collection. She was also in a Flash Crowd."

"What's a Flash Crowd, please?"

"It's this weird new hobby—people in a certain area, like a city, or a town, or a campus, sign up to be in a Flash Crowd. And then what happens is they get e-mailed instructions that they have to follow. It's strange."

"I don't understand."

"Well, Marcy told me about one event she was in. She got an e-mail that told her to show up at the Crystal Mall on the second floor in front of the Sharper Image store at two o'clock on a Sunday afternoon. When everyone was there, they had to wait to hear a Carpenters song played on the Muzak sound system in the mall. As soon as they heard it, they all had to face the Sharper Image store and play their cell phone's ring tones for two minutes. Then everybody had to split. I think she said the song was 'Rainy Days and Mondays.' "

"So that's a Flash Crowd."

"Actually that's a Flash Crowd *event*. Marcy was *in* a Flash Crowd."

"I see. So Marcy was a joiner. What else do you remember about her?"

"She painted her toenails different colors."

"Excuse me?"

"Each toe was painted a different color."

"All right. Anything else?"

"She always said she wanted to be cremated. She was afraid of being buried. She didn't like enclosed spaces."

"I see. Anything else?"

"No."

"Are you sure?"

"I don't want to talk anymore."

8

Dr. Baraku Bexley
Dr. Gwyneth June

"Hi, Gwyn."

"Bex, you old dog! How are you?"

"Well, I got up this morning, so I'm counting today as a winner."

"No argument there. You're here for the animal-shelter case?"

"Yes."

"Tough one."

"Yes. Are they all still here?"

"Yeah. Although the families are raising a ruckus and want the bodies released."

"How much longer can you keep them?"

"Well, I'm required to keep them until all the medical/legal autopsies are done and all interested parties—that would be you, and Brawley, and maybe the Good

Humor man at this stage—have determined there is no need for retention."

"And where are you now?"

"The autopsies are completed. I'll probably have to release them to the funeral homes tomorrow."

"Okay, then let's get this over with."

"Do you want my report first or do you want to see the bodies first?"

"Your report."

"Before we start, can I ask you something?"

"Gwyn—"

"Oh, come on, Bex. Who's here?"

"You know I can't—"

"Have I ever betrayed you? You know I would fall on the sword before I let you get into trouble for anything you told me."

"You're embarrassing me."

"Am I lying?"

"Oh, all right. Go ahead. Ask your question."

"Why'd she do it?"

"I don't know."

"What do you *think*?"

"It's complicated. . . ."

"Is she crazy?"

"That's what I'm trying to find out. I can't say with certainty that she was insane at the time of the crimes. That's for a jury to decide. But whether or not it even gets to a jury is essentially up to me."

"What's she like?"

"Sorry, Gwyn, that's enough."

"Oh, okay. Spoilsport. The report?"

"The report."

"The full house?"

"No, just the pertinents."

"Six bodies. Three female. Three male. All were found in an animal-shelter gas chamber. Death was due to inhalation of toxic gases and suffocation. Mostly carbon monoxide."

"*And* suffocation? As a separate determinant for cause of death?"

"Well, it's a little tricky."

"How so?"

"By the time the gas started flowing, they were all already near death from suffocation."

"What do you mean?"

"I'll get to that in a minute."

"All right. Any marks on the bodies?"

"Puncture wound on the back of the neck. Some scrapes and bruises. Probably from being dragged into the chamber. I understand the killer—sorry, the *alleged* killer—is small?"

"Yeah. She's a tiny thing."

"Well, then, she's pretty goddamned strong for someone so petite."

"Toxicology results?"

"Routine stuff for the most part—acetaminophen, ibuprofen, an antibiotic, some THC residue from the pot smokers of the bunch, some low blood-alcohol levels. However . . ."

"Yes?"

"All six victims also showed a high level of pancuronium bromide in their blood."

"Pavulon?"

"Yes."

"She paralyzed them to get them into the chamber."

"Seems so."

"Jesus."

"And they were conscious too. Remember your med-school pharmacology classes, Bex? *Pavulon: trade name for the muscle relaxant pancuronium bromide. Pavulon produces complete paralysis but with no alteration of consciousness.*"

"Yes, that's right. Jesus. So, they were all suffocating and near death even before she dragged them into the chamber. Jesus."

"You already called Him, Bex, and it doesn't look like He's a-comin'."

"Where was the injection site?"

"Back of the neck."

"She snuck up on them."

"Seems so."

"Anything else?"

"Yeah, but I doubt that this has anything to do with the case."

"Go on."

"One of the guys was HIV positive but didn't know it."

"How could you tell?"

"No therapeutic antiviral drugs in his blood."

"He could have known but not acted on it. . . ."

"I suppose. But it's all moot now. Although I did have to use biohazard precautions when working on him. So will the embalmer."

"Can I see the bodies?"

"Sure. Follow me."

Dane Lyman, *AM Live*
District Attorney Brawley Loren

"Welcome back to *AM Live*. I am here with District Attorney Brawley Loren, the chief prosecutor in the notorious Waterbridge Animal Shelter multiple-murder case. Good morning, D.A. Loren."

"Good morning, Dane. Happy to be here."

"So, D.A. Loren, what can you tell us about Tory Troy and the animal-shelter case?"

"Well, as you know, I cannot reveal details of an ongoing investigation, but I can tell you that a vigorous prosecution of Ms. Troy will proceed as planned and that we are confident of a conviction on all counts."

"Is it true that she is undergoing a psychiatric examination?"

"Yes, that's true. That information has been in the papers."

"What can you tell us about that?"

"The examination is being conducted by a psychiatrist named Baka . . . Baraku Bexley, but that's all I know."

"What specifically is the purpose of his examination, Counselor?"

"Dr. Bexley has been charged with determining if Ms. Troy is fit to stand trial."

"What do you think? Is there a chance that she won't have to stand trial?"

"There is the possibility that Dr. Bexley may find her mentally unfit to stand trial. If that happens, I will go to the judge and request a second examination. I can tell you this, Dane. If I have anything to do with it, this young lady is going to be judged by a jury of her peers."

"Speaking of Ms. Troy, what can you tell us about her?"

"She's single, twenty-eight, lives with her mother. She had been working at the animal shelter about a year when the crimes occurred."

"Can you talk about the crimes she's charged with?"

"She is charged with murdering her six coworkers by gassing them to death in the chamber the animal shelter uses for euthanizing unwanted animals."

"That is horrible, isn't it?"

"Yes, it is. And that is why we are working diligently to bring her to justice."

"Well, she hasn't been convicted yet, Counselor. She has only been charged, right?"

"Yes, of course."

"We're out of time, but I'd like to thank you for filling us in on this terrible crime."

"You're welcome. Thanks for having me."

"When we return, Kathy is in the kitchen with Chef Lorenzo. We'll be right back."

10

Tory Troy
Dr. Baraku Bexley

"Can we get back to talking about your coworkers? Do you feel up to it now?"

"I'm fine."

"Good. Let's talk about Philip."

"Philip worked in the front."

"Go on."

"He was clerical."

"Meaning?"

"He filled out paperwork and kept records."

"What was he like?"

"Very religious."

"How so?"

"He went to Mass every morning."

"Really? Every morning?"

"Yes. St. Rose's."

"How did his spirituality make you feel?"

"I didn't say he was spiritual, I said he was religious."

"What's the difference?"

"Spiritual people always try to do the right thing. Religious people are hypocrites."

"What makes you say that?"

"Because the most bigoted, mean-spirited, racist, homophobic, sexist, misogynistic, cruel people I know are all devout churchgoers."

"That's something of a blanket generalization, Tory, isn't it?"

"Not really. I know people who wouldn't miss Sunday Mass but think nothing of telling 'nigger' jokes—sorry, Doc—or buying stolen merchandise, or cheating on their taxes. Or beating their wives. Or feeling up their daughters. They think that by going to church they can do anything else they want with no penalty."

"What made you come to this conclusion about Philip?"

"One day Jake sent us to Home Depot to get some duct tape and a few other things. When we checked out, Philip gave the cashier a twenty, but the girl gave him change for a fifty. And he knew it immediately too. He just pocketed the money and walked out of the store. When we were in the car he said, 'I just made a quick thirty bucks.' He wasn't even ashamed about it."

"What did you say?"

"I asked him if he knew that the cashier would have to make up the money out of her own pocket. When he said, 'So?' I knew that he was no good. I kept my distance from Pastor Phil from that day on."

"Did you say anything to Jake?"

"No, but I went back to Home Depot that night after work and gave the manager thirty dollars of my own money."

"Do you consider yourself a spiritual person?"

"I suppose so."

"Do you have any religious beliefs?"

"I don't belong to a church, if that's what you're asking."

"Do you adhere to a moral code?"

"Yes."

"Does your moral code allow killing?"

"I see where you're going with this, Doc."

"And where is that?"

"What do you want to talk about next?"

"Very well. Let's move on to Teresa."

"Skank."

"Meaning?"

"Pig."

"She was fat?"

"No, not fat like a pig. She was a slut."

"How so?"

"Dr. Bexley. Do I really need to explain to you what a slut is?"

"Humor me, please."

"Well, she dated a lot and she had sex with every guy she went out with. Every guy. In fact, I think she had a reputation as being an easy score, because she would get phone calls from guys she had never met, asking her out. They'd call her at the animal shelter. It was pretty easy to figure out that guys who had scored with her had told their friends. And she never said no."

"How do you know that she had sex with all her dates?"

"She told me. And she did everything too. She seemed to be proud of being able to do things like deep throat and take on two guys at once. Like I said—slut."

"How did you get along with Teresa?"

"We were fine. She talked and I listened."

"Did she ever sexualize your relationship?"

"I think she was bi-curious. A couple of times I could tell she was flirting. And once she changed in front of me and seemed to spend a little more time topless than she needed to."

"Did you ever respond?"

"No. I wasn't interested. I'm straight."

"Do you recall when you injected Teresa?"

"Yes. She was second."

"Can you tell me how that happened?"

"She happened to be sitting alone at the front desk with her back to me when I entered the room with the syringe. After I injected Jake, Teresa was next only because she was the first person I ran into. It could have just as easily been Marcy or Philip or even Renaldo. My only goal was to get them all immobilized as quickly as possible."

"Did you say anything to Teresa before you injected her with the paralyzing agent?"

"No. I just quietly walked up behind her and poked her."

"What happened next?"

"Her head flew up and she sat straight up in her chair. Then she fell over onto the floor and lay there staring up at me."

"Then what did you do?"

"I went looking for Marcy."

"Where did you find her?"

"In the bathroom."

"Did you go in?"

"Yes. The bathroom had one stall and a urinal. Marcy was standing in front of the mirror, so I said hello and made like I was going into the stall. She said hi and kept touching up her lipstick. As I passed by her, I reached up and poked her in the back of the neck with the syringe. She fell down almost immediately."

"What did you do after paralyzing Marcy?"

"I went looking for Renaldo."

"And where did you find him?"

"Out on the back dock."

"What was he doing there?"

"Smoking a joint."

"He smoked marijuana during working hours?"

"Oh, yeah."

"What happened next?"

"I asked him if he could come inside and help me move a heavy box of supplies. He said sure and got up. When he headed for the back door and was in front of me, I jabbed him in the back of the neck."

"The autopsy report for Renaldo states that he had a large bruise on his forehead."

"Yeah, after I poked him, he collapsed and fell forward and hit his head on the heavy steel track of the overhead door."

"What did you do next?"

"I dragged him inside."

"So now you had Jake, Teresa, Marcy, and Renaldo incapacitated."

"Yep."

"What about Ann?"

"That was a real stroke of luck. Ann happened to be off that day, but she came in to pick up her paycheck right after I had dragged everyone into the gas chamber. She was easy. She came into the back looking for someone because the front office was empty. She was calling out, 'Hello? Hello?' and all I had to do was hide in a doorway and then jab her as she passed by."

"You didn't tell me anything about Ann."

"Not much to tell. She was married, had three kids, and worked part-time at the shelter. I think her husband was an architect, or maybe a teacher of some sort."

"There's quite a difference between those two professions."

"I know, but I never really paid all that much attention to her when she talked about her family. Her brother could have been the architect, now that I think about it."

"So you took care of Ann and dragged her into the chamber?"

"Yes."

"All that was left was . . . Philip?"

"Yeah. Father Phil."

"Tell me about what happened with Philip."

"While I was immobilizing everyone else, Phil was downstairs in the basement. The animal shelter is in an old house. The city negotiated a cheap rent from the landlord and then paid to convert it into a shelter. The house had a basement. We kept supplies and boxes of files down there."

"What was Philip doing in the basement?"

"I have no idea. He could have been jerking off for all I know. Although knowing Phil, he would probably consider that a mortal sin and completely abstain. So I'd say he was probably either inventorying supplies or looking through the records for something. Or goofing off."

"Go on."

"I waited for him to come upstairs. The way the house is designed, the door to the basement opens into the front office. I just stood off to the side and waited until he was in the room and then—pop."

"What happened after you jabbed him with the syringe?"

"He jerked bolt upright like a steel rod had replaced his spinal column. Then he dropped the files he was carrying and just crumpled to the floor."

"Did you then place him in the chamber with the others?"

"Yes."

"What can you tell me about what you were thinking, or how you were feeling, when you saw all six of your coworkers in the gas chamber, paralyzed and slowly dying?"

"I didn't feel a thing, Doc. I just wanted to get it over with."

"Did you feel any hesitation or doubt about what you were planning on doing?"

"Nope. Not one bit. And I'm sure that's going to go into your report and be highlighted in yellow, right?"

"What makes you think that, Tory?"

"No remorse. That must mean I was crazy, right? Only someone who is completely insane could rationally plan out six murders and carry them out without even blinking, right?"

"Not necessarily. You could be feigning indifference. You could be lying to me."

"I suppose that's true. And if you find me competent, and then a jury thinks I was insane, then I will have essentially gotten away with murder, right?"

"Tell me the truth, Tory. Did you have any misgivings about what you were going to do next? Any at all?"

"Like I said, Doc. It didn't bother me a bit. All I wanted to do was get it over with."

11

Dr. Baraku Bexley
Judge Gerard Becker

"Good morning, Your Honor."

"Good morning, Dr. Bexley. Please come in. Have a seat."

"Thank you."

"How's the family?"

"They're terrific, Judge, and thanks for asking."

"I always liked your wife. Halle was one of the best law clerks I ever had. What's she doing now?"

"She has a practice in Madison. Family Law. She switched from Corporate some years ago."

"Good for her. Give her my best, will you?"

"I will do that, sir, and thank you."

"So. Tory Troy. The Waterbridge Animal Shelter murders."

"Yes, sir."

"Where are you with her?"

"I've made some progress with the evaluation interviews, Judge."

"Anything you can share with me now?"

"I can tell you that I am leaning toward declaring her competent, sir. We still need to delve deeper into a few areas, and I have some tests to administer, but so far I have not seen convincing evidence that she is incapable of standing trial and participating in her own defense."

"She is forthcoming with you?"

"Very much so. Once in a while we touch a nerve and she clams up, but she'll usually open up to discussing the trigger topic at a later session."

"Loren is making quite a bit of noise about this case."

"Ah, Brawley. Did you see him on *AM Live* last week with Dane Lyman?"

"Yes, I did, and you won't be seeing Brawley Loren on TV again."

"You issued a gag order?"

"I did indeed."

"I think that's for the best. He should not be out there trying to stir up public opinion and polluting the jury pool."

"My thoughts precisely."

"Anything else, Judge?"

"Off the record, Bex. Was she crazy when she did it?"

"I don't think so, Judge. And I don't think she's crazy now. Her motives might be a little twisted, but that's a long way from being incompetent to stand trial."

"Well, I'll leave it in your good hands. I will not seek to speak with you again about this case until you issue your competency report and we meet in court to either set a trial date or institutionalize Ms. Troy."

"Okay, Judge. I'll keep your office informed of my progress."

"Thank you, Bex."

"You're welcome, Judge. My best to Cynthia."

12

Dr. Baraku Bexley
Mrs. Viviana Troy

"How nice to see you again, Mrs. Troy."

"Hello, Doctor. Nice to see you too. How's Tory?"

"She's as good as can be expected. She is managing all right in the hospital, although she has lost a little weight."

"Oh, my. Is she not eating enough? Do they not feed her? Should I send her food?"

"Oh, no. The institutional food system is much like the military's, Mrs. Troy. The motto is, take all you want, but eat all you take. They don't allow wasting food. So plenty of food is available to Tory. I just think she doesn't have much of an appetite lately, which is perfectly understandable."

"I suppose."

"Would it be all right if we talked again?"

"About Tory?"

"Yes, ma'am."

"All right."

"Before we start, do you have any questions for me? Is there anything I can help you with?"

"Did she do it, Doctor?"

"Yes, ma'am. I'm afraid she has admitted committing the murders and has gone into detail as to how she carried them out."

"Could she be lying to you?"

"Yes, I suppose so. But she has quite a bit of verifiable information that no one but the killer would know."

"Then why isn't she being sentenced to prison . . . or death?"

"Because we are a long way off from the final resolution of her case. First I have to determine if she is mentally fit to stand trial. If I decide that she is, then she will go on trial and I'm certain her lawyer will plead not guilty by reason of insanity. And then it will be up to the jury to decide if she was insane when she committed the crimes."

"We couldn't afford our own lawyer."

"Yes, I know. The court appointed one for Tory as soon as she was indicted. Carolyn Payne. She's really quite good. If this goes to trial, Tory will be in good hands."

"I only met her for a minute. Will I be able to speak to her at some point?"

"Of course. I'm sure Ms. Payne will be in touch to set up a series of talks with you."

"Is there anything I can do now?"

"I'm afraid not, Mrs. Troy. Your daughter is in the

middle of a process, and it must play out. All you can do is wait and try not to worry."

"Can I ask you one more question?"

"Of course."

"Did Tory do what she did because I never told anybody about what her father was doing to her?"

"There's no real way of knowing that, Mrs. Troy. But you should not blame yourself for what has happened. Tory is an adult, and she made the decision to do what she did on her own."

"Yes, I know. It's just that I wonder what would have happened if I had reported my husband to the police and stopped what he was doing."

"It's impossible to know, Mrs. Troy. Your husband might have snapped and killed you both. You must take comfort in knowing that you did what you thought was best at the time. It does no one any good to second-guess decisions like that. I have known many women who have been in similarly traumatic situations and have reacted exactly as you did. All right?"

"Yes, I suppose."

"Good. Now can we get to my questions?"

"Yes, I'm sorry for wasting so much time on this."

"Not at all. I am happy to do what I can to put your mind at ease as best possible."

"Thank you."

"Could we talk about Tory's high-school years, please?"

"All right. She was very popular all through high school. She had many, many friends. . . ."

13

Tory Troy
Dr. Baraku Bexley

"Before we begin, is there anything you'd like to talk to me about, Tory?"

"Yes. I don't like you talking to my mother about all this."

"Can't be helped. Next?"

"Why not?"

"Tory, I am going to speak to your mother whenever I feel I need to, as well as anyone and everyone else in your life who might be able to help me better understand you. There is nothing you can do or say to change that, and so I suggest you put it out of your mind."

"What happened to the animal shelter?"

"It's closed. Since the day of the murders."

"For good?"

"Probably not. I think it will eventually reopen."

"What about the animals?"

"All the animals that were at the shelter when the staff were killed were euthanized. All new drop-offs are being referred to the Easton shelter."

"People aren't going to get back in the car and drive to Easton. They're just going to leave the animal on the porch of the shelter."

"Yes. That has been happening. But every afternoon, a van from the Easton shelter drives by and picks up any abandoned animals left there. Anything else?"

"Did any of them . . . did . . ."

"Yes?"

"Did any of the people I worked with have their funerals yet?"

"Two. Marcy and Ann. The others are next week."

"I don't suppose there's a chance I could go to any of them, is there?"

"Assuming the judge would even grant you dispensation for a custodial field trip, do you think you would be welcome at the funerals of the people you killed?"

"Probably not."

"Do you sincerely want to go to their funerals? Explain your thinking to me."

"Oh, I don't know. It's just that it seems kind of rude for me not to be there. After all, I did work with the people."

"Tory, do you realize how irrational such a comment sounds? You are exhibiting a disconnect between the reality of what happened and your perception of those events."

"Maybe I am crazy, eh, Doc?"

"Let's move on, shall we?"

"Fire away."

"The last time we spoke, you expressed your desire on the day of the murders to get it over with as quickly as possible."

"Yes."

"Can you tell me what happened after you successfully paralyzed all your coworkers with Pavulon? According to my notes, you dragged them all into the gas chamber."

"That's right."

"Were they all conscious?"

"Well, their eyes were open, but it actually was like they were asleep."

"After you had them all in the chamber, then what did you do?"

"I stepped out of the chamber, closed the door, and bolted it."

"And then?"

"And then I did exactly what I told you we did when we did the animals."

"Could you indulge me and go through it again, please?"

"No. Check your notes."

"That's not being very cooperative."

"Tough."

"Okay, then. Let's move on. After the timer went off and you knew they were all dead, what did you do next?"

"I opened the door."

"And?"

"I stood there looking at them for a little while. That's how I got caught."

"Yes, could you talk about your arrest, please?"

"Well, it seems as though my timing couldn't have been worse. At the precise moment that I opened the door and I could see their six bodies on the floor, Tommy walked into the room."

"How did he get in?"

"He has a key to the shelter. He came by to pick up his CD player. My luck, right?"

"You had locked the door?"

"Yeah."

"So then what happened?"

"I think he said, 'Fuck!' kind of under his breath. I turned around and saw him standing there staring at the bodies. He then looked at me and his face was as white as your shirt. Before I could do anything, he ran out the front. I saw him fumbling with his cell phone. Within minutes the place was surrounded by cops."

"What did you do?"

"Nothing. They stormed in, I did what they told me to do, and here we are."

"You did not attempt to flee?"

"Why would I?"

"Many people might reflexively try to get away."

"Have you ever watched *The West Wing*, Doc?"

"Actually, yes. It's one of the few TV programs I do watch."

"There was an episode during the first season about a deranged woman who jumped the fence around the

White House and was immediately taken into custody by the Secret Service."

"Yes?"

"Well, later, one of the agents said something like, 'If they jump the fence, they're going to jail. How they behave when we get to them will determine how long they go away for.' "

"Your point?"

"I'm answering your question about why I didn't try to get away. When cops point guns at you and tell you to freeze, you obey. Without discussion. My mama didn't raise no fools, Doctor Bexley."

"Kudos to Viviana Troy."

"You betcha."

"What was going through your mind as you were being arrested?"

"What do you mean?"

"What were you thinking about . . . what was your state of mind?"

"I wasn't scared, if that's what you're asking."

"That's not what I was asking, but why did that come immediately to mind?"

"What do you mean?"

"When I asked about your state of mind, the first thing you thought to deny was fear."

"So? What does that mean?"

"You spoke about your *absence* of fear instead of the *presence* of guilt, or remorse, or sadness."

"Yes."

"Did you not feel any sense of loss? These were

people you had worked with for quite some time. You knew them. Did you consider any of them personal friends?"

"Yes . . . no . . . I don't know . . . I suppose."

"And yet you executed them, and then did not feel any regret over their passing. At your hand."

"Yes."

"Could you explain this to me?"

"Explain it?"

"Yes. Tell me why you think you were so detached after killing these people."

"I don't know."

"Are you sure?"

"What do you mean, am I sure? You think I'm lying to you?"

"No, not lying. But I don't think you are being completely forthcoming with me."

"Well, I am."

"Tory, please listen carefully. You must be honest with me. If you dissemble or lie, I cannot help you."

"Oh, you're here to help me?"

"In a sense."

"How?"

"By uncovering the truth about your mental state. My findings will determine your future, Tory. Whatever happens, your fate should be based on the truth."

"The truth shall set you free."

"So they say."

"I understand."

"So, could you tell me a little more about how you

were feeling after you executed your coworkers and as you were being arrested?"

"Like I said, Doc. I wasn't afraid. And that's that. That's all I remember about my feelings as they were slapping the handcuffs on me."

"Well, then, let's move on."

"Fine with me. But one thing, Doc."

"Yes?"

"I don't want you talking to my mother about all this."

14

Defense Attorney Carolyn Payne
Seneca Stone

"Thank you for taking my call and agreeing to see me, Miss Payne."

"You're quite welcome, but I must tell you I cannot discuss either the case or Ms. Troy with you."

"I understand. But you can listen, right?"

"Yes, I can listen."

"Teresa was my lover. She was my partner. She was my entire world."

"I am sorry for your loss. I did not know that Teresa had a life partner."

"For four years. Almost five."

"I see."

"I know what you're thinking."

"Excuse me?"

"I'll bet Tory told you that Teresa was a whore, right?"

"I told you, Ms. Stone, I cannot discuss the case or my conversations with Ms. Troy with you."

"Well, she wasn't."

"What is it you want to tell me, Ms. Stone?"

"That if that bitch doesn't die from a needle in her arm, I'll kill her myself."

"You shouldn't say something like that to me, Ms. Stone. I am an officer of the court."

"I don't care."

"If I report this, you will be in for an enormous amount of trouble."

"Yeah, well, you'd have to report it first, wouldn't you?"

"And what makes you think I won't?"

"I don't really care if you do or you don't. That bitch is doomed, one way or another."

"Okay, Ms. Stone, that's it. This meeting is over. I am going to interpret your threat toward Ms. Troy as an emotional outburst without true intent. However, I can tell you this. If Ms. Troy is found competent to stand trial, and she does go to trial, and she is subsequently institutionalized, and she is later found dead in her bed, your name will be immediately given to the police. Do you understand?"

"Fuck that bitch."

"Good day, Ms. Stone."

15

Tory Troy
Dr. Baraku Bexley

"We need to talk about euthanasia, Tory."

"What about it?"

"We need to talk about what it is, and how you feel about it."

"Why?"

"Because I said so. Please, Tory, would you humor me just once and play along?"

"Why, Doctor Bexley—a chink in your professional armor? A pinch of insecurity?"

"Hardly. I'm just a little tired today, Tory."

"Oh, okay, then. What do you want to know?"

"I'd like you to talk to me about your euthanasia sessions. As many of them as you can remember."

"I worked there over a year, Doc. That's a lot of Fridays."

"Yes, I understand. But I am quite interested in the sessions that remained in your memory."

"They all blend together."

"Yes, that would be expected, but I am sure there are some milestone sessions that you still think about. Let's start with your very first Friday session as a euthanasia technician."

"What about it?"

"You surely must recall your first."

"Do you, Doctor Bexley? Do you remember your first?"

"Stop trifling with me please, and I'll thank you to desist with the innuendo. I will say it again: It seems to me that if you have memories of any of your sessions, at least your first must have stayed with you."

"It did."

"Go on."

"I started working on a Monday. At first Jake just had me feeding the animals and showing them to families looking for a pet. On Thursday, he said, 'Tomorrow might be a little rough for you, Tory. I'm expecting you to assist me with this week's session. Are you up for it?' One thing my mother always used to say about me is true: Tell me you don't think I can do something and I will do it just to prove you wrong. So when Jake started questioning me about whether or not I'd be able to handle a euthanizing session, I made up my mind right then and there that I'd do it no matter what."

"Did you do anything special to prepare yourself?"

"Not really. The night before, I took a couple of hits

of pot around seven o'clock. I smoke so infrequently that the day after I get high I still usually feel the effects. Sort of a lingering mellowness."

"'A lingering mellowness.' I have never heard it described that way before."

"So I went to bed stoned, and by the time I got to work the next morning, I was still a little buzzed."

"You said that euthanizing sessions usually took place in the afternoon."

"Yeah . . . usually around three."

"On the Friday morning of your first session, were you told when it would happen?"

"Yes. Sometimes I stopped for coffee at Dunkin' Donuts on the way to work, and I would bring a tray of large blacks into work. We had the fixings so everybody could make their own cup. Four Big Ones was usually enough. This morning, I put the tray down, and instead of pouring some into a mug, I took a whole twenty-ounce cup and went into Jake's office."

"Why did you go see him as soon as you arrived at work?"

"I wanted to know if there was anything special that had to be done for the animals on the day they were to be . . . well, you know."

"Why did you want the whole cup of coffee?"

"Maybe because I was a little nervous? Maybe because I wanted to counteract the sedation from the pot? I don't know, I just felt like a whole cup that morning."

"Okay. So, was Jake in his office?"

"Yes. He was working at his computer. I didn't knock. I just walked in and sat down."

"What did he do?"

"Nothing. He just finished what he was doing and then looked up at me. He didn't even say good morning. The first thing out of his mouth was, 'Where's *my* coffee?' "

"What did you say?"

"I said, 'It's outside in the tray with the other ones that *I* paid for and brought in.' "

"And then?"

"He just shrugged and then said, 'So?' "

"He sensed something was on your mind?"

"Apparently."

"Go on."

"I took a sip of my coffee and asked him."

"Could you be specific, please?"

"I said, 'Is there anything I need to do for the animals before . . . this afternoon?' "

"And what did he say?"

"He said, 'Like what?' "

"Your question was not clear to him."

"Obviously not. Which I can kind of understand. So then I said, 'Do I have to give them a sedative, or withhold their food, or . . . you know . . . do anything prior to the session?' "

"You felt this was a logical question."

"Absolutely. After all, people can't eat before they have surgery, right?"

"But this wasn't surgery. This was an execution."

"Yeah, I know."

"And death-row inmates eat a last meal before they are put to death."

"Well, I guess I didn't think it through."

"So what did Jake say?"

"He just looked at me for a minute, and then he shook his head. My expression must have made him think I still wasn't clear, so then he said, 'No, nothing needs to be done, Tory.'"

"How did this make you feel?"

"Depressed."

"Why?"

"It just seemed so fucking final at that point."

"Did you then get up and leave?"

"Yes, but as I was leaving he said, 'One more thing, Tory. It's probably a good idea if you don't spend too much time with the animals today.'"

"In a way, he *was* trying to prepare you."

"I guess."

"So what did you say in response to his suggestion?"

"Nothing. I just walked out of his office and went to visit the animals."

"I see."

"You see what?"

"Why didn't you take his advice?"

"Because as long as the animals I had been taking care of were still alive, I was going to do what I could for them."

"Could you tell me about the animals that were in the shelter that week?"

"Do I have to?"

"If you wouldn't mind."

"Well, I do mind."

"Why?"

"Because it's painful to talk about them."

"Please try?"

"Oh, all right . . . there were four dogs and five cats."

"Go on."

"The dogs were a Lab, a collie, a cocker spaniel, and a terrier. Two of the cats were black and white . . . one was a kitten . . . the other two cats were gray."

"May I ask you a question?"

"Go ahead."

"Did any of you who worked at the shelter ever name the animals?"

"Oh, boy."

"Tory . . . are you crying?"

"Could we pick this up later, please?"

"Of course."

16

Dr. Baraku Bexley

Medical Log: Tory Troy

While reviewing the documents provided to me by Tory Troy's Creative Writing teacher, Mr. Gabriel Mundàne, I came upon a poem titled "A Crow on the Lawn of the House I Grew Up In." The poem is reprinted below. I believe the dark tone and the illness/suicide subtext of the poem may hold meaning. The poem is not dated and, at the time of this log entry, I have not yet asked Ms. Troy when she wrote it.

A Crow on the Lawn
of the House I Grew Up In

by Victoria Troy

All the houses
on all the streets
all are burning.
There are volcanoes
in the shopping centers.
Comets crash on
schools. Fences
spit sparks. Trees
stab passersby with
poisoned branches.
All the waters are black.
A crow on the lawn
of the house I grew up in.

Diagnosis.

17

Tory Troy
Defense Attorney Carolyn Payne

"Hi, Tory. How are you? You look good."

"Are you kidding?"

"We lawyers usually say that to all our incarcerated clients."

"How do I really look?"

"Incarcerated."

"Bingo."

"I've been kept abreast of your meetings with Dr. Bexley, although for now all I'm actually told are the time and dates of your interviews. How are those going?"

"What do you want to hear?"

"The truth?"

"They're not bad, but it upsets me when he starts probing into things I don't want to talk about."

"Like what?"

"Like things I don't want to talk about."

"Tory—"

"Carolyn, please. It's bad enough having to be psychoanalyzed by Bexley. Please don't make me relive it with you."

"Tory, I need to know what's happening in order to prepare for either your trial or an appeal to set aside your institutionalization."

"Yeah, I know."

"Can you get a sense of how Dr. Bexley is thinking?"

"Yeah. I think he thinks I'm sane."

"Really?"

"Yep. In fact, if I was a betting woman, I'd give odds he's going to find me competent to stand trial."

"I see."

"So whatever it is you need to do if that happens, you should probably get started."

"How confident are you that you are correct?"

"Very."

"Okay. Let me start thinking about where we go next if he comes back with a report of competence. We'll have time to prepare for a trial, but I think I should probably start lining up witnesses."

"They're going to find me guilty, you know."

"What makes you say that?"

"Because I killed them, and Bex is going to say I'm sane, and no jury is going to let me walk. Would you, if you were on the jury?"

"Let's not think that far ahead just yet, Tory."

"Come on, Carolyn. Let's be real about this. I'm looking at a lethal injection in my future."

"If you are right, does this frighten you?"

"Not really."

"Why not?"

"I guess I'm just not afraid of death."

18

Tory Troy
Dr. Baraku Bexley

"How was your meeting with your lawyer, Tory?"

"A barrel of laughs."

"How are you feeling today?"

"Lousy."

"Why? Are you sick?"

"Yes."

"Do you need to see a doctor?"

"You *are* a doctor."

"A *medical* doctor."

"No."

"What's wrong?"

"I'm a little nauseous. And I've got a headache. It's probably the shit food in this place."

"Would you like to end today's session so you can rest?"

"Why? What do you have in store for me today?"

"Actually, we've reached the point where I need to administer some psychological tests to you."

"*Some?* How many?"

"Six."

"All at once?"

"No, of course not. We'll do them one at a time, and we can do as many in a day as you feel up to."

"Is this how you're going to be able to tell if I'm crazy?"

"We don't like to use the word *crazy*, Tory. I will determine *fit* or *unfit* for trial. Some of my colleagues use the Canadian Fitness Interview Test and base everything on the results of that test, but I prefer to use individual psychosocial evaluatory tests. I still may turn to the FIT, but for now I'd like to start with these six."

"I'm intrigued, Dr. B. I think I'd like to try taking one and see how it goes. If it's too draining and makes me feel worse, we'll reschedule. That cool?"

"Uh, yes. That is cool."

"You are too hip, Doc. Okay, then. What's the first?"

"I really should not tell you the titles of the tests, but with your intelligence and perceptive talents, the questions will make the topic immediately clear to you, so I am going to throw caution to the wind and reveal the subjects before we begin."

"Goody. What's the first?"

" 'Could You Become Assaultive?' "

"Jesus. You're jumping right to the good stuff, eh?"

"Shall we begin?"

"I suppose."

"I am going to make ten declarative statements that I want you to respond to with 'rarely,' 'sometimes,' or 'often.' Do you understand?"

"Yes. Fire away."

"Would you like some water, or do you need to use the bathroom before we begin?"

"Nope. I'm all yours."

"All right, then. Let's get started. Number one. 'I fall into moods of irritability for no apparent reason.'"

"Rarely."

"Number two. 'I don't work hard enough to improve myself.'"

"Sometimes."

"Number three. 'If someone yells at me, I yell right back.'"

"Often."

"Number four. 'I drink frequently and often get drunk.'"

"Rarely."

"Number five. 'I do things on impulse.'"

"Often. No, wait. I want to change that to 'Sometimes.'"

"All right. Number six. 'When others cross me, I don't forgive and forget easily.'"

"Can you give me a minute?"

"Take all the time you need."

"You want to know if I'm forgiving. Like if someone screws me, right?"

"I'm not allowed to discuss the questions, Tory. Would you like me to repeat the statement?"

"Yes."

"Number six. 'When others cross me, I don't forgive and forget easily.' "

" 'I *don't* forgive and forget . . .' The question is a negative. So if I say 'sometimes,' I'm saying I sometimes do *not* forgive . . . or I rarely do not forgive . . . Takes on a whole new meaning when you parse it, Doc."

"Yes, I suppose it does."

"I'm going to say 'rarely.' I'm a pretty forgiving person, so I rarely do not forgive and forget."

"Okay. Number seven. 'When I'm angry, I slam or break things.' "

"Rarely."

"Number eight. 'I engage in physical activity or use some other outlet to "let off steam." ' "

"Sometimes. When I'm stressed I'll sometimes walk the treadmill. Or masturbate."

"Number nine. 'If someone annoys me, I'm quick to tell them off.' "

"Often."

"And the final statement. Number ten. 'After an outburst I regret having lost my temper.' "

"Often."

"There. That wasn't so bad, now, was it?"

"How'd I do?"

"Now, Tory—"

"Oh, come on, Doc. What's the harm?"

"I'll tell you what. Let's complete the tests and then I'll give you a general summation of how you scored. Fair?"

"Fair. Now, can we call it quits for today? My head *really* hurts now."

"Of course. Would you like to see the nurse?"

"I suppose. Although all she'll give me is two Tylenol. What I wouldn't give for some of those Vicodin I've got stashed away."

"I'll see you tomorrow, Tory."

"Adios, Doc."

19

Dr. Baraku Bexley

Medical Log: Tory Troy

I administered the psychological test "Could You Become Assaultive?" to Tory Troy today and she scored a 19, which is an utterly average result. The protocols state that a client with a 19 shows an average amount of control when it comes to inhibiting angry feelings. She manifests a relatively high level of self-discipline regarding her anger. However, since this is the first test in a series of six, I will refrain from a preliminary evaluation at this time and will provide a more detailed interpretation later in this report.

20

Tory Troy
Dr. Baraku Bexley

"I'd like to continue with our discussion of your coworkers today, please."

"What about the rest of the tests?"

"We'll come back to them."

"Why do I have to talk about the people I worked with?"

"Indulge me, please, Tory. And by the way, how are you feeling today? Better, I hope?"

"Yeah. I threw up last night."

"And now you feel better?"

"Yes. It must have been some kind of virus, because now my headache is gone too."

"Very good. My notes show that you have already talked about Philip, Marcy, and Teresa. Perhaps you can tell me about Renaldo? What kind of relationship did you have with him?"

"I always got along with Renaldo. He was a really sweet guy. He had only been in this country for a few years. He was saving up money to bring his wife and kids over here."

"Where was he from?"

"Manacor."

"Where's that?"

"It's a small town on Majorca off the coast of Spain. The Balearic Islands."

"How was his English? Were you able to communicate with him?"

"His English was sometimes better than mine. His family had moved to Majorca when he was in his twenties, so he had gone to public schools in Spain, where English is a required course. And not just two years of it, the way we make kids here take Spanish or French. Before they could graduate they had to be able to speak and write high-school-level English. Shit. Some American high-school kids can't speak and write high-school-level English."

"What did you two talk about?"

"Not much, really. He told me about his family back home. I told him about my favorite movies and TV shows. He was fascinated by American movies and TV shows."

"What was his job?"

"He was the janitor. He spent all day mopping and sweeping and emptying pails and cleaning windows. He kept the place sparkling, I must say. He also had to clean the cages, which was probably the dirtiest job of all. But he never complained. Not once. And the cages were always spotless."

"It sounds like you were fond of Renaldo."

"I was. You know what he told me once? He told me that he put half of every paycheck in a savings account. Half. He actually lived on half his pay. When you consider his expenses—you know, rent, and utilities, not to mention food—that is an amazing achievement."

"Apparently he was quite committed to bringing his family over."

"He sure was. He had it all figured out too. He knew how much it would cost, and he even had a job at a nail salon lined up for his wife."

"And now none of that will come to be."

"Is that a question?"

"How does that make you feel?"

"I don't want to talk about that."

"Tory—"

"I don't. I *know* none of that will happen now. What else do you want me to say?"

"I want you to tell me what you're feeling. You know that you were the reason that none of Renaldo's plans will ever be realized. How does that make you feel?"

"You keep asking me that."

"Yes, I do. And I will keep asking until you tell me."

"Okay. I'll tell you. It makes me feel fucked up."

"Guilty?"

"Only in that Renaldo sort of got caught up in what happened, and maybe he shouldn't have been taken out with the others."

"Then why was he?"

"Because he was there."

"Didn't your connection with him mean anything to you? Didn't your friendship with him make you doubt what you were doing?"

"No. Like I said, he was there. So he was included."

"I see. And now, what would you say to his wife and children?"

"I wouldn't say a word. They're probably never going to make it here now, right?"

"That's awfully cold, Tory."

"You think?"

"Yes, I do. And it doesn't seem like you. It seems to me that you are posturing and that you feel a great deal of remorse about Renaldo."

"Well, you're the shrink. You oughta know better than me, I guess."

"Do I? Do I know better than you? Am I correct?"

"I'm done for today."

"Tory—"

"I'm serious, Doc. I'm done for today."

"Very well. We'll pick up tomorrow from this point."

"No we won't. I don't want to talk about Renaldo anymore. Give me a test tomorrow or I'm not saying a word."

"All right. I'll see you tomorrow."

"Yeah."

21

Dr. Baraku Bexley
Mrs. Viviana Troy

"Hello, Dr. Bexley."

"Hello, Mrs. Troy. Thank you for seeing me again."

"Anytime, Doctor. I will do anything I can to help my daughter."

"I'm glad to hear you say that, Mrs. Troy, because I am going to ask you to do something that might be a little difficult."

"Oh?"

"I would like to speak with Tory's father."

"No. Out of the question."

"May I ask why?"

"He has been out of her life for many years—and for good reason. I don't want that despicable monster to have anything to do with my daughter, especially now."

"Your ex-husband would have no contact whatsoever

with Tory. I can promise you that. On my word as a doctor."

"Then why do you want to speak to him?"

"Considering Tory's history with the man, it might be useful for me to discuss a few things with him. Let me put it this way, Mrs. Troy. Any trauma from Tory's past that could have contributed toward the state of mind she was in when she committed the crimes may serve her well."

"How would what happened to her in the past have anything to do with her fitness to stand trial?"

"It wouldn't. But it would have something to do with her mental state at the time of the crimes. And since my reports will certainly be entered into evidence, her defense lawyer may be able to . . . help the jury better understand what happened, and why it happened."

"I see."

"Do you?"

"Yes."

"Will you give me contact information for your ex-husband?"

"Yes. But I hold you to your promise, Dr. Bexley. He is under no circumstance to have any contact whatsoever with Tory."

"Understood. I will be the only one who speaks to him. The only one."

"Very well. Do you have a piece of paper?"

22

Tory Troy
Dr. Baraku Bexley

"Are you ready for your second test?"

"Ready as I'll ever be, I suppose. What's this one called?"

" 'Could You Break the Law?' "

"You're kidding."

"No, I'm not."

"Well, due respect, Doc, but don't we already know the answer to that question? I did, after all, break the law, right? Six times, according to the indictment."

"Yes, Tory, you did break the law. We know that. But many people break the law in a state of mind completely antithetical to their true personality. You did break the law, but I need to know if you could break the law when you are in what I'll have to call for now a 'normal' state of mind."

"I see."

"Do you understand?"

"Sure. I may not have been 'the real me' when I did what I did. That's what you want to find out, right?"

"In a sense."

"Okay. Fine with me. Fire away."

"Okay. This test is a little different than the first one."

"How so?"

"I will make ten declarative statements to which you will answer 'true' or 'false.'"

"Okay."

"Any questions?"

"Yeah. How'd I do on the first one?"

"You know I can't answer that."

"Yeah, I know. Took a shot."

"May we begin?"

"Shoot."

"Number one. 'I am highly sensitive when rebuffed or put down by someone.'"

"*Highly* sensitive?"

"Yes, that's how it reads."

"False."

"Number two. 'I am chronically angry, upset, and frustrated.'"

"*Chronically?*"

"Yes, chronically."

"False."

"Number three. 'I have gone through very low periods where I have felt utterly worthless.'"

"*Utterly?*"

"Yes."

"False."

"Number four. 'I am, or have yearned to be, on my own—free and independent of people and the restraints of society.' "

"True."

"Number five. 'Compared with others, my need to do risky things to find excitement is high.' "

"*Very* false."

"Number six. 'I have had episodes of boundless optimism that exceeded the reality of my situation.' "

"*Boundless?*"

"Yes."

"That means *completely* limitless, right?"

"Yes."

"False."

"Number seven. 'I have often done or craved to do things that are forbidden by society.' "

"*Forbidden?* That's a foreboding word, Doc. Have I craved to do *forbidden* things? Craved? This is a weird question."

"I'm sorry, Tory, but we cannot discuss the questions. You need to answer them on your own."

"Okay, then, false."

"Number eight. 'As a youngster, I often got my way by bluffing, bullying, or using physical force.' "

"Yeah, right. Look at me. I was even skinnier when I was a kid. False."

"Number nine. 'As a teen, I often committed petty, illegal acts like shoplifting, driving too fast, or cheating on exams.' "

"Could we go back to 'rarely,' 'sometimes,' or 'often' for this question?"

"Very funny. True or false, Tory."

"Well, the key word is *often*, so I'll say false."

"Number ten. 'I lose my temper easily.' "

"*Unequivocally* false."

"That's it. Would you like to go on to the third test or do you need a break?"

"No, I'm fine. What's the third called?"

" 'How Empathic Are You?' "

"Oh."

"What do you think? Are you up for it?"

"Ah, what the hell. Yeah, let's do it."

"Okay. This test consists of ten questions consisting of declarative statements, and for each statement you must answer using one of the following five qualifiers: 'not at all,' 'somewhat,' 'a good deal,' 'very much,' or 'exactly.' "

"Really? I get five choices?"

"Yes. It gives you a wide range of levels of agreement or disagreement with the statement."

"Okay. Take it away, Doc."

"Number one. 'In emergencies, I become emotional.' "

"Wow. A tough one right off the bat."

"Take your time."

"What are the five choices again?"

" 'Not at all,' 'somewhat,' 'a good deal,' 'very much,' or 'exactly.' "

"Do I become emotional in emergencies? That's a really good question. I'm trying to remember emergencies from my past. There really haven't been that many, thank God. Do I become emotional in emergencies? I think I'm going to go with 'very much' for this one, Doc. I put up a good front when there's a crisis, but inside I'm falling apart."

"Is 'very much' your answer?"

"Yes."

"All right. Number two. 'Even when I'm pretty sure I'm right, I'm patient enough to listen to other people's arguments.'"

"Oh, that is so true about me. Sometimes, when I'm listening to some idiotic argument, I wonder where I get the patience. I remember one time my friends and I were at a bar, and this guy kept trying to convince us that the story about Ivy League colleges taking nude posture photos of incoming freshmen in the fifties and sixties was an urban legend."

"Nude posture photos?"

"Yeah, you must have heard about them. Diane Sawyer, Meryl Streep, Dick Cavett . . . they were all photographed completely naked when they started college."

"Is that true?"

"Completely."

"Is there evidence?"

"Yes. The photos themselves still exist and are in a vault somewhere in the Smithsonian. Some journalist spent months tracking them down and interviewing former students who had posed for the pictures. The writer even saw some of the pictures."

"And this gentleman in the bar kept insisting you were wrong?"

"Yes. He went on and on about it being a big hoax and that nothing of the sort ever happened, blah, blah, blah."

"Yet you knew he was wrong."

"Yes."

"Did you argue with him?"

"Sort of. It all stayed pretty friendly, though, and was fueled by many beers and many shots."

"You patiently listened to him put forth his incorrect argument?"

"Yes."

"So, getting back to the test, what is your answer to question number two—'Even when I'm pretty sure I'm right, I'm patient enough to listen to other people's arguments'—?"

"I'd have to go with 'exactly,' Doc."

"Very well. Moving on. Number three. 'I feel deeply for the characters in tearjerker movies.'"

"That's an easy one too. I cry at movies all the time. Did you see *Titanic*, Doc?"

"Yes, I did."

"The scene where Leonardo DiCaprio lets go and drowns? And you can see his face, and his outstretched arm reaches toward Kate Winslet as he falls deeper and deeper? I'm tearing up now just talking about it."

"Yes, it was a poignant moment."

"You're not kidding. And it doesn't have to be a movie for me to start bawling like a baby."

"What else made you cry?"

"Bobby's death scene in *NYPD Blue* got to me. Big time."

"What was it about that scene that moved you most?"

"Probably Sipowicz promising Diane he'd always take care of her. Bobby and Andy were partners. The love and loyalty and commitment he felt toward Bobby, and his promise to take care of his partner's wife, was really touching."

"So do you have a response to this question?"

"Yeah. I'm going with 'exactly.'"

"All right. Continuing on. Question four. 'When I am with a depressed person, I become uncomfortable and it is difficult for me to talk.'"

"I'll go with 'very much' on that one, Doc. I don't like being around depressed people."

"All right. Question five. 'I feel uneasy when someone I know casually tells me about a personal problem.'"

"It doesn't usually bother me when people I know tell me about their personal problems, but I think the key word in that question is *casually*, so I'm going to say 'exactly.'"

"Okay. Question six. 'When a disagreement with someone becomes intense, I can't deal with it at the time.'"

"I'd have to say that's true. I've been known to walk away from a heated argument rather than deal with it right then."

"Your answer?"

"Exactly."

"Question seven. 'Others have said that I am softhearted.'"

"Who've you been talking to, Doc? Did you write these questions specifically about me?"

"Of course not. These are standard questions."

"I know. I'm only kidding. But, man, some of them are sure on target."

"So you're saying that people have described you as soft-hearted?"

"Well, actually people have called me a 'softie,' but I guess it's the same thing."

"So how would you respond?"

"Exactly."

"Question eight. 'I daydream about things (good and bad) that might happen to me.' "

"Damn. Another bull's-eye."

"You daydream?"

"All the time."

"Your answer?"

"Exactly."

"Question nine. 'The true answer to the great majority of issues is not clearly black or white—usually the truth is somewhere in between.' "

"I've believed that for a long time. I once knew a guy who used to say that everything is black or white—no grays. I never agreed with that. Nothing is that carved in stone, although one solution may have a preponderance of logic in its favor."

"What do you mean?"

"It's all a matter of perception. Let's say there are two neighbors who share a property line. One of the guys puts up a fence to keep his dog from wandering around the neighborhood and getting hit by a car, but the fence blocks the view of the other guy—who bought his house for the view of the mountains out his window. One guy's solution is another guy's problem."

"I see. So how do you respond?"

"Exactly."

"And the final question. 'I feel sad when I see a lonely stranger in a group.'"

"That's easy. Exactly."

"Okay, that concludes the third test. Since it's getting late, why don't we stop here and pick up where we left off tomorrow?"

"You're the doctor, Doc. It's almost time to eat anyway. Mental-institution food. Mmmm. That's good eatin.'"

"I'll see you tomorrow, Tory."

"Hasta la vista, baby."

23

Dr. Baraku Bexley
Crouch Troy

"Mr. Troy?"

"Yes?"

"This is Dr. Baraku Bexley."

"Who?"

"I am the court-appointed psychiatrist assigned to determine whether or not Tory Troy is fit to stand trial."

"Oh . . ."

"Mr. Troy?"

"Why did you call me?"

"Are you aware of the case, sir?"

"Only what I've read in the papers."

"If you have no objection, I would like to meet with you briefly to discuss Ms. Troy."

"Why?"

"As her father, you may be able to provide some useful information."

"What kind of useful information?"

"Background on her childhood, her schooling, her home life . . . that sort of thing."

"Her mother and I are divorced going on fifteen years, Doctor."

"I'm aware of that."

"I haven't seen or spoken to my daughter since the divorce."

"Yes, I know that too."

"Then why do you want to talk to me? You should talk to her mother."

"I'm talking to a great many people about Ms. Troy, sir, including her mother."

"Is this for real?"

"What do you mean?"

"Are you really her doctor? Tory's doctor?"

"No, sir, I did not say I was Tory's doctor. I am a doctor the court has appointed. Technically, she is not my patient and I am not treating her. But I can assure you that I am, indeed, a doctor, and I can provide complete credentials when we meet—including the court assignment."

"I don't know about this . . ."

"Mr. Troy, you have nothing to be concerned about. I am only compiling background information. You are not under subpoena."

"Do I need a lawyer?"

"No, but you are free to bring one to our meeting if it will make you feel more comfortable."

"All right. We can meet. One time. And I *will* bring

my lawyer. And I will tell you this, Doctor. We will be out the door instantly if she hears one thing she doesn't like. Are we clear?"

"Crystal."

"All right, then. How will this work?"

"Let me have your attorney's name and I'll call her to set up a meeting."

"You're definitely not a cop, right?"

"No, sir, I'm not. I'm a doctor."

"Okay. But bring those credentials you were talking about so my lawyer can get a look at them, all right?"

"Yes, sir, I will."

"Are we finished?"

"Yes, sir."

"Then good-bye, Dr. Bexley."

"Good-bye, Mr. Troy."

24

Tory Troy
Dr. Baraku Bexley

"Good morning, Tory."

"Hi, Doc."

"How are you today?"

"Tired."

"Why's that?"

"Some guy in one of the unlocked wards screamed 'Beverly!' all night long."

"Who's Beverly?"

"I have no idea, but I now loathe her with a deep and heartfelt passion."

"I don't blame you. Are you up for the next test?"

"Yes. I'd like to get them over with."

"Fine. Then let's dive right into it."

"What's this one called?"

" 'Can You Keep Yourself in Check?' "

"Boy, you sure know how to pick 'em, Doc."

"Why, thank you, Tory. Shall we begin?"

"Go ahead."

"This is a 'rarely,' 'sometimes,' or 'often' test, Tory."

"Oh, good. My favorite."

"Ready?"

"Go ahead."

"Number one. 'You grow quite impatient when you must wait in line.' "

"Quite?"

"Quite."

"As in 'very'?"

"Yes."

"I do get impatient when I have to wait in a line—who doesn't? But 'quite'? I don't like this question."

"Why not?"

"It's too hard to make the decision whether or not my impatience is 'quite.' "

"That's part of the process, Tory. Evaluating your own responses to the various answers to the question should provide you with some insight and reveal the correct answer. For you, that is."

"I thought you weren't supposed to help?"

"I'm not. Let's just call that a methodology clarification."

"Okay, then. 'Quite impatient,' huh? I'll say 'sometimes.' "

"Number two. 'You work very hard, play very hard, and try to be the best at what you do.' "

"Well, I do try to be the best that I can be . . . you

know . . . like that old army commercial? But 'very hard'? That's too extreme for me. I'll say 'sometimes.' "

"Number three. 'You easily become annoyed when held up by someone in traffic.' "

"Easily?"

"Yes."

"Rarely."

"Number four. 'You are more of a go-getter than most of your friends.' "

"Sometimes."

"Number five. 'You slam and break things when angry.' "

"Again with a breaking-things question?"

"Tory . . ."

"All right. Rarely."

"Number six. 'It irritates you when people don't take their job seriously.' "

"Often."

"Number seven. 'You snap at strangers when you become annoyed—for example, while driving, shopping, or working.' "

"Rarely."

"Number eight. 'You become angered when you fail at things you attempt to do.' "

"Sometimes."

"Number nine. 'When angry, you speed up and do things like driving, eating, and walking faster.' "

"Rarely. I slow down, actually."

"Number ten. 'You don't easily forgive and forget someone who offended you.' "

"And here we have another forgiveness question. I'll say rarely."

"That's it."

"That wasn't too bad."

"Ready for the next test?"

"Can we do it tomorrow?"

"Of course."

"Thanks, Doc. See you tomorrow, then."

25

Dr. Baraku Bexley
Crouch Troy
Attorney Marilyn Costanza

"Good afternoon, Mr. Troy. Counselor."

"Dr. Bexley."

"Before we begin, Doctor, I must insist on a few ground rules on behalf of my client."

"This is not a deposition, Counselor. Why would you feel the need for ground rules?"

"Because I told her I didn't want to talk about certain things and she's just doing her job."

"Very well. What are your concerns, Counselor?"

"We will not answer any questions about my client's relationship with his daughter prior to his divorce from Viviana Troy."

"May I ask why?"

"You may ask, but we will not answer that question. If I was informed correctly, you told my client that you wished to obtain background information about his daughter's childhood, schooling, and life at home. Is that correct?"

"Yes."

"Well, then, I must insist that you maintain those parameters in your questioning."

"Fine. Anything else?"

"No questions about my client's current personal life."

"I see. Anything else?"

"Not right now. Why don't we get started and we'll see how it goes."

"All right. Let's begin with this, then. Mr. Troy, could you tell me what Tory was like as a child?"

"She was always studying."

"She liked school?"

"Very much. She always got straight As."

"Do you recall what her favorite subjects were?"

"In grade school?"

"Yes."

"She liked science a lot. Stuff about dinosaurs especially. She knew all the names of the dinosaurs."

"Did she have many friends when she was young?"

"I wouldn't say she had a lot of friends, but I know that she was very close with the friends she did have."

"Do you remember what she was like in school? Anything her teachers may have said about her? How she got along with her classmates?"

"She was always very well-behaved. Her report cards always said that she was quiet in class and never got into fights. And she always raised her hand before talking."

"Did she ever talk to you about her schoolwork?"

"Doctor . . ."

"That's an innocent question, Counselor."

"It's okay, Marilyn, I'll answer it. Yes, she always told me about her classes and tests and everything else that went on in school."

"I see. Did you ever help her with her homework?"

"Doctor, that's enough."

"May I ask why?"

"You're veering too close to asking questions my client has stated he does not wish to answer."

"How so?"

"You're now asking about his personal interaction with his daughter, and if he answers one, you'll certainly ask many more. Those questions are off-limits. So, I'm sorry, but that's enough."

"Yes, Counselor, it is enough. Obviously, I am not going to learn anything of merit from Mr. Troy with you hovering over him like a mother hen guarding her brood, so why don't we end this here and now?"

"I am offended by your characterization, Doctor. I am simply protecting the interests of my client."

"Well, I apologize if I offended you, but it strikes me as quite odd that there even exists the *need* for you to protect your client. I told him during our phone conversation that I was not a member of law enforcement and that this was not a deposition. What does he have to hide that you and he are so concerned about 'protecting' him?"

"That's enough. Crouch, we're leaving."

"Thank you for your time, Mr. Troy."

"You're welcome, Doctor. And would you tell Tory . . . would you give her my best and tell her I am praying for her and that I hope everything works out for her?"

"I will do that, sir."

"Thank you."

"Can I ask you one last question, Mr. Troy?"

"I don't know. Can he, Marilyn?"

"Go ahead and ask your question, Doctor. I'll determine whether or not he should answer it."

"I see you wear an eye patch, and I know how you lost your eye. Tell me, do you have a prosthetic eye?"

"Go ahead, Crouch. You can answer it."

"No. I never got one."

"Why not?"

"I never wanted to forget why I am wearing this patch."

"I see."

"Is that it, Doctor?"

"Yes, Counselor. That is most assuredly it."

26

Tory Troy
Dr. Baraku Bexley

"Can we talk about Jake today, Tory?"

"No tests?"

"Perhaps later."

"All right. What do you want to know?"

"What was Jake like?"

"You mean as a boss?"

"As a person."

"As a person, he wasn't too bad."

"And as a boss?"

"An obnoxious prick."

"How so?"

"He gave in to the stress of the job."

"Meaning?"

"He let the job change his personality. He seemed to have this 'boss' persona that he put on whenever he was at work. It was like he was a different person."

"Could you give me an example?"

"He acted like he wasn't one of us—he wouldn't talk about anything non-work-related."

"For instance?"

"One day, Marcy brought in a photo album of her and her friends. You know, vacation pictures, family stuff . . . her friends and her just goofing around."

"Sounds like fun."

"It was. We were all just sitting around flipping through the pages, laughing, making fun of some of the pictures, when Jake walked in. We had just come to a picture of Marcy and one of her friends—I think it was a girl named Sarah—goofing around at a pool party. They had pulled off each other's bikini tops, and someone had snapped a picture just before they covered their breasts with their hands."

"They could both be seen topless?"

"Yes, but it was no big deal. They were both small on top, and it really wasn't pornographic at all or even erotic. The picture showed what happened at that moment—two twenty-something girls fooling around at a pool."

"But Jake could see Marcy without her top on, right?"

"Yes."

"From your description of Jake, I might guess that did not go over too well with him."

"You're not kidding. Boy, did he freak out."

"How?"

"He took one look at the picture, turned bright red,

and started yelling about how this was a place of business, and who said you could bring a picture like that into work, and stuff like that."

"He was embarrassed."

"Yeah, I suppose that's what it boiled down to. But he didn't have to go off the deep end like that."

"What happened then?"

"Marcy slammed the album shut, burst into tears, and ran into the bathroom."

"Did you say anything to Jake?"

"Yeah. At first I actually considered flashing him, but all I did was call him an asshole."

"What was his response?"

"Nothing. He just stomped into his office and slammed the door."

"How did this make you feel toward Jake?"

"Pissed off."

"Because he made Marcy cry?"

"No. Because he couldn't be a regular guy, and laugh along with the rest of us, and just be grateful that he was treated to a glimpse of Marcy he wouldn't have gotten to see in a million years."

"What else can you tell me about Jake?"

"He played piano, and he loved pizza. He once told me he could play the Beatles 'Martha My Dear' perfectly on the piano."

"If I recall correctly, Jake played the Beatles' 'Helter Skelter' during euthanasia sessions?"

"Yes."

"Isn't 'Martha My Dear' about Paul McCartney's pet sheepdog?"

"That's what they say."

"How about the animals?"

"What about them?"

"How was Jake with the animals?"

"Neutral."

"Meaning?"

"He wasn't *anything* with the animals. He didn't even have a pet at home—which I always thought pretty strange for a guy who managed a municipal animal shelter. I remember once going into a chain pet store and seeing a big poster with the numbers and kinds of pets each employee had. That always seemed to me to be the absolutely perfect thing to do. The poster, I mean. We never did it at the shelter, but we should have."

"Did everyone at the shelter have a companion animal?"

"Yeah. Some of them had more than one."

"Why do you think Jake didn't have a pet?"

"Who knows? Maybe he just took the job to have a job. Not everybody is personally into the stuff they work on all day. I once knew a guy who managed a jewelry store and who knew everything there was to know about jewelry. Rick. He did repairs, appraisals, set work—everything—and yet he didn't even wear a wedding ring. He told me sometimes customers would ask him why he didn't have a bracelet, or fancy rings. He used to shock the shit out of them by telling them that he wasn't into jewelry. He said the inevitable follow-up question was always, 'Then what are you doing here?' His stock answer was always, 'I've got a mortgage.' Maybe that's why Jake worked at the animal shelter. Just for the money."

"Anything else about Jake?"

"You know what, Doc? I'm starting to get one of those headaches again, and it feels like it's going to turn into something nasty."

"Would you like to stop for the day?"

"Do you mind?"

"Not at all. I'll see you tomorrow."

"Thanks."

"Not a problem. I hope you feel better."

"Yeah. Me too."

27

Tory Troy
Dr. Baraku Bexley

"How are you feeling today?"

"Better."

"Headache gone?"

"Almost. Now it's just a dull ache in my neck, and pain radiating into my jaw."

"Pain in your jaw?"

"Yeah, but it's TMJ, not a heart attack. I know this pain."

"All right. But let me know if you experience any alarming symptoms, okay?"

"Roger that, Doc."

"Ready for another test?"

"Ready as I'll ever be, I suppose. What's this one called?"

" 'What Are Your Dreams Telling You?' "

"Oh, yeah. This should be fun. I think."

"Once again, this is a 'true' or 'false' test. I will make ten declarative statements and you will answer 'true' or 'false' based on your own dream experiences."

"Okay."

"Ready?"

"Yes."

"Number one. 'I sometimes gain a better understanding of myself through a dream.'"

"True."

"Number two. 'My dreams are generally pleasant.'"

"Here we go again. *'Generally'*?"

"Yes."

"True."

"Number three. 'I sometimes solve a problem through a dream.'"

"True."

"Number four. 'I can recall my dreams at least twice a week.'"

"True. Sometimes more than that, actually."

"Number five. 'I have the same dream about eight or nine times a year.'"

"False. Actually *totally* false. I never have the same dream. It's always something new."

"Number six. 'I have disturbing dreams or nightmares eight or nine times per year.'"

"False. I never have nightmares."

"Number seven. 'A bad mood from a dream sometimes lingers into the next day for several hours.'"

"False. Within a few minutes after getting up, my dreams are gone with the wind."

"Number eight. 'I dream in color.' "

"True. But I also dream in black and white. Does that matter?"

"No. The question does not rule out *not* dreaming in color."

"Okay."

"Number nine. 'I cry, scream, or shout in my dreams about two or three times a year.' "

"Jeez, Doc. I certainly would not want to know someone who answers 'true' to that one."

"What is your response?"

"False."

"And the final question. 'I abruptly awaken from a dream about once a month.' "

"False."

"Very good. Thank you."

"What's next?"

"Well, if you are up for it, I would like to discuss a meeting I had recently regarding you and your case."

"Yeah, I'm up for it. Who with? Who was the meeting with?"

"Crouch Troy."

"Orderly!"

"Tory—"

"Mention him again and I am leaving. And I will never speak to you again."

"I'm sorry, Tory, but you cannot dictate the parameters of my questioning. I promise I will be solicitous of your feelings."

153

"How could you possibly bring that scumbag into this?"

"Now, Tory—"

"Don't 'Now, Tory' me. . . . He's a creep, and you must know by now what he did to me and my mother. Why would you involve him in this?"

"Because what he did to you and your mother most likely had a major impact on the person you are now, and since it is my job to determine your mental competence, I must understand how you came to be the woman you are today."

"I will not talk about him. I won't. I don't want anything to do with him. And if you push, I'll play 'sick' and I'll remain 'sick' for weeks."

"Tory—"

"I'm not kidding, Dr. Bexley. Believe me. I will not talk about him. If you think I'm not serious, just try me."

"Tory, I understand. All right. Calm down. Consider the subject closed. I will not bring him up again. Okay?"

"Do you mean it?"

"Absolutely. But if you don't mind, I would like to pass along a message to you from your father."

"A message? What could that asshole possibly have to say to me?"

"He asked me to tell you that he was praying for you and that he hoped everything worked out for you."

"Great. I'm touched."

"I'm only the messenger, Tory."

"I know, Doc. I'm sorry if I got a little, uh, 'ornery' with you."

"Not a problem. Would you consider doing another test, then?"

"Sure. It'll take my mind off what you just told me. What's it called?"

" 'Does Anger Get the Best of You?' "

"Ha! That's great! After I explode at you, you're going to test me on my anger-coping skills. Excellent! Carry on."

"I'm glad I was able to get a chuckle out of you. Ready?"

"Ready."

"For this test, please answer 'true' or 'false' to the twelve declarative statements I will make."

"Okay."

"Number one. 'I am usually the one to stand up for the rights of other people.' "

"I'd have to go with 'true' on that one. It pisses me off to no end when I see someone being bullied."

"Okay. Number two. 'It irritates me when peers or family members tell me what to do.' "

"Irritates? I'll say false. It actually kind of amuses me, since I'm going to do what I want to do regardless of what anyone says."

"Number three. 'Expressing anger to someone who annoys you is emotionally healthy.' "

"Hell, no. It's not emotionally healthy, it's god-damned dangerous."

"You're saying 'false'?"

"Yes."

"Number four. 'It bothers me very much to be considered "second best." ' "

"No way. I remember this old Italian guy once told me that the secret to being happy was to be content with what you had, and with who you were. I'll never forget that. He used to say—with an Italian accent, of course—'There will-a always a-be people with a-more and a-less-a than you.' That is so true."

"False?"

"False."

"Number five. 'Most of the time, I am willing to fight for what I want.' "

"That's probably true."

"Is it, or isn't it?"

"Okay. True."

"Number six. 'I would have no qualms talking back to an authority figure such as a guard or police officer.' "

"That is completely false. I don't believe in mouthing off like that. It shows a lack of respect."

"Number seven. 'I like to direct the actions of others.' "

"Me a leader? No way. False."

"Number eight. 'I probably would try to get even with people who had been bossy or pushy toward me.' "

"Whoa."

"What's wrong?"

"That one hits a little close to home."

"How so?"

"The whole 'getting even with people' thing—is that

156

what I did? Did I 'get even' with the people I worked with?"

"Is that how you see it?"

"I don't know."

"Well, we can come back to that if it concerns you. For now why don't we try to get through this test."

"Okay. I'm going to say false."

"All right. Number nine. 'If I'm upset with someone, I don't hesitate to let him or her know about it.'"

"I hold a lot of that stuff in, Doc. I'll go with false."

"Number ten. 'People will take advantage of you if you're humble.'"

"Sad, but true."

"True?"

"Yes."

"Number eleven. 'A person who is spontaneous in releasing anger is better adjusted than one who is slow to express it.'"

"That is such bullshit. I think someone who is spontaneous in releasing anger is an out-of-control jerk."

"I'm going to go out on a limb here and guess that your answer is false?"

"Bingo."

"And the final question, number twelve. 'I would feel glad if someone told off a person I found obnoxious.'"

"That's probably true. I would take pleasure in seeing some creep told off."

"That's it, then."

"How'd I do?"

"Tory . . ."

"Oh, come on, Doc. That's the last test, and you said you'd give me an idea of how I did when we were finished. Remember?"

"Well, I need to study the full results before coming to any conclusions, but I can tell you that on this test you scored a four, which indicates that you have an average degree of hostility that you'd be willing to vent against others."

"Is that good?"

"The higher the score, the less control the person has of his or her social animosity. Thus, the lower the score the better."

"So I am in control. Most of the time."

"Apparently."

"That's pretty ironic, isn't it, Doctor B?"

"How so?"

"The test says I can control my anger, and yet I am locked up for killing six people. Maybe that means I wasn't angry when I killed them. Can someone commit murder without being angry at their victims?"

"That's a good question. What do you think?"

"I think probably yes. After all, that's what I did, right?"

"You were not angry at your coworkers? Even a little? Didn't you say that it upset you that none of them—let me check my notes—*realize how they earn their money?*"

"Yeah, I guess so."

"Not much irony in manifesting anger through violence, now, is there, Tory?"

"No."

"Are you all right?"

"So where are we, Doc? What happens next?"

"My testing is completed and I will now study the results. I do think I will need a few more sessions with you before I reach my decision on whether or not you are competent to stand trial, though. Also, there are a few more people I'd like to talk to."

"How's it looking, Doc?"

"I'm not allowed to say, Tory. You know that."

"Well, you don't have to, my friend. I know I'm competent and you know I'm competent. And you also know that no jury on earth is going to acquit me. I'm looking at a lethal injection in my future."

"You should not presume anything, Tory. The resolution of situations like this are often stunningly surprising."

"Perhaps. But if I was a bettin' woman, I sure wouldn't like my odds."

"Are you a betting woman?"

"No. Never have been and probably never will be."

"Well, then, my only advice is to hope for the best, but prepare for the worst."

"Thanks, Doc. That's exactly what I've been doing. Do you remember what I told you in our very first session?"

"Yes."

"Well, I'm *still* thinking about suicide. A lot."

"Tory—"

"Time's up, Doc. See you soon."

"All right. See you soon."

28

Dr. Baraku Bexley
Halle Bexley

"Did I tell you that Judge Becker was asking about you?"

"Yes."

"Good. At least I'm not going completely senile."

"You look tired."

"I am. Today I told Tory Troy that I had completed my testing of her."

"Did you?"

"I'm not sure. I'm tempted to give her the Fitness Interview Test."

"In addition to the six tests you've already given her and on top of your personal interviews?"

"Yes."

"Are you that ambivalent about your conclusion?"

"No. In fact, I'm utterly convinced she is mentally competent and fit to stand trial."

"Then why waste time with more tests?"

"I guess I'm just nervous about my findings being challenged on appeal."

"Honey, listen to me. You know you're correct. And you know she's fit. You know you've done your job. Am I right?"

"Yes, you are."

"Then write your report, and move on."

"I suppose you're right."

"You know I am."

"All right, then. I'll call the judge in the morning and tell him I'll have a report for him within a few days. I'm going to sleep."

"Good night, honey."

"Good night."

29

Dr. Baraku Bexley
Lester Jackson

Psychological Report for Victoria Troy

"Good morning, Dr. Bexley."

"Good morning, Lester."

"You finished the Troy evaluation?"

"Yes. I'd like to dictate the report to you, and I'm hoping you can get me a formatted copy within the next couple of days."

"Not a problem. I can drop it off at the house Wednesday—two days after Labor Day? That all right?"

"That'd be great."

"It's done."

"Okay. Shall we get started?"

"Fire away, Doc."

"Psychological Evaluation, Woodward Knolls Psychiatric Institute, Old Saybrook, Connecticut. Name: Victoria parenthesis Tory close parenthesis Abigail Troy—"

"You're using Victoria . . . or Tory?"

"Except for here, I decided to use Tory when I cite her full name. She hardly ever uses Victoria."

"Okay."

"Dates of evaluation: August fifth through eighth, twelfth through fourteenth, nineteenth through twenty-first, 2002. Case number 71653-90262. Building number two. Ward nine. Admission date: Friday, 2 August, 2002. Date of report: Monday, 26 August, 2002."

"All standard format, right?"

"Yes. Use the template in the Word Project Gallery."

"Okay."

"Purpose for evaluation: This is the first admission to this facility for this twenty-eight-year-old single female who has a college degree, a certificate in Animal Euthanasia, and who works for the Waterbridge Animal Shelter. She attended St. Francis of Assisi Grammar School in New Haven, Connecticut—graduated 1988; St. Mary's High School in New Haven, Connecticut—graduated 1992; and the University of Bridgeport in Bridgeport, Connecticut—graduated 1996 with a Bachelor of Arts in American Literature and a minor in Psychology. She successfully completed an Animal Euthanasia Technician course—funded by the shelter—and received certification from the state of Connecticut."

"She minored in Psych?"

"Yes."

"Did that affect the interviews? Did she see through any of the questions?"

"Yes to both. She was very sharp."

"Okay. Go on."

"She was remanded to the custody of the facility after being arrested and charged with the felony murder of her six animal-shelter coworkers. She has been held in the locked detention ward of the facility since her admission on 2 August 2002. The purpose of this court-ordered evaluation was to determine the patient's fitness to stand trial for the above-mentioned felony charges. The question that needed to be answered was, Is Tory Troy mentally competent to a degree rendering her capable of understanding the charges against her and participating in her own defense?"

"Do you want me to answer the phone?"

"No, let the service take it. We need to get through this."

"Okay."

"Preliminary results were reported in the patient's progress notes on 8 August 2002. The current report will supplement and elaborate upon those preliminary findings."

"Do you want the August eighth report attached to this?"

"Yes."

"Okay."

"Assessment procedures. Patient was examined physically upon admission to the facility and was found to be in good health, although slightly underweight—five feet five inches, one hundred nine pounds. Blood pressure, blood sugar, cholesterol, and temperature were all normal. Medical reports attached."

"She's tiny."

"Yes, she's very petite."

"Where are the medical files?"

"In the locked folder *Med Reports* on my hard drive."

"The password still *Hippocrates*?"

"Yes. But all lowercase."

"Okay."

"Continuing on. The patient is highly intelligent, perceptive, and very verbal. She is aware of her situation and acknowledges the possibility of standing trial and being found guilty. She fully understands that she might be sentenced to death under current Connecticut state sentencing laws if she stands trial and is found guilty. Since her admission, patient has been administered alprazolam—Xanax—two milligrams b.i.d., and zolpidem—Ambien—ten milligrams at bedtime. Six psychological tests were administered verbally to the patient over a period of four days, combined with a clinical interview and a mental status examination. Tests were administered by Dr. Baraku Bexley and interpreted by same."

"Do you want any of the tests reproduced in this report?"

"No."

"Okay."

"Background information. Tory Troy was sexually and physically abused by her biological father until her early teens. She lashed out physically against her father toward the end of the period of abuse and stabbed him in the eye with a nail file. The father lost the eye. Her mother, Mrs. Viviana Troy, also a victim of physical abuse, divorced her husband fifteen years ago. Mrs. Troy and the patient have continued to live together. Mr. Crouch Troy, Ms. Troy's biological father, was interviewed for this evaluation but was noncooperative."

"Daddy wouldn't talk to you, eh?"

"We spoke briefly, but I knew we'd be going nowhere when he showed up for the meeting with a lawyer."

"Really? Guess you made him nervous."

"She watched him like a mother hen. After she told him not to answer a couple of questions, I cut the interview short. I've had no more contact with Crouch Troy."

"Was he wearing an eye patch?"

"Yes. And I asked him about it."

"About the patch?"

"No, about why he didn't have a prosthetic eye."

"Really? What did he say?"

"He said he didn't get one because he never wanted to forget why he was wearing the patch."

"How noble. Hey, maybe there's hope for the guy yet."

"Maybe. Continuing on. Ms. Troy had been working at the Waterbridge Animal Shelter for eleven months when the murders occurred."

"Ms.?"

"No . . . change that to . . . just delete the *Ms.* and refer to her as *Troy*."

"Okay."

"Troy does not have a history of serious substance abuse, although she has experimented with illicit drugs. Her experiences with drugs and alcohol were mostly random and short-lived, in a pattern known as 'recreational,' although at the time of her arrest, she was not deliberately abstaining from either alcohol or drugs. She has acknowledged smoking marijuana and experimenting with pharmaceuticals. She has acknowledged purchasing prescription painkillers—Percocet, Vicodin, Oxycontin—from friends and also being given prescription pain medications as a gift from friends. All were used to get high, and the patient did not mix the drugs with alcohol or take an excessive or dangerous amount. Troy has no history of 'doctor shopping' drug-seeking behavior, and there are no reports of emergency-department visits for acute drug intoxication."

"Your typical party girl?"

"Not really. I got the sense she experimented more out of curiosity than out of an urge to get . . . wasted. She's a writer, and maybe she was looking for new artistic horizons."

"I thought writers were mostly alcoholics."

"Some were . . . and still are, I suppose. She never abused alcohol, though."

"Okay. Go on."

"At the beginning of her evaluation, Tory Troy admitted to having a supply of eighty-seven hydrocodone hcl pills—trade name Vicodin—hidden somewhere known only to her. She has admitted thinking about taking the entire lot of pills to commit suicide. She manifested intermittent signs of depression during the evaluation but seemed to be able to return to a positive state of mind, and was even quite cheerful at times."

"She was suicidal? So was Hemingway."

"In addition to determining the patient's fitness to stand trial, her suicidal ideations prompted this evaluator to determine whether or not the patient was self-destructive. The conclusion of this evaluator is that the patient is posturing and would be unlikely to actually commit suicide. She was placed under a suicide watch for the first week of her admission, but it was subsequently canceled. Since there is no possibility of Troy being released on bond, any suicide attempts would occur within the Woodward Knolls Institute. Staff observations of the patient, all of which were compiled during the course of this evaluation, reported that Tory Troy is polite, cooperative, and pleasant. She obeys all instructions, takes all medication as instructed, and does not act out or verbally abuse the staff."

"Sounds like a good patient."

"She is. Mental-status examination. Results of mental status examination revealed an alert, attentive individual who was able to maintain cohesive conversation and who was not easily distracted. The patient was well-groomed. Patient was oriented perfectly to time, place, and date. Patient seemed to avoid excessive eye contact. Her deportment was appropriate for a face-to-face interview. She sat comfortably upright with her back against the back of the chair and her hands clasped on the table in front of her. Her speech was appropriate in volume, rate, modulation, prosody, and tone. Her grammar and vocabulary were suggestive of above-average intelligence, and her interaction with this evaluator suggested above-average social skills. At various times throughout the questioning, the patient manifested a clever sense of humor."

"Hang on a minute, Dr. Bexley. I have to change pads."

"All right."

"Okay. Sorry. Go on."

"The patient's attitude was candid and compliant. Her mood was stable. Her memory functions were intact. Her thought process was sound, and her thinking was well-organized. Her expression of her ideas and thoughts was focused and complete. She manifested no perceptual disorders. She manifested no delusion or paranoia. She did manifest and discuss suicidal ideations. Her level of personal insight was higher than normal. She seemed to understand and be able to identify her significant stressors. Her social judgment was good, although this contrasts markedly with the charges against her."

"I have to interrupt, Doc, to tell you that this girl does not sound like a cold-blooded killer. Is there any chance she didn't do it?"

"She admitted the murders."

"Oh. Okay. Sorry. Go on."

"Summary and recommendations. Results of psychological evaluation reveal a history of physical and sexual abuse against the patient perpetrated by her biological father. Any psychosocial scarring from this abuse seems to have been repressed by the patient for the past fifteen years. A further assessment of the patient's mental state at the time of the murders with which she is charged, and how this state of mind was modulated by the patient's past, is not the purview of this report. Defense counsel will be required to support a plea of not guilty by reason of insanity. The answer to the question, Is Tory Troy mentally competent to a degree rendering her capable of understanding the charges against her and participating in her own defense? is yes. This report is to determine the patient's mental competence for trial, and it is the finding that she is competent to stand trial. Okay. That's it."

"Respectfully submitted, Baraku Bexley, M.D., Ph.D.?"

"Yes."

"Okay, Dr. Bexley. I'll get on this ASAP and I'll see you Wednesday at your house. Ten copies enough?"

"For now. Thank you very much, Lester."

"My pleasure, sir. See you Wednesday."

"Okay."

"Oh . . . one more thing."

"Yes?"

"Why'd she do it?"

"She loved animals."

"Really? Then why the hell did she go to work as a euthanasia tech?"

"At this point, she's the only one who can answer that. And right now her answer is, 'I don't know.'"

"Okay, Doc. See you Wednesday."

"Okay, Lester. Wednesday."

30

Defense Attorney Carolyn Payne
District Attorney Brawley Loren
Judge Gerard Becker
The Jury Pool

"Juror ID 861-227?"

"Here."

"How are you?"

"Fine, thank you."

"I'd like to ask you a few questions."

"All right."

"How do you feel about animals?"

"What do you mean?"

"Do you have a pet?"

"No."

"Do you like animals?"

"Not particularly."

"Thank you, you're excused."

"Juror 701-909?"

"Here."

"Have you read any of the newspaper articles about my client and the crimes she has been charged with?"

"Yes."

"Do you think you would be able to objectively listen to all the evidence and come to a fair verdict?"

"I think so."

"Do you think she is guilty?"

"Well, didn't she admit to killing all those people?"

"Yes, she did."

"Well, then she's guilty, right?"

"Would you consider the possibility that she might have been insane at the time of the murders?"

"Insane?"

"Yes."

"Like, crazy . . . out of her mind?"

"Unable to understand the full consequences of her actions at the time of the murders."

"No."

"Thank you. You're excused."

"Juror 107-774?"

"Right here."

"Good morning, ma'am."

"Good morning."

"Do you work, ma'am?"

"Yes."

"And what is it you do?"

"I'm a hospice nurse."

"I see. So you deal with terminally ill patients on a daily basis?"

"I don't 'deal with them,' sir. I take care of them."

"Of course. My apologies. Do you administer medications to your patients?"

"Yes."

"Morphine?"

"Yes."

"Dilaudid?"

"Yes."

"Oxycontin?"

"Yes."

"Your patients are in extraordinary pain, are they not?"

"No, we keep them very comfortable."

"I'm sorry. I wasn't clear. Let me rephrase my question. The illnesses your patients are suffering from cause a great deal of pain—is that correct?"

"If left unmedicated, yes. The pain levels of terminal patients would be considered excruciating. Some have used the word *catastrophic* to describe certain levels of end-stage pain."

"Isn't it true that the narcotic pain medications that I mentioned can suppress breathing?"

"Yes."

"If you note that a terminal patient's breathing is becoming shallower and that their respiration is becoming more difficult, do you reduce the levels of their pain medication accordingly?"

"No."

"Why not?"

"Because we do not allow patients to suffer."

"But isn't it possible that by maintaining the same high

levels of narcotic pain medications, you could further slow their breathing and possibly even hasten their deaths?"

"I don't want to answer that."

"Your Honor?"

"Juror 107-774, could you tell the court why you do not want to answer that question?"

"I just don't, Your Honor."

"I'll need more than that, dear."

"The District Attorney is asking me if I perform euthanasia, Judge."

"I see. May I read something to you?"

"Please."

"When I was given this case, I did some preliminary research into euthanasia. I found something on the euthanasia.com Web site that might alleviate your concerns about answering the D.A.'s question. *What euthanasia is not: There is no euthanasia unless the death is intentionally caused by what was done or not done. Thus, some medical actions that are often labeled 'passive euthanasia' are not a form of euthanasia, since the intention to take life is lacking. These acts include not commencing treatment that would not provide a benefit to the patient, withdrawing treatment that has been shown to be ineffective, too burdensome, or is unwanted, and the giving of high doses of painkillers that may endanger life when they have been shown to be necessary. All those are part of good medical practice, endorsed by law, when they are properly carried out.* Does that change your thinking, ma'am?"

"Not really, Judge. I am aware of the doctrine espoused in the excerpt you cited, but it is still me up here answering a specific question, not engaging in some abstract discussion. So I still do not want to answer his question."

"I see. Well, then, is there anything you can tell the court that might help us understand what you do when faced with the situation the D.A. has described?"

"Yes, Your Honor, I will say this. We administer to our patients the medications prescribed for them by their doctors. We do not . . . supersede the physicians' orders regarding the dosages or the spacing of doses."

"Very well. That's good enough for me. Move on, Counselor."

"Do you have a pet, ma'am?"

"Yes. A dog."

"Would you put your dog to sleep if he was suffering from a painful, terminal illness?"

"Yes."

"That's all I have, Judge. She'll do."

"Thank you. Juror 107-774, please see the clerk for your juror information packet. Who's next?"

"Juror 863-725?"

"Here."

"Would you please remove your sunglasses."

"Sorry."

"How old are you, please?"

"Twenty-three."

"And do you work?"

"Yes."

"What is it you do?"

"I'm in college. And I work as a waitress."

"Where?"

"The Olive Garden."

"Do you have a big family?"

"Yes."

"Are your grandparents still alive?"

"No, they all died."

"I see. How old were you when your last grandparent passed away?"

"Twenty-two. It was just last year."

"And who was it that died?"

"My grandmother."

"Maternal?"

"What does that mean?"

"Was it your mother's mother or your father's mother?"

"My mother's."

"Could you tell me about how she died?"

"She had liver cancer but my mother was taking care of her at home, and then one day she started throwing up blood, and we called 911, and they rushed her to the hospital in an ambulance, but she died later that night."

"You say, 'We called 911.' Were you present during all this?"

"Yes."

"How so?"

"I was with my mother at my grandmother's house when she started puking—sorry—throwing up blood."

"Were you the one who called 911?"

"Yes."

176

"Did you go with your grandmother in the ambulance?"

"No, my mother went with her and I followed them in my mother's car."

"Were you with your grandmother when she died?"

"Yes."

"Could you tell me about that, please?"

"What's to tell? She was lying on a gurney, and they had an oxygen mask on her face, and the next thing I knew she started gasping and trying to sit up, and then she fell back. And that was it."

"Did they try to resuscitate her?"

"No. She had a DNR—you know, an order against it."

"I see. How did watching your grandmother die make you feel?"

"I really didn't feel much of anything, to tell you the truth. Ever since she got really sick, she was mostly out of it. They had her on all kinds of pills, and anytime I went to see her she was either sleeping or raving about something."

"She was delusional?"

"I don't think so. I think she was just really high."

"Do you have any thoughts about your grandmother's final days?"

"What kind of thoughts?"

"The way she spent her final months . . . If you could choose how to spend your final days, would it bother you if what happened to your grandmother happened to you?"

"Hell, yeah."

"How so?"

"She suffered, even with all the pills. I don't want to go out like that. I want it to be quick. Bang. Like a heart attack or stroke. And if it's my time, I don't want to survive it. I don't want to end up paralyzed or not able to talk, or be some vegetable in a coma."

"If you were diagnosed with a painful, terminal disease, would you consider suicide?"

"Probably."

"I have no more questions, Judge. She's fine."

"Juror 745-111."

"Yes?"

"What do you do for a living?"

"I'm the mayor of Wesley, Connecticut."

"A mayor couldn't get out of jury duty?"

"I didn't even try, Counselor."

"We appreciate your diligence, Your Honor."

"May I make a request, Counselor?"

"Of course."

"Out of respect for His Honor, and acknowledging that this is, indeed, his courtroom, would you kindly address me as Madame Mayor?"

"Of course. My apologies to you and the court."

"Proceed, Counselor."

"Yes, Your Honor."

"Madame Mayor, do you support the death penalty?"

"Yes, I do."

"Well, you are in agreement with seventy-one percent of the American population. If you ascended to the governorship of your state, what would it take for you to seriously consider commuting a death sentence?"

"I would not consider commuting a death sentence."

"Ever?"

"No, sir."

"May I ask why?"

"Because I wouldn't have that power. Plus, I believe it vitiates our judicial system."

"How so?"

"I'm sure I do not have to tell you, Counselor, of the many protections and checks and balances of American jurisprudence."

"And?"

"By the time someone is sentenced to death in our court system, I believe that there has been adequate opportunity for the presentation of evidence that would exculpate him or her. Thus, I do not believe it is an executive's place to debase such a process by a last-minute negation of the verdict and sentence."

"But I'm sure you've heard of people wrongly executed? People who were innocent but were put to death before the evidence to save them could be presented?"

"Of course, but those cases are few and far between and, overall, the death penalty has been applied fairly in the overwhelming majority of cases."

"There are many judicial scholars who would argue that point, ma'am, but let's move on."

"Nothing's perfect, Counselor."

"Fine. Do you support a woman's right to choose?"

"Yes."

"Do you support partial-birth abortions?"

"No."

"Why not?"

"Because at that late stage, a baby is viable. I only support abortion up until the fetus is viable. Once the baby can live outside the mother, even with advanced medical technology assisting, abortion is then murder."

"Would you support legislation outlawing partial-birth abortions?"

"Yes."

"What happens as technology improves, and babies born four or five months premature can survive and lead healthy lives?"

"Then I would use viability as the benchmark and prohibit abortion accordingly."

"It is quite possible, then, that based on your doctrine, in the future, abortions would only be allowed in the first trimester."

"Yes."

"Do you believe abortion protesters who kill abortion doctors are justified?"

"No."

"Are you married, Madame Mayor?"

"Yes."

"Do you have children?"

"Yes."

"Are your parents still alive?"

"No, they're both dead."

"That's all for me, Your Honor. We'll thank the

mayor for her time, but we choose to pass on her services as a juror."

"Very well. Move on."

"Yes, Your Honor. Juror 400-806."

"That's me."

"Good morning, sir."

"Hello."

"Have you been following the newspaper reports of the animal-shelter murders?"

"Oh, yeah."

"You say that with a certain 'definiteness.' "

"Really? I do?"

"Yes."

"Well, I have been following the stories in the papers."

"Why have you been so interested in the case?"

"Why? What do you mean?"

"Have you regularly followed other local crime stories with the same enthusiasm?"

"No."

"Then what is it about the case of Tory Troy that has captured your interest?"

"My brother."

"Your brother? What about your brother?"

"The Sunday after Tory Troy was arrested, he gave a sermon about the murders. From then on, I've been reading all the stories in the newspapers about it."

"Your brother is a priest?"

"Yes."

"Have you and he discussed the case?"

"Yes."

"Has your brother given you his opinion about what happened?"

"Yes."

"Did your discussions with your brother influence your own opinion about the case?"

"Yes."

"If you were on the jury, and Tory Troy was found guilty, would you be able to sentence her to death by lethal injection?"

"No."

"If you could determine her sentence, what would it be?"

"Life in prison with no chance of parole."

"What if everyone else on the jury was for the death penalty?"

"Then I guess we'd have a hung jury."

"Thank you, sir, you're excused."

31

Judge Gerard Becker
Defense Attorney Carolyn Payne
District Attorney Brawley Loren
The Jury

"Ladies and gentlemen, thank you. Being on a jury is an exciting civic experience, and a responsibility and privilege of being an American. This case is a very serious one. Six people are dead, and the defendant has been charged with their murders. Your job will be to listen carefully to all the evidence and come to a conclusion. Victoria Troy is being tried for all six murders at one time, in one trial. Six premeditated Murder One charges. Your verdict will be one of the following: guilty, or not guilty by reason of insanity. You will also be responsible for a sentencing recommendation. The statutes address the magnitude of the crimes and proscribe specific sentences for a guilty verdict. If you find Ms. Troy guilty, you will be required to choose from three sentences: twenty-five years to life with no parole for each murder, sentences to run concurrently; or life in prison without parole; or death by lethal injection. I do have the judicial authority to set aside your sentencing recommendation. Are there any questions? Ma'am?"

"Thank you, Judge. Are we going to be sequestered?"

"I thought about it, but I have decided against sequestering. And from the looks on all your faces, I can tell that this is a popular decision. I see no purpose in locking you all away in a hotel for however many days or weeks it takes to get through this trial. You have all read the newspaper accounts of the crimes; many of you know people involved in the case. I have great trust in the wisdom of the American jury, however, and I do not believe we need to treat jurors as if they are fragile and will be corrupted by information in the mainstream culture. I will, however, ask you all not to read newspaper, Internet, or magazine accounts of the ongoing trial, and I will also ask you to not watch televised reports of the trial. Yes?"

"How will we avoid all that, Your Honor? And what happens if we are exposed to something on the news? Or if someone says something to us? Will we get in trouble?"

"No, of course not. But remember that your job is to evaluate the evidence. You all need to keep in mind that nothing you hear outside this courtroom is considered evidence. Do you understand? I'll repeat it. *Nothing you hear outside this courtroom is considered evidence,* and it cannot factor into your decision as to the guilt or innocence of the defendant. Sir?"

"What if we get sick, or need to use the bathroom during the trial, or there's some kind of emergency in our family?"

"None of you need to worry. Regarding personal comfort: Two bailiffs will be stationed at either side of the jury box. All you need to do is raise your hand and a bailiff will immediately come to you. If you need to use the bathroom or do not feel well, you will tell the officer. I am very solicitous of the well-being of my jurors. I have trained my court attendants to be able to communicate with me with a system of hand signals. If one of you needs a bathroom break, and the need is so urgent that you will not be able to wait until the next recess, I will immediately call a recess, and the first thing I will order is the vacating of the jury box. Within seconds, you will all be in the private jury room, which has two nicely appointed bathrooms. A bailiff will be stationed outside the jury room, and as soon as everyone is comfortable, one of you will notify him and we will reconvene. Suffering through testimony with intestinal distress or a full bladder is not going to happen in my courtroom. This I promise you. The Connecticut court system has a reputation for treating its jurors with respect and assuring their comfort. That reputation is deserved. And please do not worry about interrupting the proceedings. As you will quickly learn, both defense and prosecution counsels will have no qualms whatsoever about calling for a recess, no matter where we are in the trial. Does this calm your worries? Good. Any other questions?"

"Family emergencies, Your Honor?"

"Yes. I'm sorry. I did not address that issue. All of you

will be given a private emergency phone number that you can give to two members of your family. And I use the term *family* loosely, by the way. Significant others and close personal friends count. The two people you choose are completely up to you. This phone number is staffed every minute of the entire court day. If there is a family emergency, someone can call this number, state the problem to the officer who takes the call, and within minutes one of my bailiffs will be informed of the situation and I will call a recess. If the emergency requires the termination of your services as a juror, you will be dismissed and an alternate will be appointed in your place. Any more questions? No? Good. We will convene Monday morning at ten A.M. for opening statements. Thank you, and you all have a nice weekend."

32

Tory Troy
Defense Attorney Carolyn Payne

"They impaneled the jury."

"Yeah, I heard. How's it look?"

"Seven men, five women. Youngest is twenty-three; oldest, sixty-four. Two blue-collar workers, two stay-at-home moms. Plus a hospice nurse, an accountant, a pharmacist, a stockbroker, a teacher, a journalist, a surgeon, and a college student."

"What do you think?"

"It looks like a relatively balanced bunch."

"No matter."

"What do you mean, Tory?"

"They're going to find me guilty."

"You don't know that."

"Oh, come on, Carolyn. I was caught with the smoking gun, so to speak. Actually, the smoking gas chamber. Plus, I've been declared fit to stand trial. Why in the world would a jury acquit me, or even say I was insane at the time of the murders?"

"We've got a slew of experts available, if need be, to speak to those very issues."

"You're going to use my father, aren't you?"

"I haven't decided on whether or not to call him to testify, but I will tell the jury about his abuse of you and your mother. In fact, I bring it up in my opening statement."

"Are you calling my mother as a witness?"

"Yes."

"No."

"Tory—"

"I don't want her put through that."

"She can be very helpful in making the jury understand the trauma you endured as a child. And if they are aware of the abuse you suffered at the hands of your father, they might be more predisposed to consider the possibility that you were, in fact, insane when you committed the murders. Do not dismiss the power of post-traumatic stress as a defense strategy."

"It wasn't just hands."

"Pardon me?"

"You said 'the abuse you suffered at the hands of your father.' It wasn't just his hands."

"Yes, I know. I was speaking figuratively."

"Oh, he made good use of his hands, that's for sure. But that's not all he used."

"I am hoping you will testify to that, Tory."

"You really think it's a good idea for me to testify?"

"Yes. In this case, the only way the jury is going to warm to you as a person is if they get to hear you speak and see you as something other than a tiny brunette at the defense table flanked by me and two guys in dark suits."

"I don't know . . ."

"Tory, listen to me. You had better get your head in the game, sweetheart. I'm getting the unsettling feeling that I am going to be representing an apathetic client. And that will not play well with the jury."

"It won't matter."

"Stop saying that."

"I'll stop saying it, but it still won't matter."

"Let's talk about the witness list."

"Okay."

"Since you've agreed to testify, you will almost certainly be the prosecution's first witness. Loren will grill you, probably pretty hard, and then request the right to re-call you. They'll probably follow you with Tommy."

"Yeah, that figures."

"With Tommy, they're immediately going to establish that you were seen standing over the bodies by an eyewitness."

"Yes. But why are they going to all that trouble? I admitted doing it."

"Not to the legal system you didn't. Our plea is not guilty by reason of insanity. They need to prove for the record that you did it. We then need to stipulate that there is obvious evidence that you committed the crimes but that you should not be held responsible for the murders because you were insane at the time."

"Can I ask a question?"

"Of course."

"What would happen if I changed my plea to guilty?"

"I would, of course, strongly advise against it, but if you did, since this is a death-penalty case, we would move right to a Supreme Court review of the case."

"No appeal?"

"A review, and then sentencing."

"So if I plead guilty, I would either be sentenced to prison with no chance of parole or to death by lethal injection."

"Correct."

"My inner goddess is talking to me, Carolyn."

"Oh, really? And what is the goddess saying to you?"

"She keeps talking about sacrifice."

"How so?"

"She keeps reminding me that if I willingly sacrifice myself, it would save my mother from going through the ordeal of testifying."

"The goddess is right, but let me ask her this: What would Viviana Troy want?"

"She'd want to testify on my behalf."

"That's right."

"But dredging up all that shit from the past . . ."

"She'll get through it. And the reason I know she'll get through it is because she told me so."

"You talked to my mother about this?"

"Many times, Tory. Many times."

"And she said she'd testify and talk about my father?"

"Without hesitation."

"I'm not feeling very well."

"Would you like to stop for today?"

"Yes."

"All right. I'll see you tomorrow. And think about what I said."

"I will."

33

Defense Attorney Carolyn Payne

Case Notes: Tory Troy

I was recently contacted by Dr. Baraku Bexley, the court-appointed psychiatrist who declared Tory Troy competent to stand trial. He told me that during his review of a number of writings by Tory Troy provided to him by her college Creative Writing professor, Gabriel Mundàne, he came upon a story titled The Baby's Room *that he thought I might find interesting. The story is about a young mother who loses her daughter to SIDS. I include the text of the story in this file for review by second- and third-chair attorneys on this case. If its subject suggests any additional strategies for Ms. Troy's defense, I would welcome a report.*

The Baby's Room

by Victoria Troy

The last Night that She lived
It was a Common Night
Except the Dying—this to Us
Made Nature different
EMILY DICKINSON

IN THE BLINK . . .

Sarah opened her eyes and saw that the digital clock next to her bed read 6:15.

She had missed one of Annie's feedings.

The baby monitor was silent, though, and Sarah was surprised that her four-month-old daughter had slept through her five o'clock feeding. Sarah figured that her darling Annie Bananny was just overtired because she had kept her up a little later than usual last night. Sarah's parents had come by, and they could never stand having Annie taken away from them when they visited.

She hated to have to go in now and wake her from a sound sleep just to feed her, but if she waited much longer, she'd throw off her schedule for the whole day and she knew that Annie would be cranky and probably wouldn't go down for her afternoon nap.

Sarah threw off the covers and swung her legs off the bed. Even though her husband, David, had been dead for a year, she still had not been able to use the whole bed for herself. She still slept on "her" side of the mattress; she still made the bed every day; and she still changed the sheets and pillowcases once a week. She knew it was bizarre to change the pillowcase on David's pillow every week, but it somehow comforted her and so she indulged herself.

Sarah sat on the edge of the bed for a moment, stared at the carpet between her bare feet, wiggled her toes, and tried to wake up. Coffee. That was what she needed. Huge amounts of coffee. But first, she had to take care of Annie.

Sarah slid down the right half of her nightgown and squeezed her full, milk-laden breast. A drop of milk appeared at the end of the engorged nipple.

Sarah got out of bed, slid her feet into slippers, and slipped on a heavy red robe. Scratching her ear, she padded down the hallway to Annie's room. She could see through the window at the end of the hall that the sky had clouded over during the night and, as she neared the baby's room, she could hear rain start to pelt the vinyl siding.

She passed the bathroom without going in. Sarah always waited until she checked on Annie before she allowed herself to use the bathroom. Her routine was to peek in the crib, stroke Annie Bananny a little to let her know she was there, whisper a few endearments to her, and then tell her she'd be right back. She would then go pee, get a soft towel from Annie's shelf in the linen closet, and return to the baby's room, where she would breast-feed her daughter in the padded oak rocker that her mother had given her as soon as she had heard that she was pregnant. Sarah still teased her mom that the furniture delivery truck was already in the driveway before she hung up the phone after telling her that she was expecting.

Sarah paused at the door to the baby's room. An early gray light was just beginning to filter in through the white damask curtains, and she could see Annie's small form in the crib.

Sarah walked over and bent over the side of the crib, hoping to see Annie's eyes open so she wouldn't have to wake her by jostling her or picking her up.

Annie's eyes were still closed.

Sarah bent over and saw that Annie was not moving in her sleep but instead lying perfectly still, wrapped all the way to her neck in her pink *Beauty and the Beast* sleeper. Sarah's heart began to race and she could feel a film of cold sweat break out on the back of her neck. She placed the back of her hand against Annie's cheek and gasped when she felt how cool the skin was. Sarah let out an uncontrollable wail of terror, grabbed Annie's small body with both hands, and pulled her roughly out of the crib.

"Annie!" she cried, as she stared into the baby's face. "Annie! Wake up! Please! Wake up for Mommy!"

No response.

Outside, the wind picked up and the cold rain began to beat more heavily against the windows of the baby's room.

IMAGES FROM A NIGHTMARE

Sarah rushing, grabbing, pacing; Sarah watching, standing, watching; Sarah jumping, crying, spinning; Sarah screaming; Sarah fainting.

. . . *rushing* down the hall carrying Annie in her arms;

. . . *grabbing* the phone and punching 911 so hard she snapped off a fingernail all the way down to the cuticle, leaving her nail bed spurting blood and not even feeling it;

. . . *pacing* the living room with Annie in her arms, waiting for the ambulance;

. . . *watching* as the two EMTs ripped open Annie's *Beauty and the Beast* sleeper and shoved a tube down her tiny throat;

. . . *standing* in the rain outside the entrance to the emergency room at the hospital as the two men unloaded the gurney and wheeled Annie through the automatic doors;

. . . *watching* helplessly from the corner of the trauma room as what seemed like a hundred people descended on Annie and tried desperately to bring her back to life;

. . . *jumping* in shock as a doctor applied tiny little

electrical paddles to Annie's tiny little chest and shouted, "Clear!";

. . . *crying* as she watched a nurse with the brightest red hair she had ever seen pull a white sheet up over Annie's face;

. . . *spinning* hearing a doctor say matter-of-factly, "Let's call it. Time of death, seven-sixteen A.M.";

. . . *screaming* as she looked down and saw Annie's *Beauty and the Beast* sleeper on the trauma-room floor, covered in the blood from her own torn fingernail;

. . . *fainting* as a young woman with genuine compassion in her eyes asked her, "Are you all right, ma'am?"

ANNA AND GEORGE

Sarah's parents, Anna and George, came to the hospital after a physician's assistant named Erika called them and gave them the bad news.

They had both been up, but still in their robes. George had been sitting in the living room watching the *Today* show, and Anna had been standing at the kitchen counter adding items to a grocery list. George took the call and was so stunned, he couldn't hang up the phone. It simply slipped from his hand and landed on the floor next to his recliner. Anna, knowing that most phone calls at seven-thirty in the morning usually meant trouble, came into the living room and gasped when she saw the look on her husband's face.

"Annie's dead," he said in a flat monotone. "That was the hospital. We have to go pick up Sarah."

"Dear God," Anna whispered, already crying. "How much can one woman be expected to take?"

THE LAST DAY THAT HE LIVED . . .

It had been a year since Anna and George had lived through the death of Sarah's husband.

David, a tall blond who everyone had said looked a little like a young Robert Redford with a mustache, had been sitting at his desk at work when he suddenly stood up, grasped both sides of his head, screamed, and collapsed. David had then had a violent seizure on the floor behind his desk, and by the time the EMTs got to him, he was already dead. They had worked on him, of course, and they had even used lights and sirens to take him to the hospital, but the two guys in blue from the American Ambulance Service had known as soon as they saw him that it was already too late. The autopsy would determine that David had died of a cerebral aneurysm. A critical artery in his brain had burst and he had died within minutes.

Sarah had been home watching *Oprah* when she got a call from David's boss. She was in a good mood because she had been to the doctor that morning and he had told her that she was definitely pregnant—about five weeks or so. Sarah couldn't wait to tell David. She had already taken a home pregnancy test, and the two of them had sat nervously on the edge of the bed waiting for the digital countdown timer on David's Casio watch to chime. The test had been positive, but they didn't want to let themselves get too excited until the pregnancy was confirmed by a doctor. Today it had been confirmed, and now Sarah was just waiting for David to get home so she could give him the good news and they could celebrate with pizza and nonalcoholic wine.

The phone rang about four-thirty.

"Hello?"

"Hello, is this Sarah?"

"Yes, who's this?"

"Hi, Sarah, this is Bill Curtin from MedTech."

Sarah immediately tensed up. Bill Curtin was David's boss, and she instantly knew that the only reason he would be personally calling her was if something bad had happened to David.

The first thing she thought of was an accident at work. MedTech made sophisticated surgical equipment and tools, and it was David's job as a senior design engineer to troubleshoot production problems once a piece of equipment hit the assembly line. This often necessitated his going out onto the factory floor and working with some of the assemblers to fix a glitch or modify a manufacturing procedure. Sarah knew that some of the machinery could be dangerous, and she immediately imagined David's hand mangled in a lathe or his leg crushed by a roll of steel stock that had slipped its bonds and rolled over him.

"Sarah, I have some bad news."

Sarah clenched her teeth and realized that she had been holding her breath since she had heard Bill's name. She forced herself to release her breathing and loosen her jaw.

"Is it David? Has he been hurt at work?"

"Sarah, is there someone there with you that I can speak to? I really don't want you to be alone right now."

"God damn you, Bill!" Sarah shouted into the phone. "WHAT HAS HAPPENED TO MY HUSBAND?"

"David's on his way to the hospital, Sarah. St. Stan's. They took him by ambulance. He apparently had some kind of stroke while sitting at his desk and that's all I know. Would you like someone to come over and stay with you? Do you have anyone you can call? I'm on my way to the hospital right now myself. Would you like me to pick you up?"

"No, no, Bill. Thank you, but I'll call my father. And, really, thank you for calling. I'm sorry I shouted at you."

"No problem, Sarah. Jesus, I'm sorry to have to be the bearer of such horrible news, but I'm sure David will be all right. Just· don't go getting yourself so worked up that *you* get sick, okay? David needs you now, you know."

"Yes, I know, Bill. Thanks again for calling. I have to call my father. Bye."

Sarah hung up the phone, and she knew.

Deep in that silent place where a woman feels things no man could possibly feel, she knew. Deep in the sacred recesses of what we have, for lack of a better word, for centuries called the soul, Sarah also knew. In some mysterious and shrouded part of her being, Sarah suddenly and undeniably felt an emptiness in that place where her beloved David had lived.

Sarah stood with her hand on her belly for a full two minutes before she could pick up the phone again and call her father.

When they got to the hospital, George did all the inquiring, shielding Sarah from the painful ordeal of having to find out where her husband was and what had happened to him. After what seemed like forever, a young resident named Dr. Taylor came into the small room where Sarah and her father were waiting and sat down on the arm of the sofa, directly across from the two chairs where father and daughter sat next to each other.

It took Dr. Taylor precisely forty-one seconds to tell the two of them that David had been brought in, blah, blah, blah; we pronounced him, blah, blah, blah; there was nothing we could do, blah, blah, blah; I'm very sorry for your, blah, blah, blah . . . before his beeper went off. He apologized, said I have to take this, and then excused himself from their presence.

Throughout the good doctor's speech, Sarah had sat perfectly still, numbly staring at the cover of the beat-up *People* magazine on the table in front of her. The cover had a gorgeous photo of actress Molly Ringwald on it, and all Sarah could think of was, look at how red her hair is, I wonder if our baby will have red hair? Look at how red her hair is, I wonder if our baby will have red hair? Look at how red her hair is, I wonder if our baby will have red hair? Look at . . . look at . . . red hair . . . I wonder?

THE BLUE NOTEBOOK

Sarah and Annie's ride to the hospital had been terrible.

Sarah's ride home with her parents might have been worse.

Sarah sat huddled under a blanket in the corner of the backseat. She was barefoot, and her hand was painted with the blood from her torn finger. She refused to respond to either her mother or father, and she sobbed nonstop from the front door of the hospital until her mother put her to bed in the room she had grown up in.

A couple of hours later, Anna tried to get Sarah to come downstairs and eat a little something, but her daughter just lay there, under the quilt, in a fetal position. Anna saw that the pillowcase was drenched, but when she tried to move Sarah so she could change it, Sarah let out an anguished wail that sounded like something that might emanate from a wounded animal, so Anna just left the room and let Sarah lie in her own tears.

This day, the day Annie died, Anna and George had to handle all the arrangements for the funeral. A woman named Mrs. Tomkins from the hospital called around noon that day and asked for Sarah.

"This is her father, George. Sarah can't come to the phone right now. Can I help you, please?"

"Yes, sir, this is Mrs. Tomkins from St. Stan's. I am very sorry for your loss, and the reason I'm calling is to find out the name of the funeral home you've chosen for your granddaughter's burial. Since the death occurred early in the day, it will be possible for the funeral director to pick up Annie's remains sometime today and begin preparations for the funeral. Do you have that information for me?"

George was momentarily speechless. He and Anna hadn't given a moment's thought to the "arrangements," as they are so delicately called. They had been grief-stricken, of course, at the loss of their precious Annie Bananny, but for the past several hours they had been more concerned with their Sarah, their darling little girl who now lay upstairs in her childhood bed in a dark room with dried blood on her hand, mute and emotionally paralyzed. They had also spent the morning calling the rest of the family and trying to contact Sarah's doctor. Now, here it was, mere hours after their hearts had been gutted and filled with ice, and suddenly the practical demands that death unavoidably made on a family had reared up, insisting on being dealt with.

"To tell you the truth, Mrs.—what did you say your name was? Tomkins? Yes, I'm sorry—Mrs. Tomkins, we have not had a chance yet to make those arrangements. Would it be all right if I made some calls and got back to you as soon as I could?"

"Yes, that would be fine, sir, except that the morgue crew changes shifts at three and it would be better if your granddaughter's body could be picked up before then. It would make things go a little smoother if the attendant that brought her down also turned her over. But whatever you need to do, you go ahead and do it, and I will wait for your call. If there is anything at all I can do to help, please do not hesitate to ask. And again, I am deeply sorry for your loss."

George thanked her and hung up the phone. Anna stood leaning against the counter with her arms crossed. Her eyes were rheumy and red, and George saw that she had a stunned look on her face that instantly reminded him of the look some of his friends had gotten during the war when the stress of battle just completely overwhelmed them and their critical faculties essentially shut down.

"We have to call Neal at Saunders. Now."

Anna looked at him and nodded. She then turned around and began rinsing out the coffee cups that had been lying in the sink. George noticed that her back heaved every few seconds and he reminded himself that he needed to put the trash and the recycling bin out tonight. Have to put out the trash, he thought, as he rummaged through some papers on the counter looking for the little blue spiral notebook where they kept all their important phone numbers.

IN SARAH'S ROOM

"No, she hasn't gotten out of bed since we brought her home around eight this morning. No, I don't think so. Anna? Has Sarah gotten up to go to the bathroom? No, Doctor, she hasn't. No, I really don't think we'll be able to get her in to see you. She hasn't even moved for the past ten hours, for heaven's sake. How would we possibly get her up and into a car? No, I don't know if she's been sleeping or just laying there. Sometimes she has her eyes open but she just stares. Yes. Yes, I can get to a pharmacy. Are you sure it's wise to try and give her tranquilizers? Yes, I know she can't continue in this state. Okay. Okay. Greene's Pharmacy on Main. Okay. Yes. One every four hours, even if we have to open her mouth and shove it down her throat manually. Jesus, Doc. Yes, I know. Yes. Okay. Yes, we will. Thank you. Okay. Bye."

George hung up the phone and turned to his wife. "He says we have to sedate her, that she's in a fugue state that's primarily due to shock and that she has to get some deep sleep or she may end up so catatonic that it'll take days, or even weeks, for her to snap out of it. He wants me to pick up a prescription for her at Greene's."

Anna nodded and went to get her husband's jacket and keys.

Just as Anna was reaching for George's blue Members Only windbreaker in the kitchen closet, Sarah, mother of the recently deceased Annie Bananny, daughter of Anna and George, widow of David, screamed from her childhood bedroom with such agony and horror in her voice that Anna dropped George's jacket and then fainted dead away against the broom-closet door.

George ran to his wife, kneeled beside her, and gently slapped her pale cheeks. "Anna! Anna! Jesus Christ, wake up! Sarah needs us." Upon hearing her daughter's name, Anna's eyes popped open and George helped her struggle to her feet. "Are you all right?" he asked her, and when she nodded yes, they ran upstairs, where Sarah was still screaming at the top of her lungs.

Upon entering the bedroom, they found Sarah sitting on the edge of the bed, holding her head in her hands, screaming so forcefully her face was a bright crimson.

She is going to have a goddamned stroke if she doesn't stop right now, George thought to himself, and immediately ran to the bed, sat down next to his daughter, and embraced her with a hug that completely enveloped her in his big arms.

"Sarah!" he shouted.

The screaming continued.

"SARAH!" he barked even louder.

Sarah stopped screaming and allowed herself to be embraced by her father. George began rocking his sobbing little girl, and the memory of doing exactly the same thing with her when she was eight and terrified of the dark flashed into his mind.

Anna stood in the doorway and watched father and daughter each try to deal with the most horrible tragedy either of them had ever had to endure. Even the death of Sarah's husband, David, from a cerebral aneurysm when Sarah was one month pregnant had not been as bad as the death of Annie.

Outside Sarah's bedroom window there was an old oak tree that had been there since before Anna and George had even bought the house. Its leafy branches had kept the sun out of Sarah's eyes in the summer, and its wide trunk had protected her from storm winds and spitting snow in the winter. Tonight, all the leaves on the old tree were gone, and out of the corner of her eye, sheltered in her father's arms, Sarah could see nothing but undulating black bones starkly silhouetted against the backdrop of a bloody red sunset sky.

SEEING THE ROCK IN THE WATER

One Easter Sunday, when Sarah was visiting her parents in Brookvale, she walked down to the beach and out onto a rock promontory that extended hundreds of yards into Long Island Sound. The day was cold and out on the craggy stones the wind was biting and annoying.

Sarah liked the place, though, and always tried to walk down there when she visited her parents.

On this chilly Easter, Sarah did something spontaneous while standing out on the bluff overlooking the dark gray sea. She impulsively picked up a large rock that looked like a basketball with a flat bottom, and hurled it into the sea.

Sarah watched, mesmerized, as the rock spun high through the air and hit the water with a loud *kerplunk* and a bigger splash than she had expected. The rock disappeared from her sight almost immediately in the dark water, but in her mind's eye, Sarah watched as it floated slowly down to the sea bottom, gently buoyed by the water, until it landed in the sand, stirring up, Sarah imagined, a big cloud of greenish, muddy muck.

Years later, as Sarah lay in her childhood bed on the day Annie Bananny died, she could see the rock in the water as clearly as she could see the tree branches outside her window. The rock was still there, Sarah knew, and not a week had gone by that she had not thought of that rock sitting there at the bottom of Long Island Sound, passing winters and summers in the same immutable silence.

DR. SUNDERLAND

George pulled into the parking garage and drove up two levels. He stopped in front of the door leading to the hospital elevators and got out. He helped Sarah out of the backseat and held her arm until Anna came around to the driver's side and took over. George got back in the car and drove off to find a parking space as Anna slowly walked Sarah into the parking-garage elevator lobby.

Dr. Sunderland practiced at the psychiatric clinic at St. Stanislau's Hospital, and he had insisted on seeing Sarah as soon as she was capable of getting there. It had been eight days since Annie had died, and Sarah had stayed with her parents through the funeral and the burial and still had not been able to leave and go home to her own house. George had taken care of picking out the coffin and had made the decision on his own not to have a wake. He had felt it would be easier on Sarah to just have a Mass and then a ceremony at the cemetery instead of having to sit through four hours of staring at the tiny white casket propped up at the front of the room, surrounded by what he was certain would look like all the flowers in the whole world.

Today, Sarah had finally agreed to see Dr. Sunderland. The psychiatrist had been highly recommended by their family doctor, who had really been able to do nothing more than prescribe Valium and advise Anna and George to try to get Sarah to eat something.

Anna had been giving Sarah ten milligrams of Valium three times a day, and telling all the friends and family members who kept calling that she was not up to having visitors. Anna had also been taking Sarah to the bathroom, bathing her, dressing her, and trying to get her to take some soup and drink some fruit juice every day at breakfast, lunch, and dinner. For the first few days after Annie's death, Sarah had refused to eat or drink anything. Anna had put her in a black dress for the funeral and bathed her and washed her hair, but it really didn't disguise the hollow eyes and her blank expression. Even the pearl earrings couldn't help.

In the past couple of days, though, Sarah had been sipping the soup and there was an occasional glimmer of alertness in her eyes. This was a definite improvement, since most of the time she had just lain in her old bed and sobbed for hours at a time.

Finally, this morning, Sarah had given her father a small nod when he asked her yet again if she'd see Dr. Sunderland. George was relieved but he wasn't quite convinced that even the highly recommended Dr. Sunderland would be able to do much of anything to help his daughter.

"I understand you lost your husband last year, Sarah. Is that correct?"

Sarah nodded.

"And now you've lost your daughter as well."

A momentary flash of anger crossed Sarah's face.

"Yes."

"Your father tells me you haven't been eating."

"I'm not hungry."

"I see."

Sarah stared at her hands.

"Do you want to talk about anything, Sarah?"

Sarah raised her head and looked directly into Dr. Sunderland's eyes.

"You're kidding, right?"

"What do you mean?"

"Do I want to *talk* about anything? Is that what you asked me? What could I possibly want to talk about? How about we talk about how my thirty-one-year-old husband died instantly sitting at his desk at work when an artery in his brain exploded? Should I talk about that? That's probably too depressing, don't you think? I suppose you probably aren't really interested in David's death, right? You want me to talk about Annie, don't you?"

Dr. Sunderland crossed his leg and shifted in his chair to find a more comfortable position. He said nothing.

"Well, I don't want to talk about Annie. I can't. I just can't."

Dr. Sunderland stared at Sarah's grim face for a moment and then scribbled something on the pad he had in his lap and stood up.

"Sarah, I'd like you to call someone who I think can help you. Let's face it. You don't want to talk to me because you think I haven't got a clue as to how you're feeling. My professional pride makes me believe otherwise, but *my* feelings are not what's important here. Getting you healthy is what I'm most concerned about."

Dr. Sunderland handed her a slip of paper with a phone number on it.

"This is Catherine Connolly's phone number. She's a clinical psychologist who specializes in helping parents cope with the loss of a child. She has a lot of patients who have lost children to SIDS. She holds a support group meeting every Wednesday and I think you should attend at least one of them. It's up to you, of course, but I would strongly recommend you go. Being with people who have already gone through what you are now experiencing could be extremely helpful."

Sarah looked down at the paper with the number on it. She felt emotionally overwhelmed and ready to burst into tears at any moment. She felt guilty about the way she had snapped at the doctor and by the burden she knew she was being on her parents. She felt excruciatingly empty when she thought of Annie. She felt scars that still ached from David's death. She felt all of these things at the same time and did not know how to handle any of them.

"Would you consider attending one of Catherine's meetings, Sarah?"

Sarah nodded without looking up. From where he was standing, Dr. Sunderland could see two impossibly large tears sliding down Sarah's cheeks in a perfectly straight line, leaving a line of wetness as they rolled toward her chin. The soft morning light through his high office windows made one of these tear streaks glisten brightly and, to Dr. Sunderland, the line of moisture on Sarah's right cheek reminded him of the garish face paint of a circus clown—one of those sad clowns that kids are so afraid of, he thought to himself. Not the laughing ones. Dr. Sunderland wasn't quite sure if funny clowns painted tears on their faces.

THE PRAYER

The cemetery had been flooded with bright sunlight on the day of Annie's funeral. Sarah sat beside her daughter's tiny coffin, wearing a black dress and pearl earrings. Throughout the service, she was completely still, just sitting there in the black folding chair on top of the garish fake grass that was always laid out for graveside ceremonies. After the service was over, but before the coffin was lowered into the ground, Sarah's family and friends passed by her and whispered their condolences. Sarah never even looked up at the parade of solemn faces that floated by, instead continuing to stare at the white casket covered from head to toe in tiny white roses. David's friends from MedTech were there, as were Sarah's high-school girlfriends. David's parents, Donna and Frank, were so overcome with grief they could not even approach Sarah or her parents. As George helped Sarah to her feet, he could see the other two grieving grandparents being helped to their car by David's two brothers.

As Sarah was walking to the limousine, her arm entwined tightly in her father's, a woman friend of Sarah's mother came up to Sarah and took her hand. "You need this," she whispered in Sarah's ear, as she slipped her a folded piece of paper. "It's a very special prayer to St. Joseph. It can't bring your daughter back, but it might bring you peace. I hope it helps, my dear, and I am so, so sorry."

Sarah did not respond to the woman, who she later

learned was Connie, the wife of her mother's hair-dresser, but she did place the paper in her pocket. Days later, she found it. At first she didn't want to read it, but then her curiosity got the best of her and she opened the cream-colored sheet.

"PRAYER TO ST. JOSEPH"

Introduction

This *Prayer to St. Joseph* was found in the fiftieth year of Our Lord and Savior Jesus Christ. In 1505, it was sent from the Pope to Emperor Charles when he was going into battle. Whoever shall read this prayer, or hear it, or keep it about themselves, shall never die a sudden death, or be drowned, or shall poison take effect on them; neither shall they fall into the hands of the enemy, or shall be burned in any fire or shall be overpowered in battle. Say reverently for nine mornings for *anything you may desire.* It has *never been known to fail,* so be sure you really want what you ask for.

Oh, St. Joseph, whose protection is so great, so strong, so prompt before the throne of God, I place in you all my interests and desires.

Oh, St. Joseph, do assist me by your powerful intercession, and obtain for me from your divine Son all spiritual blessings, through Jesus Christ, Our Lord.

*So that having engaged here below your heavenly
power, I may offer my thanksgiving and homage to
the most loving of Fathers.*

*Oh, St. Joseph, I never weary contemplating you and
Jesus asleep in your arms; I dare not approach while
He reposes near your heart.*

*Press Him in my name and kiss His fine head for me
and ask Him to return the kiss when I draw my dying
breath.*

St. Joseph, Patron of Departing Souls, pray for me.

Sarah read the prayer twice, mysteriously thrilled by
the bold promise that it would grant *any* wish of the pe-
titioner. She of course knew that even this "magic"
prayer would not give her back her Annie (or could it?),
but she hoped that the prayer might be able to help her
cope and possibly allow her to break through the surface
of the dark, cold waters she had been drowning in since
that unimaginably horrible morning in the baby's room.

Sarah took a deep breath, put her legs up onto the
window seat, and began to read the prayer again.

EATING

The first real food that Sarah ate after Annie's death was
an entire box of Entenmann's cream-filled cupcakes and

215

eleven popcorn rice cakes. She devoured this feast at ten a.m. the day after her visit to Dr. Sunderland and was immediately sick to her stomach. She spent the next two hours vomiting into a basin and sitting on the toilet with explosive diarrhea. She had initially tried kneeling in front of the toilet to vomit, but her bowels were so agitated and unpredictable that she knew that she would eventually make a disgusting mess all over the floor if she did not sit on the bowl and use a basin instead. The strangest thoughts kept running through Sarah's mind during this agonizing two hours. She would suddenly and unexplainably get incredibly horny for a few minutes, noticing between intestinal spasms that her nipples were hard as bullets and that her vagina had lubricated; and then just as quickly, the sexual feelings would pass and she would be overcome with laughter and find herself trying to giggle between the deep and foul breaths she needed to take during the breaks from vomiting.

After she felt a little better, Sarah washed her face, brushed her teeth and used mouthwash, and went in and lay down on her childhood bed, where she immediately began counting the red lines in the wallpaper. Not the blue lines and not the yellow lines. The red lines. There were exactly one hundred and seventy-six red lines in the wallpaper in her childhood bedroom. After Sarah was confident that this number was precise (she assured herself of that by counting them twice), she began counting the blue lines. She decided to save the yellow lines for the following Tuesday.

A MESSAGE

Sarah had two unusual experiences on the second Sunday after Annie's death.

The first occurred in Stop & Shop. Sarah was leaning against a shopping cart in the book department and browsing through a self-help book on how to handle trouble when she got an overwhelming and literally *breathtaking* sense of not only the presence of her deceased husband, but also the nearness of God.

Sarah had to put the book down and fight back tears, so overwhelmed was she by the power of this experience.

The second event, several hours later, took place at her parents' home. Next to her father's recliner in the living room was a small table: The *TV Guide* was on it, as well as a Bible, a pocket calendar, a small legal pad, a mug of pens and pencils, and a pile of magazines George was currently reading. On top of the stack of magazines, her father had placed a box of Kleenex.

Sarah fell asleep in this chair and was awakened by the magazines and the Kleenex box striking her left arm. The whole pile had fallen over, neatly cascading into a stairlike configuration, with the Kleenex box gently coming to rest on her left arm. There was absolutely no way this stack could have fallen over due to being misbalanced or crookedly placed. The stack of magazines was steady enough to place a full glass of any beverage on top of it and not have the liquid in the glass budge.

When the falling magazines awakened Sarah from her nap, she once again had an extremely powerful sense of being sent a message, the gist of which was, *Don't worry. We're here for you.*

GROUP

On the third Wednesday after Annie's death, eight women of all shapes and sizes sat in a circle on brown folding chairs in a corner of the auditorium in the Jewish Community Center on Davenport Avenue. One of these eight was Sarah. The ninth chair was empty and was for the leader of the group, Dr. Catherine Connolly. Dr. Connolly arrived one minute before ten and walked completely around the group, introducing herself to each woman before she even took her coat off or sat down.

Sarah tried to muster a smile when Dr. Connolly put her hand on her shoulder and said to her, "You must be Sarah," but the best she could come up with was something that resembled an anemic grimace.

"Thank you all for coming today, ladies. This is the SIDS Support Group and I am Catherine Connolly. We all share something that none of us ever thought in our wildest nightmares that we would have to go through. We have all lost a baby to SIDS. My Brandon was seven months old when he died. I went in to wake him one morning and . . . well, you all know the rest of the story. Not a day goes by that I don't think of him and wonder about how his life would have turned out if he had lived. Would he have been a good student? What would have been the name of his first girlfriend? Would he have gotten married in a summer month, or a winter month? Would my first grandchild have been a boy or a girl? I still feel the pain, and the loss, and there are days when I cannot even get out of bed. This overwhelming grief is a big part of why I started this group. After the pain did not diminish over time, I realized that there were probably other mothers who were going through the exact same thing. I started this group as a way to try and help."

Dr. Connolly reached down into her briefcase and pulled out a sheet of light-blue paper.

"Sudden Infant Death Syndrome," she began, "or SIDS for short, was called crib death for a long time because that was where these poor babies died: in their own cribs, at home, in their sleep. An apparently normal infant with no known health problems would just *die* one night, and no one would be able to explain why. These babies were usually between two weeks and one year old when they died, and to this day we still don't really know the underlying causes for SIDS. Oh, sure, the doctors at the hospital can tell you *what* killed our babies—it's usually respiratory failure, cardiac arrest, or circulatory shutdown—but they can't tell us *why* these apparently normal, healthy infants go *into* respiratory arrest, or experience circulatory failure. Seven thousand babies a year die of SIDS in the United States, and some of these babies have been found to have more immune cells in their lungs than healthy babies. Researchers are looking to this as a clue to the cause of SIDS. But they're also questioning if SIDS babies die because they're put to sleep on their stomachs, or if it's because their mattresses were too soft, or even if it's because their rooms were too hot. We still just do not know. And this dreadful inability of medical science to answer our questions and solve the mystery as to why our babies died makes closure impossible, and, unfortunately, makes these support groups necessary."

A thin black woman in a blue dress named Claire raised her hand. Catherine nodded at her.

"How long ago did your son die, if you don't mind my asking?"

"No, I don't mind at all. Next Thursday, it will be exactly twenty-two years and seven months since my Brandon died."

Sarah, who had spent the entire time that Dr. Connolly was talking counting the creases in her palm, looked up and stared at the psychologist. The phrase "twenty-two years and seven months" kept repeating in her mind like a surrealistic, depraved mantra that she could not escape.

For the next fifty-two minutes, Sarah did nothing but listen to that sick mantra and try to keep track of precisely how many creases there were in her left palm.

THE RETURN HOME

Almost one month after Annie's death, Annie Bananny's grandfather carried two big Filene's shopping bags out to the driveway and put them down behind his car.

He opened the trunk and placed the bags inside, next to each other. The brown bags with the purple letters contained clothes that he and Anna had brought for Sarah from home, plus some brochures from a SIDS group Sarah had attended one meeting of, and a brand-new pink baby's T-shirt with a bunny on it.

Dr. Sunderland and Dr. Connolly had both agreed that it was time for Sarah to return home. She couldn't live with her parents for the rest of her life, and it was only postponing the inevitable by allowing her to stay. Of course, Anna and George would have allowed Sarah to move in with them permanently if she had wanted to, but her doctors felt that it would be best if she returned home and tried to regain some semblance of a normal life.

The ride home was terrible. Sarah was anxious and edgy and kept snapping at her mother, who was futilely trying to soothe and comfort her but only succeeded in aggravating Sarah.

Sarah refused to allow her parents to come into the house with her. She had not been home since she had left the house that awful morning with the ambulance. She had been out of her parents' house many times—to go to the store, to visit doctors, to walk the beach, to go to the bank—but she had not been able to return to her own house. George had been going over every day to get her mail, turn on the lights, pick up some clothes and a few other things Sarah needed, and make sure everything was all right. He had not gone into Annie's room, except to close the door.

Sarah stood in the driveway and watched as her parents drove away. When they were out of her sight, she took a deep breath and turned to look at the house.

It looked the same.

The curtains were familiar; the black mailbox was familiar; the bushes needed trimming; the porch light was slightly crooked—everything looked the same.

Sarah picked up her bags and walked around the garage to the back door. This was the entrance she and David always used to enter the house.

She pulled on the screen door and propped it open with her hip, the way she always did, as she fumbled for the key to the doorknob. The hinge on the screen door made its old familiar screeching sound and, for what was probably the five thousandth time, Sarah made a mental note to spray some WD-40 on it.

She inserted the key, turned the knob, and pushed open the door.

She automatically reached around the jamb with her right hand and flipped on the overhead light.

Everything was the same. Except for one thing.

On the kitchen table was a seven-inch stack of mail. Sarah gasped when she saw the precariously balanced pile of letters. Tears flooded her eyes and she leaned back against the counter. She knew that her father had been taking in her mail and bringing it to her. But George had been compassionate in what he had allowed Sarah to see. Bills, magazines, junk mail. That was it. He had left the remainder of the mail on the kitchen table.

The seven-inch stack of letters (exactly one hundred and sixty-seven pieces of mail, Sarah would later count) were sympathy cards, spiritual bouquets, and personal notes of condolences. Eventually Sarah would open and read every one. It took her three weeks, but she ultimately wrote a personal thank-you note to every one of the one hundred and sixty-seven people who had written to her.

Today, however, Sarah walked right through the kitchen and directly into the living room. She sat on the sofa and, for the next hour and eleven minutes, stared at the color photo on the TV of her and David at their wedding, and the small framed photo of Annie, taken moments after her birth, that stood next to it. It was dark when she finally got up and went to the bathroom.

It was near midnight before Sarah finally got to bed. She had taken a hot shower, eaten some soup, and watched a couple of TV programs that she had never seen before.

She had not even looked at the door of Annie's room as she walked the upstairs hallway.

When she finally did go to bed, she lay awake until four A.M.; counting sheep; counting shadows; counting pink T-shirts with bunnies on them; counting *Beauty and the Beast* sleepers; counting cardioresuscitation paddles; counting silent, sad women sitting in brown folding chairs; counting magazines in a stack; counting ambulances; counting Kleenex boxes; counting comets; counting pills; counting red lines; counting blue lines; counting (finally) yellow lines; counting prayers to St. Joseph; counting letters to Annie Bananny; counting baby bottles; counting rocks in the water; counting cerebral aneurysms; counting screams; counting cream-filled cupcakes; counting parking spaces; counting rice cakes; counting possibilities; counting days; counting years; counting fruitcakes; counting Christmas trees; and, of course, counting Christmases.

A VISION OF ANNIE

As Sarah lay in bed trying vainly to count away her pain, a vision unfolded in her mind.

Sarah inexplicably saw herself again standing in the baby's room, still clutching the silent Annie to her breast, gasping in fear and trying desperately to pray her little Bananny back to life.

As Sarah lay under the light-blue comforter and watched this unspeakably horrible drama once again play itself out, she was astonished to see a sudden bright light envelop the body of her silent infant daughter. From the heart of the light, Sarah watched as a tall woman slowly appeared, and she had the unexpected thought that the young lady looked exactly like the actress Sandra Bullock.

But Sarah knew who the woman really was. This woman was the spirit of her Annie: Sarah was being blessed with a vision of her Annie grown into the woman Sarah knew she would never become. Sarah was now seeing the adult Annie, a miracle even more crushing to her by what Sarah knew to be the truth, that her Annie would *never* grow up and become the lanky, russet-haired beauty she now saw before her.

As Sarah continued to watch this dreadful drama, the older Annie smiled and gently placed an ethereal hand on her weeping mother's shoulder. Annie said nothing, though, and soon the light surrounding her grew brighter and brighter, ultimately becoming a blue nimbus so blazing that Sarah had to shield her mind's eye from the brilliance. Sarah then saw Annie once again smile and then begin to fade from view.

Just before Annie completely vanished into the light, Sarah sensed her daughter's final thoughts: *Oh, my land of rootless trees!* Sarah heard in her mind as a soft whisper, *Who would have ever thought there'd be orchids?*

And then, finally, Sarah slept.

Sarah opened her eyes and saw that the digital clock next to her bed read 6:15.

She had missed one of Annie's feedings.

The baby monitor was silent, though, and Sarah was surprised that her four-month-old daughter had slept through her five o'clock feeding. Sarah figured that her darling Annie Bananny was just overtired because she had kept her up a little later than usual last night. Sarah's parents had come by, and they could never stand having Annie taken away from them when they visited.

She hated to have to go in now and wake her from a sound sleep just to feed her, but if she waited much longer, she'd throw off her schedule for the whole day and she knew that Annie would be cranky and probably wouldn't go down for her afternoon nap.

Sarah threw off the covers and swung her legs off the bed. Even though her husband, David, had been dead for a year, she still had not been able to use the whole bed for herself. She still slept on "her" side of the mattress; she still made the bed every day; and she still changed the sheets and pillowcases once a week. She knew it was bizarre to change the pillowcase on David's pillow every week, but it somehow comforted her and so she indulged herself.

Sarah sat on the edge of the bed for a moment, stared at the carpet between her bare feet, wiggled her toes, and tried to wake up. Coffee. That was what she needed. Huge amounts of coffee. But first, she had to take care of Annie.

Sarah slid down the right half of her nightgown and squeezed her full, milk-laden breast. A drop of milk appeared at the end of the engorged nipple.

Sarah got out of bed, slid her feet into slippers, and slipped on a heavy red robe. Scratching her ear, she padded down the hallway to Annie's room. She could see through the window at the end of the hall that the sky had clouded over during the night and, as she neared the baby's room, she could hear rain start to pelt the vinyl siding.

She passed the bathroom without going in. Sarah always waited until she checked on Annie before she allowed herself to use the bathroom. Her routine was to peek in the crib, stroke Annie Bananny a little to let her know she was there, whisper a few endearments to her, and then tell her she'd be right back. She would then go pee, get a soft towel from Annie's shelf in the linen closet, and return to the baby's room, where she would breast-feed her daughter in the padded oak rocker that her mother had given her as soon as she had heard that she was pregnant. Sarah still teased her mom that the furniture delivery truck was already in the driveway before she hung up the phone after telling her that she was expecting.

Sarah paused at the door to the baby's room. An early gray light was just beginning to filter in through the white damask curtains, and she could see Annie's small form in her crib.

Sarah walked over to the crib and bent over the side, hoping to see Annie's eyes open so she wouldn't have to wake her by jostling her or picking her up.

Annie's eyes were still closed.

Sarah bent over and saw that Annie was not moving in her sleep but instead lying perfectly still, wrapped all the way to her neck in her pink *Beauty and the Beast* sleeper. Sarah's heart began to race and she could feel a film of cold sweat break out on the back of her neck. She placed the back of her hand against Annie's cheek and gasped when she felt how cool the skin was. Sarah let out an uncontrollable wail of terror, grabbed Annie's small body with both hands, and pulled her roughly out of the crib.

"Annie!" she cried, as she stared into the baby's face. "Annie! Wake up! Please! Wake up for Mommy!"

No response.

Outside, the wind picked up and the cold rain began to beat more heavily against the windows of the baby's room.

"Annie! Wake up for Mommy! Please wake up!" Sarah was now screaming into Annie's tiny face.

The rain began to slap harder against the windows and the side of the house.

Sarah stood desperately clutching her precious baby girl as the tears slid uncontrollably down her face. Her heart pounded in her chest and she was gripped with a terror she had never before felt in her life.

And it was at that precise moment, just when Sarah believed that she would be utterly and irrevocably crushed under the weight of this newborn, unimaginable grief, it was then that darling little Annie Bananny opened her eyes and smiled sweetly up at the impossibly wide and newly luminous eyes of her mother.

34

Tory Troy
Defense Attorney Carolyn Payne

"I read your novella."

"You too?"

"What does that mean?"

"Nothing. It's just that Dr. Bexley took a pile of my stuff from my old writing teacher, and he insisted on talking about some of them. Which one did you read?"

"*The Baby's Room.*"

"Oh, yeah. The SIDS story."

"What can you tell me about your intentions for this story?"

"My intentions?"

"Yes. What were you trying to say when you wrote the story?"

"'*Trying* to say?' Guess I didn't pull it off, eh?"

"No, I'm sorry. You did. I have my ideas about the story, but I'd like to hear you tell me about it."

"Well, I guess it's about the sheer terror that love can trigger."

"Terror?"

"Sure. The mother in the story loves her daughter so much that she lives a full-blown, fully realized nightmare in the millisecond it takes to blink an eye. I think only love might be capable of such cataclysmic power."

"They say imminent death does the same thing. Makes people experience an enormous influx of memories in a heartbeat."

"The 'life passing before your eyes' thing?"

"Yes."

"Maybe. But that's the person's entire life. In my story, love spurs Sarah to experience a specific incident . . . a possibility. It's not her whole life, it's just how she and her life would change if Annie had died."

"I see. Do you think that's really possible?"

"Hell, yeah. I've never experienced it myself, but I know people who have been through it. People I trust. One guy I know told me he relived his entire life in the two minutes that he was underwater and drowning when he was fourteen years old."

"Where do you think these experiences come from?"

"Utica."

"Excuse me?"

"Sorry. It's a joke."

"Oh. One thing people have never said about me is that I have a quick sense of humor."

"No. Don't feel that way. It was disrespectful of me to make a joke about a serious question. It's just that 'Utica' came immediately to mind because I once read somewhere that that's what Stephen King used to say when they asked him where he got his ideas."

"I see."

"Oh, come on, Carolyn, I'm sure you've got a great sense of humor. Watch. You know what the difference is between a pregnant woman and a lightbulb?"

"No. What's the difference?"

"You can unscrew a lightbulb."

"Tory!"

"Please. Spare me the feigned shock. I see you trying not to laugh. Don't worry about it. I will not think anything less of your professionalism. Honest. You know what's funny, though? Steve Martin used that joke in the movie *My Blue Heaven* to prove to Joan Cusack that she didn't have a sense of humor and, unlike yourself, she did *not* try to stifle her laughter. She—well, her character—really couldn't find the humor in the joke. Which kind of made it funnier. Although you're much funnier than her."

"Thanks. I'm almost flattered. Let's move on, shall we? We are only a few days away from the start of your trial."

"I know."

"Am I correct in assuming that our plea will not be changed before the trial begins?"

"I don't know, Carolyn."

"You're not still thinking about pleading guilty, are you?"

"I might be."

"Tory, you need to dig in and look at your situation objectively. At least with an insanity plea, there's a chance at life."

"If I plead guilty, who sentences me?"

"The judge. In some states, capital punishment sentencing powers have been taken away from judges. Not here, though. Judge Becker will be the one who decides your fate."

"Do you think he'd give me the death penalty?"

"That's a good question. I really don't know."

"Come on, Carolyn. Give me your best guess."

"Well, from what I know of Judge Becker, he would not want to sentence you to death, but he would feel compelled to do so. If you plead guilty, the full weight of your crimes comes to bear. Where we are now is in this weird gray area of jurisprudence. Everyone knows you did it, but it has not been conclusively established that you are *legally* liable for your crimes. If you plead guilty, any question of sanity or insanity at the time of the crimes goes out the window. You are admitting you did it, and you are agreeing to accept the penalties that will be doled out to you. That's death or prison. No chance at institutionalization. Plus there's no chance for an appeal either, although there will be a mandatory State Supreme Court review of the case—which will allow the ruling to stand, I'm sure."

"Do you think he'd give me the death penalty?"

"Well . . ."

"Carolyn, answer me. Do you think he'd give me the death penalty?"

"Yes."

"Lethal injection, right?"

"Yes."

"When do I have to let you know?"

"As soon as possible. Judges do not like going through the time and expense of beginning a trial if the case is going to be resolved with a plea."

"All right. I'll tell you tomorrow."

"Tory, I would advise against changing your plea to guilty. You will do what you will do, but factor in my opinion as you make your final decision, okay?"

"Okay."

"See you tomorrow."

"Ciao."

35

Tory Troy
Psychiatric Nurse Chiarra Ziegler

"Here's your Ambien, Tory."

"I really don't need a sleeping pill anymore, Chiarra."

"I know you don't. But your orders haven't been changed, so it's my job to give it to you and to watch you take it. You or your lawyer should talk to one of the staff docs and have them cancel the Ambien if you really don't need it."

"Do you think they would?"

"They might. But if there is anything these guys want the patients here to do, it's sleep. So don't count on it."

"Thanks. I won't."

"Tory, can I ask you a question?"

"As a nurse or as a friend?"

"Friend."

"Sure. Go ahead."

"What happened?"

"You mean with the six?"

"Yes."

"You know what happened, Chiarra."

"No, I mean what happened with *you* that you would do such a thing?"

"You know what's an even more difficult job than animal euthanasia technician?"

"What?"

"Animal euthanasia technician."

"Excuse me?"

"The same job—but at a veterinary hospital."

"Why?"

"Because there, they have to euthanize people's *pets*. And a lot of the time, the owners want to be in the room."

"In the gas chamber?"

"Vets mostly use lethal injection. They only do one animal at a time."

"Oh. That must be horrible—standing there and watching the poor thing die."

"I know a couple of E.T.s who work at animal hospitals. I have literally been in tears from some of the stories they've told me. Kids hugging their dog . . . old ladies with tears rolling down their cheeks as the cat who has been their only companion for fifteen years is 'put to sleep' . . . goddamned euphemisms."

"That's so sad. I don't think I could do it. In fact, I don't even think I could do what you do."

"Someone has to."

"So . . . what happened . . . you know, with you."

"I'm not really sure, Chiarra. I try to understand, but . . . I think my cat had something to do with it."

"Your cat?"

"Yes."

"What do you mean?"

"Do you really want to hear this?"

"Yes. I do. I am now officially on my break, so we have twenty minutes. If the story is longer than that, I'll have to hear it in installments."

"No, it won't take longer than that. There's really not that much to tell."

"I'm all ears."

"When I was a kid . . . like early teens . . . after my father left . . . I had a cat named Gandalf."

"From *The Lord of the Rings*."

"I actually got it from *The Hobbit*."

"Okay."

"Gandy was a great cat. He and I were together constantly. I remember he used to know when I wasn't feeling well. Like, if I had a headache, he would jump up onto the bed or the arm of my chair and lick my forehead. Gandalf was always healthy. All his life."

"He licked your forehead?"

"Yeah. Can you believe that? And he would walk over to his dish if I even *thought* about feeding him."

"That's amazing."

"One day he threw up. Cats are always throwing up, so I didn't think anything of it. But then he threw up again, and it was bright yellow. Like the yolk of an egg."

"I've had cats, Tory. I know what that means."

"Yup. Kidney problems. That's one of the first signs. So I brought him to the vet, and the blood work showed that his kidneys were on their way out."

"How awful."

"The vet told me that I needed to bring him into the office twice a week for intramuscular infusion of fluids. That would take some of the pressure off his failing kidneys and buy him some time. After a few weeks of that, he taught me how to do it myself, and I gave Gandy the fluids at home."

"You had the IV bag and the syringes at home?"

"Yeah. Once a day I infused him. I would lay him down on a towel and inject him in his side. He would stay quiet the whole time. I think he was really nauseous during his last couple of weeks."

"Was he eating?"

"No. When he was first diagnosed I gave him baby food. Then I switched to a protein gel in a tube. I would place a glob of it on his tongue and he would instinctively swallow it. He didn't want it, though."

"Then what happened?"

"The vet always used to tell me that I would know when it was time. One day, Gandalf had to stop and lie down halfway across the room to his litter box. He was so weak and nauseous, he couldn't even walk the entire way without resting. Then when he did manage to make it to the box, he could only step into it before he started peeing with his butt hanging over the edge. He peed all over the carpet because he didn't even have the strength to take another couple of steps into the litter."

"That is so sad."

"That was the day I knew. That was when I knew that I was prolonging his suffering by letting him go on the way he was. He was terminally ill, and near death, and I was keeping him alive because I didn't want to let go."

"I'm gonna cry."

"Well, I did cry. I picked him up one last time, and held him in my arms, and I could smell the ammonia on his breath because his kidneys couldn't process the toxins out of his bloodstream anymore."

"The poor thing."

"He was all skin and bones. I put him on a blanket and called the vet. I told him I had to bring him in that day and that all I wanted to do was give the carrier to someone in the office and leave. I couldn't bear to see him taken out of the carrier in the waiting room, and I did not want to be with him when they euthanized him. I still feel guilty about that. He said he'd take care of it, and that was that. I cried all the way home from the vet's."

"I'm not surprised."

"And that's why. Or at least I think that's why. I don't really know, Chiarra."

"For someone who was so upset about having to put down a pet, you picked a pretty strange career choice, don't you think? I mean . . . animal euthanasia technician—the whole job is killing animals."

"I know."

"What the hell were you thinking?"

"I don't know. I really don't. I got hired by Jake—and to give him his due, he did explain the job—and the next thing I knew I was going to school for my E.T. certificate."

"Why didn't you say no when he asked you to take the course?"

"I don't really know. I think I was probably caught up in the notion that E.T.s help to mercifully end the lives of animals that would die anyway—but they'd die in a much uglier way. And I still believe that."

"I have to ask. How did you manage to get through all those Fridays?"

"Oh, I don't know ... maybe the same way the guards—the decent ones—herding the Jews into the ovens at Auschwitz managed to get through all *their* Fridays. You go numb. Except that *every* day was Friday in the concentration camps."

"Jesus, Tory, that's depressing."

"Yeah, I know. By the way, how long can you hang out?"

"Well, I finished my med rounds—your Ambien was my last stop—so I've got a few minutes. If you don't mind, that is."

"Are you kidding? You're my only friend in this place."

"So tell me. Is there anything you want to talk about?"

"Oh, I don't know ... Do you have any thoughts on the foreign trade deficit? Tom and Nicole? The best sushi bars in town?"

"Ha-ha, very funny. Come on, Tory. Seriously. Is there anything on your mind?"

"Okay, I'll tell you what's been going through my

mind lately, Chiarra. I haven't even told this to Carolyn. Or my mother. Especially my mother."

"What is it?"

"I feel lost. Just utterly lost. I don't understand anything anymore. . . . Actually, it's more like I *can't* understand anything anymore. I try to see myself through someone . . . *anyone* else's eyes—Bexley's, my mom's, you—and I can't recognize the person I see."

"I'm sorry, Tory . . . I'm not following you."

"I know. I'm not making any sense. I'm sorry."

"Don't worry about it, honey. Try to relax. Want me to turn on the TV?"

"No. I'll read a little. That usually helps."

"Okay, then. I'll be back a little later."

"All right. Later."

36

Court Transcript:

Tory Troy

Defense Counsel Carolyn Payne

District Attorney Brawley Loren

Judge Gerard Becker

Court Personnel

The Visitors' Gallery

The Jury

"Mr. Loren? Opening statement?"

"Yes, Your Honor. Thank you. Good morning, ladies and gentlemen. My name is Brawley Loren, and I am the Connecticut District Attorney prosecuting this case. I represent the interests of the state in the matter of *State of Connecticut v. Victoria Abigail Troy*. I'll keep this short and to the point. The facts of this case are plain. One Friday afternoon, the defendant, Victoria Troy, snuck up behind each of her six animal-shelter coworkers and injected them in the back of their necks with a powerful drug that completely paralyzed their bodies, including their lungs, yet allowed them to maintain consciousness. The drug she used was pancuronium bromide—a drug the defendant once sold to hospitals when she worked as a pharmaceutical sales representative. What happens when someone is injected with pancuronium bromide is that the victim begins to immediately suffocate, while retaining complete awareness of what is happening to him or her. Six times she stabbed with her syringe. Six times she watched her victim crumple to the floor. And after all six of her coworkers were incapacitated, their lungs unable to move, she then dragged each of them into the animal-shelter gas chamber—the euthanasia chamber—and turned on the gas. Just for good measure, I suppose. She must have wanted to make sure they'd all definitely die. The evidence against the defendant is overwhelming. Her fingerprints are on the syringes. A coworker saw her standing at the open door of the chamber, staring down at the bodies. And she has pleaded not guilty by reason of insanity. So there is no question that she committed six felony murders. The only question is, will you accept the excuse that she was insane at the time of the murders and incapable of knowing that what she was doing was wrong? That's the only question you each have to answer before you vote guilty or not guilty. I, for one, already know the answer to that question. I trust in your good judgment and wisdom to arrive at the same conclusion as have I. Thank you."

"Thank you, Mr. Loren. Ms. Payne?"

"Yes. Thank you, Your Honor. Good morning, ladies and gentlemen. I am Defense Counsel Carolyn Payne, and I represent Tory Troy. My grandfather once told me something that has always stayed with me. You can tell a great deal about a society, about a culture, by two things: how they treat their elderly, and how they treat their animals. Now, you might think that we treat animals pretty well in America. After all, every major grocery store has an entire aisle devoted to pet food. Pet owners can buy health insurance for their puppy, and some families visit the vet's more than their own doctors. Their people doctors. But there is a dark side to the animal situation in America. And that dark side is the plight of the unwanted. Stray animals that wander our streets, many of which end up at understaffed, underfunded public animal shelters where they are kept caged for a time—usually a very *brief* time—and then euthanized. Put to sleep. Put down. *Killed*. We have trained people for that terrible job. They're called animal euthanasia technicians. Tory Troy is an animal euthanasia technician. Her job was to eliminate animals that no one wanted, that no one was willing to take care of, that no one cared about. Except Tory. Tory cared about the animals that were brought to the Waterbridge Animal Shelter. She cared about them deeply. But she did her job. Why? Because she knew that the alternative for these animals that no one wanted was even more horrible than being put to death: starvation, abandonment, sickness . . . and worse. She did her job. And she prevented a great deal of suffering. But one day, she couldn't take it anymore, and she snapped. The overwhelming horror of her job consumed her and destroyed her ability to think rationally, logically, compassionately—and she lashed out. Was Tory Troy sane at the time she committed six murders? How could she have been? How could this sensitive, smart, compassionate woman have been in full possession of her faculties when she did what she did? We believe that, after hearing the facts of this case, including Tory's story told by Tory herself—especially the abuse she suffered at the hands of her father when she was a child—you will conclude that the only fair and honest verdict you can render is not guilty by reason of insanity. Thank you."

"Thank you, Counselor. We will recess for lunch for one hour."

"All rise."

37

Court Transcript:

Tory Troy

Defense Counsel Carolyn Payne

District Attorney Brawley Loren

Judge Gerard Becker

Court Personnel

The Visitors' Gallery

The Jury

"The prosecution would like to call to the stand Victoria Abigail Troy."

"Hang on. Mr. Loren? Ms. Payne? Approach the bench, please."

"Yes, Judge?"

"What are you doing, Mr. Loren?"

"Sir?"

"The prosecution is not permitted to call the defendant as a witness."

"That's true, sir. But she wants to testify, and she asked that I question her. *And* she asked that I call her first."

"Ms. Payne?"

"It's true, Your Honor."

"Did you advise your client that not only does she not

have to be questioned by Mr. Loren, but that she need not even take the stand?"

"I did, Your Honor."

"If I ask Ms. Troy that question, will she give me the same answer?"

"Absolutely, Judge."

"This is highly irregular, Ms. Payne."

"I know, sir, but Tory . . . Ms. Troy wants to take the stand, and she wants to be questioned by Mr. Loren. Completely against my advice, but she's the boss."

"And you're all right with this, Mr. Loren?"

"Unequivocally, Judge. I want very much to question Ms. Troy about the crimes with which she is charged."

"I'll bet you do, Brawley."

"Ms. Payne. To me, please?"

"Sorry, Your Honor."

"Very well. As long as I have your assurance, Ms. Payne, as an officer of the court, that you have made her rights clear to her, as well as explained the possible consequences of her testifying, I will allow it."

"Thank you, Your Honor."

"Thank you, Judge."

"Step back. Ladies and gentlemen of the jury. We are breaking from standard procedure somewhat in that the defendant has agreed to testify for the prosecution, and to be called first. Mr. Loren, you may proceed."

"Please raise your right hand and place your left hand on the Bible. Do you solemnly swear or affirm that the testimony you are about to give in this court will be the truth, the whole truth, and nothing but the truth?"

"I do."

"Please state your name for the record."

"Victoria Abigail Troy."

"Thank you."

"Good morning, Miss Troy."

"Mr. Loren."

"Please tell the court what it is you do for a living."

"I am a certified animal euthanasia technician."

"And what is that?"

"Your Honor, can I speak to you, please?"

"Step back, Counselor. What is it, Ms. Troy?"

"Judge, I'm not feeling well. I'm nauseous, and I have a headache, and I feel hot and dizzy."

"Can you continue your testimony?"

"I don't think so. Not today, Your Honor. I'm sorry, but I really feel like I'm going to lose it. I'd like to lie down."

"Very well, then. We'll adjourn for today."

"I appreciate it, Judge. I wouldn't do this if I felt all right. I want you to know that."

"Thank you, Ms. Troy. We can reconvene when you're feeling better. Counsel, approach the bench."

"What's this all about, Judge?"

"The defendant is ill. I'm adjourning for today, and we will reconvene when she feels better."

"Are you kidding? My office has spent a great deal of time and expense preparing for this case, and you adjourn after we ask our first question?"

"That's enough, Counselor."

"I want her examined by a doctor to confirm that she isn't faking."

"Oh, come on, Brawley, give it a rest."

"Attorney Payne, please address the bench."

"Sorry, Judge."

"So that's it? We have to wait until she gets over her . . . *illness*?"

"That is correct, Counselor, and please take caution with your tone. Step back. This court stands in recess until further notice. We are adjourned."

38

Juror Number 4
Juror Number 3

"Do you believe she was really sick?"

"Why? Do you think she was faking? Pass the pepper, please."

"I don't know. But the D.A. only got to ask her one question before she suddenly got too sick to continue. It just seems awfully convenient."

"I don't think we're supposed to be talking about this."

"Why not? We're going to talk about it in the jury room, right? Why can't two jurors talk about it outside the room if no one else can hear us?"

"I suppose . . ."

"And as long as we don't breathe a word of this to anyone who is not a juror, I can't imagine that we're violating anything."

"The judge may feel differently about that."

"Do you want to change the subject?"

"No. We can talk about it if you want."

"Did you see what she was wearing? That lavender cowl-neck sweater? It looked like cashmere."

"It was. It was a Cynthia Rowley. I think I saw Angelina Jolie wearing the same one in a picture in the *Star*. Or the *Enquirer*, maybe. Or maybe it was Sandra Bullock."

"How can she afford designer clothes?"

"I don't know. Maybe it was a gift?"

"Nice gift. And she's got generous friends if it's true. A sweater like that has got to run close to three hundred dollars. Hey, wouldn't it be something if that top was a gift from one of the people she worked with?"

"Oh, that's too sick to even think about."

"No. Think about it. The only people who would know would be the relatives and friends of the person who gave it to her. It would be like she was spitting in their face. Like a secret message."

"I can't imagine she would do something that deliberately hurtful."

"Why not? She killed six people, right? What's more 'deliberately hurtful' than that?"

"I suppose. But still . . ."

"I have to ask. Are you leaning one way or another?"

"It's got to be guilty or not guilty by reason of insanity, right?"

"Yes. This risotto is to die for."

"I don't know."

"No early feelings toward one verdict or another?"

"Well, sometimes I think that a person couldn't be sane and do what she did. But then I think about how she planned the murders, and paralyzed them all with the Pavulon, and dragged them in one at a time. It was so . . . systematic. How could an insane person do that?"

"She couldn't. That's why my mind is already made up."

"Before you hear any testimony? You're kidding!"

"Nope. Grated cheese?"

"No, thanks."

"You don't like grated cheese?"

"I love grated cheese. It's just that I'm lactose-intolerant and I forgot my Lactaid."

"She's guilty as sin and she should die for her crimes."

"So let me get this straight. You heard her response to one question, which, if I recall, was what she did for a living, and you have already concluded that she is guilty and should get the death penalty?"

"You got it. I'm a no-nonsense girl, my fellow juror. I see what I see, and I know what I know. And this chick is guilty."

"That just seems so . . . rash. And unfair."

"Why unfair?"

"Because the purpose of a trial is to give anybody accused of a crime a chance to defend themselves. Right? You're not giving her that chance."

"Let me put it this way, Judge Judy. She admitted doing it. In my mind, that immediately leads to *case closed*. I don't buy that somebody can be not guilty because they were insane at the time of their crimes, and then they suddenly snapped back into sanity as soon as they finished. It just does not make any sense at all to me. So, if I remove the possibility of a not-guilty-by-reason-of-insanity verdict from the table, then the only thing left to consider— and I'm only talking about me now, remember—is the sentence. And since I am pro-death penalty, I say she should die for her crimes. Like I said. Case closed."

"How can you be so nonchalant about sentencing somebody to die?"

"It's easy. I just think about the six dead people and their families."

"Well, if your mind is made up, and mine isn't, what's going to happen in the jury room if I want to vote for not guilty?"

"One of three things. One: Everyone in the room will agree with you, and the verdict will be not guilty. Two: You will change your mind and agree with everyone else, and the verdict will be guilty. Or three: We'll have a hung jury. The depth and passion of each juror's commitment to their decision will determine how hard they fight. And how long we remain locked up in that room."

"What if I decide she was insane and, therefore, not guilty, and everyone else agrees with me?"

"Then we're hung, sweetie pie. Because this girl *ain't* changing her mind."

"Well, then, I guess we just wait and see what happens after the testimony is over, right?"

"Right as rain. Man, this risotto is extraordinary. Waiter? Excuse me?"

"Yes, ma'am?"

"I hope I'm not asking you to divulge state secrets or anything, but could you tell me what are the dominant flavors I'm tasting in this risotto?"

"Happily, ma'am. That is our Italian Glory Risotto, and what you're tasting is a blend of provolone and ricotta cheeses, garlic sautéed in extra virgin olive oil, a soupçon of butter, and fresh basil. The chef also adds a dash of white pepper to the rice as it's cooking with the other ingredients. And I have to specify *white* pepper. I have direct orders. After he created the dish, our chef told us all, 'There is a difference between white pepper, black pepper, and red pepper. My Italian risotto uses *white* pepper.' "

"Well, please extend my compliments to the chef. This is absolutely delicious."

"That I will do, ma'am. And I offer his thanks. Will there be anything else?"

"No, just the check, please. Thank you. Unless you want more coffee?"

"No, I'm fine."

"Just the check, then. Thank you. Wasn't that nice of him to tell us what was in the risotto?"

"I tasted the basil, but the ricotta was a surprise. That's probably why it was so creamy. And something else just occurred to me."

"What's that? More about the verdict?"

"No. It occurred to me as we were listening to the waiter that the risotto had two kinds of cheese in it. Plus butter."

"Oh, no. Your lactose thing!"

"Yes. Which means I have approximately one hour before I will be spending a great deal of time on the . . . uh, the 'witness chair.'"

"That's funny! The witness chair! Very clever."

"So I hope you will forgive me if I leave immediately. This should cover my share of the bill. If it's more, I'll give it to you tomorrow at the courthouse. But I really have to leave."

"Go. I'll take care of the bill."

"Thanks. See you in court."

"Good luck with your . . . uh, 'testimony.'"

"Very funny."

"Sorry. Now I just hope I can get a cab."

"Let me know if I can do anything to help."

"Thanks. See you soon."

39

Tory Troy
Defense Counsel Carolyn Payne

"So, my dear, what was that all about? You look okay to me."

"Why, Attorney Payne—are you suggesting that I was faking? I'm aghast at such a notion!"

"Yes, I'm sure you are. I'm simply asking what that was all about. Postponing a trial because the defendant doesn't 'feel well' is, to be blunt, a royal pain in the ass. Especially after she has taken the stand and answered precisely one question."

"Pretty slick, huh?"

"So you *were* faking?"

"I really did feel a little queasy. Honest. But let's just say I exaggerated my symptoms a little."

"May I ask why?"

"Because Brawley Loren is a dick."

"You'll get no argument from me there, but what

good does it do you to antagonize the D.A. and delay your trial?"

"*No* good. But I don't care. You and I both know what's going to happen. And it's not a happy ending."

"Tory, you shouldn't talk like that. And you certainly shouldn't think like that."

"You know what's been happening to me lately, Carolyn? I've been seeing dying faces."

"Even though I'm not sure I should ask—please, do tell what in the name of heaven *that* means."

"Did you ever see someone walking on the street, or browsing in a store, and you immediately—almost reflexively—think to yourself how healthy their face looks? Like when you see a teenager who has a clear complexion, bright eyes, perfect teeth, great hair . . . they just radiate health, you know?"

"Tory, it's only normal for young people to look healthy. *You* look healthy."

"Yeah, I know that. But there's more to it than that. They almost *glow* sometimes."

"Okay . . . and?"

"Nowadays, if *I* see someone that the rest of the world would think looks healthy, I suddenly get a flash of what their face will look like moments before their death."

"Jesus Christ, Tory. How morbid is that?"

"I can't help it. All of a sudden I see them ravaged by cancer, or kidney failure, or some horrible disease."

"That's twisted."

"You think I'm imagining it on purpose?"

"I don't know if you're consciously trying to imagine

what these people will look like with a disease but, for some reason, your mind is instantly leaping to thoughts of disease and death when you see someone healthy-looking. I'll bet it has something to do with your current . . . situation. Your, you know, state of affairs."

"You think because I'm on trial for killing my coworkers that I'm seeing dead people. Like in the movie?"

"Well, that kid actually *did* see dead people. Bruce Willis, anyway."

"Right."

"Oh, I'm awful."

"Why?"

"The thought that just popped into my mind was, Well, that's one and the same thing."

"Carolyn! You aren't a Bruce Willis fan?"

"Not in his bald, post-Demi years. I'm more of a *Moonlighting/Die Hard*-era Willis fan."

"Is it the baldness?"

"Not really. I don't mind baldness. Baldness can be sexy. Masculine. Sean Connery? Patrick Stewart? It's more the attitude, I think. He's obviously not hungry anymore, and that comes across to me these days. He seems like a nice guy, though."

"I think I know what you mean."

"Tory, is this 'death vision quest' trip you're on bothering you? Do you feel all right to testify?"

"I don't have a choice, Carolyn. Good old Dr. Bex said I was fit to stand trial, so any mental 'issues' that come up now are almost certainly going to be . . . what's the word . . . invalidated?"

"Not necessarily. I can go to the judge and ask for a continuance so you can talk to another psychiatrist if you think it will help."

"You think he'd grant it?"

"Hard to say. He might. His immediate willingness to postpone yesterday because you didn't feel well shows that he obviously has some benevolent feelings toward you. Plus there's something else. This is a huge case for him. Six felony murders. I am certain he is already strategizing about how he can protect his rulings and limit the possibility of appeal based on something *he* does wrong. So I'm betting he will err on the side of caution. So, do you want to talk to someone else?"

"No."

"Are you sure?"

"Yes."

"Okay, then, do you have any idea as to when you think you'll be, uh, 'healthy' enough to resume your testimony?"

"I'm ready now."

"Tory, it's four in the afternoon."

"No, I don't mean *right now*. I mean, I'm ready whenever."

"Have you seen the staff doctor?"

"Yes. And he has seen me."

"What did he say?"

"That it was probably a twenty-four-hour virus."

"I see."

"Those twenty-four-hour viruses are a bitch."

"Apparently. And they seem to know when the

twenty-four hours are up too. Smart little buggers, aren't they?"

"That's funny, Carolyn. And you said you didn't have a sense of humor!"

"Yeah, right. I'm putting in a request to be a stand-up comedian in my next life."

"What happens now?"

"I'll tell the judge you'll be ready to resume your testimony tomorrow morning."

"Okay. And thanks."

"For what?"

"For everything. I can only imagine what it's like to try to defend someone you know is going to lose."

"I never said that."

"You didn't have to."

"I'll see you tomorrow, Tory. And please, could you do me a favor?"

"What?"

"Would you try to have at least one positive thought sometime tonight?"

"I'll try. But no guarantees."

"You're killing me, Tory. You know that, don't you? You're killing me. Have a good night."

"Well, we'll see about that, won't we?"

"Killing me. Guard!"

"Bye, Carolyn."

"Bye, Tory."

40

Court Transcript:

Tory Troy

Defense Counsel Carolyn Payne

District Attorney Brawley Loren

Judge Gerard Becker

Court Personnel

The Visitors' Gallery

The Jury

Tomoyuki Nakamura

"I'd like to remind you, Ms. Troy, that you are still under oath."

"Yes, Your Honor."

"Thank you. You may proceed, Counselor."

"Good morning, Ms. Troy. In your previous . . . *ab-breviated* testimony, you stated that you were a certified animal euthanasia technician. Is that correct?"

"Yes."

"Could you tell us, please, what that job entails?"

"I euthanize sick, violent, and unadopted animals at an animal shelter."

"So you kill animals for a living."

"I do not consider it 'killing' animals."

"Why not?"

"Because there is no malice. The word *kill*—and I'm speaking only for me now—the word *kill* to me suggests deliberate, *murderous* intent, and that is the furthest thing from my mind when I do my job."

"Do you always parse your words so carefully, Ms. Troy?"

"When they are important enough, sir, I do, yes."

"Then would you please tell the court the difference between *killing* animals and what you do."

"The end result is the same, of course. The animal is dead. But I consider what I do—what I *did*—to be releasing them from a life in which no one will take responsibility for them. This is humane, not cruel."

"I see. Do you like animals, Ms. Troy?"

"I love animals."

"It would seem that euthanizing animals would be the last job in the world an animal lover would want."

"Is that a question?"

"Strike that. Do you think it is hypocritical for an animal lover to take a job killing animals?"

"No."

"So you don't think it's hypocritical."

"No."

"Not in the least."

"I said no."

"Could you do us the privilege of enlightening us as to your thinking, please?"

"Objection. Badgering. *Sarcastic* badgering too, Judge."

"Scale it back a notch, Mr. Loren."

"Sorry, Your Honor. Would you explain your thinking to the court, please?"

"I'll try. I once read something that horrified me. It said that almost three-quarters of the animals that are brought to animal shelters—surrendered, we call it—have to be euthanized. This means that only one out of four animals in shelters finds a home. What this says to me, Mr. Loren, is that there really is no interest in, first, finding homes for all these animals, and, second, getting our animal population under control. And so we end up just exterminating them. And that's where I come in."

"So you see yourself as an exterminator? Don't exterminators get rid of pests, Ms. Troy?"

"Bad choice of words, Counselor. Yes, I exterminate unwanted and sick animals, but I do so with an eye on the big picture."

"And what is that 'big picture,' please?"

"What would happen if we did not do what we do."

"And what does that mean?"

"Let's hypothesize a little. Let's say that animal euthanasia was abolished tomorrow. Would that solve the unwanted-animals problem? Hardly. Suddenly, cities everywhere would be faced with thousands of dogs and cats with no homes and no food. Who would feed these animals? Would taxpayers sit still for massive tax increases to provide shelters and care for all these animals? Would you, Mr. Loren? Cities don't have enough room in their shelters for *people*, for heaven's sake, let alone animals. So, after a time, what would happen? Starving, sick, crazed animals would be roaming our streets, rummaging through Dumpsters and garbage cans, desperately looking for anything at all to eat. People would be afraid to walk around for fear of being attacked by savage, feral animals."

"Oh, come now, Ms. Troy. Isn't that a bit far-fetched? Something of an extreme scenario?"

"Hell, no! Sorry, Judge. It absolutely is *not* far-fetched! These animals exist. And since they are living creatures, they need to eat. And if they don't get enough food, they will scavenge. It will be a survival thing, Mr. Loren. Some experts believe that in a situation as I have just described, rogue animals could even turn to killing and eating their own."

"Animal cannibalism?"

"Precisely."

"So how did all that factor in to your decision to become a certified animal euthanasia technician?"

"I evaluated the situation calmly, and, I hope, rationally, and came to the conclusion that, when faced with a problem with two bad solutions, you go with the lesser of two evils. So I consider what I do merciful."

"Do you ever feel guilty about it?"

"No, I do not."

"Could you elaborate on that a little, please?"

"What do you mean?"

"As an ancillary part of our preparation for your trial, Ms. Troy, we talked to many people in all walks of life about what your job entailed. Many of them had the same response: 'How could a person go to work and kill animals as part of their job?' The public obviously considers what you do to be abominable. Don't you feel even the least bit guilty about what you do?"

"Again with the guilt? People think that way because they are ignorant. And also because they want nothing to do with accepting responsibility for the companion-animal problem in this country. I feel sorrow, but not guilt."

"I see. Very well. Your Honor, if I may, I would like to move on to another witness at this time, while reserving the right to call Ms. Troy later."

"Attorney Payne, do you have any questions for the defendant?"

"Not at this time, Your Honor."

"Very well. Ms. Troy, you may step down. Please remember that you are still under oath. Call your next witness, Mr. Loren."

"The Prosecution calls Tommy Nakamura."

"Please raise your right hand and place your left hand on the Bible. Do you solemnly swear or affirm that the testimony you are about to give in this court will be the truth, the whole truth, and nothing but the truth?"

"I do."

"Please state your name for the record."

"Tommy—uh, Tomoyuki Nakamura."

"Thank you."

"Good morning, Mr. Nakamura."

"Good morning."

"Tell us what you do for a living, please."

"I'm a student. And I work part-time at the Waterbridge Animal Shelter. Sundays."

"And what are you studying in school?"

"I'm a biochemistry major."

"I see. Are you married?"

"No, sir. I'm single."

"Do you know the defendant?"

"Yes."

"How do you know her?"

"She's the C.A.T. at the animal shelter."

"C.A.T.?"

"Certified animal euthanasia technician."

"Of course. You leave the *E* for *euthanasia* out of the acronym?"

"Yes. Well, I do anyway. Actually, most of us do."

"How long have you known her?"

"Since I started working there part-time, about seven months, I'd say. I can find out for sure if you need the exact date."

"No, that's fine. Could you please tell the court about the Friday afternoon you visited the shelter and discovered that your coworkers had been murdered?"

"Objection."

"Overruled. It has been stipulated that Ms. Troy admitted the murders and that six people were killed, Counselor. Proceed, Mr. Loren."

"Mr. Nakamura, could you please tell the court what you saw that afternoon?"

"I work at the shelter on Sundays. I staff the front desk and take in any animals that people drop off. I write them up, feed them, and place them in a cage. It's not all that busy on Sundays, so I usually bring some studying, and I always have my CD player with me. I listen to it with headphones, but since I'm right in front of the front door, I can see anybody who comes in, and the phone blinks red when it rings, so I don't miss anything. The Sunday before the day of the murders, I left my CD player at the shelter when I went home that night. I was a little upset with myself because it had a new CD in it that I had just bought, and I wanted to listen to it again that night."

"What CD was that?"

"Paula Cole. *Amen*."

"Excellent album."

"You know Paula Cole?"

"Sure. *Harbinger*. *This Fire*. She's—"

"Mr. Loren?"

"Sorry, Judge. Please continue, Mr. Nakamura."

"So, like I said, I left behind my CD player, and I originally planned to pick it up between classes the following day, but I couldn't."

"Why not?"

"I just got too busy with school."

"Well, what about the rest of the week? Why did you wait until Friday to go get it?"

"I live with my parents, and on Monday night their water heater burst and flooded the basement. For the next few days, any free time I had was spent helping them clean up the basement and throw stuff out. We were without hot water for almost three days by the time the plumber got there."

"Could you please tell us about the Friday afternoon you returned to the shelter to pick up your CD player?"

"Class ended at eleven forty-five—Human Physiology—and I didn't have anything else that afternoon, so I went to McDonald's and had lunch. Then I saw a movie, and then I drove to the animal shelter. Do you want to know what I ate?"

"No, that won't be necessary. Were you alone?"

"Yes, sir."

"What movie did you see?"

"*Road to Perdition.*"

"Any good?"

"It was excellent."

"What time did it start?"

"It was a twelve forty-five show. I go to the early show because it's cheaper."

"What time did you arrive at the animal shelter?"

"It was around three, I think."

"Go on."

"The door was locked, which was very strange."

"How so?"

"It shouldn't have been locked at that time of day. They always locked it for lunch from twelve-thirty to one-thirty, but at three o'clock, it should have been open."

"So what did you do?"

"I used my key and went in."

"What did you see when you first entered the building?"

"Nothing. I mean, there was no one at the front desk,

which was a little unusual, but not alarming. Sometimes everyone was busy in the back and the desk was left unmanned for a couple of minutes."

"So what did you do next?"

"I went into the front office and picked up my CD player."

"Where was it?"

"In Marcy's desk drawer. She probably found it on her desk when she came in Monday morning and put it away for me."

"What did you do next?"

"I put my CD player in my knapsack and walked into the back to say hello to everybody before I left."

"And then?"

"Then I saw Tory."

"Go on."

"She was standing at the door of the euthanasia chamber."

"Was the door open?"

"Yes."

"Could you see inside the chamber?"

"Yes."

"Please tell the court what you saw."

"They were all dead."

"Who are 'they,' Mr. Nakamura?"

"All the people who worked at the shelter. Everybody."

"Marcy, Ann, Philip, Teresa, Renaldo, and Jake?"

"Yes."

"What did you do then?"

"I said, 'Fuck!'—sorry, Your Honor—and pulled out my cell phone."

"And then?"

"I started running out of the shelter. I dialed 911 as I ran."

"Did Ms. Troy see you?"

"Yes."

"Did she say anything to you?"

"No. She just looked at me."

"What happened next?"

"I jumped in my car and sat there until the police came."

"Why didn't you drive away?"

"Because the 911 operator told me to find a place of safety but to remain at the shelter. So I did."

"Then what happened?"

"The cops came."

"How many?"

"Two cars with two cops in each."

"And then?"

"They jumped out of the cars with their guns drawn, ran into the shelter, and then they were inside for quite a while."

"Did anyone speak to you?"

"Yes. Later. After the detectives arrived."

"And when did that happen?"

"A car with two detectives showed up within a couple of minutes after the cops got there."

"Did you see the defendant being taken into custody?"

"I didn't see them arrest her inside the shelter, if that's what you mean. I saw them put her in the cop car, though."

"What happened next?"

"I talked to the detectives for a little while, and then they told me I could go."

"Did you see them remove the bodies from the animal shelter?"

"No, sir."

"That's all I have for Mr. Nakamura, Judge."

"Ms. Payne?"

"Mr. Nakamura, what do you recall about the look on Ms. Troy's face when you saw her standing at the door of the gas chamber?"

"The look on her face?"

"Yes. Did she look angry? Or sad? Or afraid?"

"No, ma'am."

"How *did* she look?"

"Just blank. I mean, her expression was just blank, like she was just staring at a wall or something. Like she was in neutral."

"I see. Thank you. That's all I have, Judge."

"You may step down, Mr. Nakamura. Thank you."

"Thank you, Your Honor."

"This court will stand in recess until tomorrow morning at ten A.M. Court adjourned."

41

Viviana Troy
Defense Counsel Carolyn Payne

"But I *am* afraid, Miss Payne. I've changed my mind. I don't want to testify in court."

"Why are you afraid, Mrs. Troy?"

"That man frightens me. And please call me Viviana."

"D.A. Loren?"

"Yes."

"You don't have to worry, dear. The judge is a wonderful man who is very protective of his witnesses and his jurors. It's the lawyers he has a problem with."

"What will they do to me when I testify?"

"They won't *do* anything to you. You will simply have to answer some questions. That's all."

"What kind of questions?"

"Well, you'll probably have to answer some questions about Tory."

"Will I have to talk about Crouch?"

"Yes, you probably will."

"Will they ask me about what he did to her?"

"Actually, dear, *I* will probably have to ask you some questions about that. The abuse your daughter endured at the hands of your husband may have contributed to her mental state and had something to do with her willingness to kill her coworkers. We have to be sure the jury understands the trauma she suffered when she was young. I will try to use what happened to Tory to *help* Tory."

"Won't Mr. Loren want to talk about that?"

"Probably not, since he is not going to want to give the jury an opportunity to feel sympathy for her. No, the questions about Crouch will have to come from me, but I promise you they will not upset you too much."

"All right. I trust you, Miss Payne."

"Thank you, Viviana. That means a lot to me."

"How long will I be on the stand?"

"Less than two hours all told, I expect."

"And you like this judge?"

"Yes. A great deal. Judge Becker is a stern but compassionate man. He will not allow lawyers to manhandle witnesses, and I personally have witnessed what happens when he gets his ire up with an attorney."

"What does he do?"

"One time, he had a defense lawyer put in jail for the night because he snapped at him somewhat abruptly. Judge Becker immediately declared him in contempt of court and the guy spent the night in a jail cell. The judge slammed down his wooden gavel so hard I thought he was going to crack the top of his bench."

"What did the lawyer do that made the judge mad?"

"He got very aggressive with a teenage girl who had been in a car with a drunk driver when the driver hit and killed a young boy. The lawyer was defending the kid who was driving."

"What happened?"

"Well, the girl hadn't even been drinking, but because she had been in the car, she was subpoenaed to testify. She was dumb to have gotten in the car with him in the first place, but she really had nothing to do with the accident. The driver's lawyer started attacking the girl—you know, accusing her of distracting him, egging the kid on to drive fast . . . that kind of stuff—and the girl broke down in tears. She just fell apart. The judge reprimanded the lawyer, who, like I said, snapped at him and interrupted him—to try to defend himself, I guess. The next thing he knew he was behind bars."

"Oh, my."

"I know that lawyer too. Usually he's smarter than that. But that day, he began arguing with the judge while Becker was still talking, and that was that. The one thing lawyers learn right out of law school is never interrupt the judge. *Never.* The judge is the God of the courtroom. Sometimes, in the heat of a trial, some lawyers forget that."

"Did the lawyer get out of jail?"

"Oh, yeah. The following morning the judge let him go. It was sort of funny, because the judge ordered him released at eight in the morning and he had to be in court by ten, so he had to rush home, shower, change his clothes, and get back to the courthouse in time. And because he had been in a cell all night, he had not been able to prepare for the following day's testimony. Needless to say, that case did not go very well for my friend."

"I'm still very nervous, Miss Payne."

"You have nothing to worry about, Viviana. And just keep in mind that everything you will do will be to help your daughter."

"All right. Thank you. I'll try to stay calm."

"You'll be fine. I promise you that, and the judge will see to it."

42

Court Transcript:

Tory Troy

Defense Counsel Carolyn Payne

District Attorney Brawley Loren

Judge Gerard Becker

Court Personnel

The Visitors' Gallery

The Jury

Dr. Gwyneth June

"Please raise your right hand and place your left hand on the Bible. Do you solemnly swear or affirm that the testimony you are about to give in this court will be the truth, the whole truth, and nothing but the truth?"

"I do."

"Please state your name for the record."

"Gwyneth June."

"And would you please tell the court your occupation?"

"I am a forensic pathologist for the state of Connecticut. Non-field."

"What does 'non-field' mean?"

"I do not go to crime scenes. I perform autopsies on untimely death victims at the Hartford lab."

"And what are 'untimely death victims,' please?"

"Murder victims, sudden deaths, unattended deaths, suicides. Pretty much almost any death outside of a health-care facility or a hospice."

"I see. Were you the pathologist of record for the six murders for which the defendant is being tried?"

"Yes."

"And what were your conclusions as to the causes of death of the six victims?"

"They all died from suffocation."

"And what caused them all to suffocate to death?"

"Paralysis of the lungs, primarily; inhalation of toxic gas—carbon monoxide—as a secondary cause."

"Lung paralysis and carbon monoxide poisoning."

"Yes."

"Did you do toxicology screens?"

"Of course."

"And could you tell us what drugs, or substances, if any, were found in the bodies?"

"The findings were routine, except for the pancuronium bromide. The Pavulon. The specifics of what was found in each body are in my lab reports."

"We'll get to the Pavulon in a moment, Doctor. Permission to admit Dr. June's toxicology reports into evidence, Judge?"

"Granted."

"Dr. June, what else can you tell us about your autopsy findings that you would consider relevant to this case and important for the members of the jury to know?"

"There are two findings that I consider important. The first is that each victim exhibited a small puncture wound in the midpoint of the posterior of the cervical spine."

"There was a hole in the back of their neck."

"A puncture. Yes."

"And what made this puncture hole, Doctor?"

"A hypodermic syringe."

"A needle."

"Yes."

"This leads me to ask you about your second important finding, please."

"Each of the victims evidenced a measurable level of pancuronium bromide in their blood. Pavulon."

"And what is Pavulon, Dr. June?"

"It is a paralytic agent. A paralyzing drug."

"And what is Pavulon used for?"

"Mainly to immobilize patients before surgery."

"You say to immobilize patients. Does it make them unconscious? Knock them out?"

"No. That is done by standard anesthesia. Paralytic drugs prevent the patient's body from moving involuntarily during surgery, but it is not an anesthetic."

"So, at the time of their deaths, the six victims were paralyzed?"

"Yes."

"And conscious?"

"Yes."

"How long would they have remained conscious after they were injected with the drug?"

"At least a few minutes. Until they blacked out from lack of oxygen and then died."

"So, then, Dr. June, based on your findings, the six victims in this case were paralyzed, suffocating, and wide awake when they were dragged into the gas chamber and the gas was turned on."

"Yes."

"No further questions, Your Honor."

"Does Defense Counsel have any questions for this witness? Ms. Payne?"

"Not at this time, Your Honor."

"You may step down, Dr. June."

43

Tory Troy
Psychiatric Nurse Chiarra Ziegler

"Hey, Chiarra."

"Hi, Tory."

"You know what occurred to me last night?"

"What's that?"

"That I'm grateful for music."

"You're grateful for music? Grateful? What does that mean?"

"I've been listening to a lot of classical stuff lately. My mother sent me a bunch of CDs. And Carolyn gave me a two-CD set of twenty-four Shostakovich piano preludes and fugues. Played by Keith Jarrett. I usually don't go for the more modern composers, but I'm loving these CDs."

"Well, good, Tory. I'm glad music provides something of a respite for you. We do so love when our patients are—what's the word?—placid."

"Placid? Is that what I am?"

"Well, you do seem somewhat more relaxed."

"It's because of the trial."

"What do you mean?"

"It's moving right along now . . . and for some reason, the fact that the end is a foregone conclusion has made me less . . . anxious."

"Tory—"

"It is, Chiarra . . . we both know it. . . . Anyway, I guess that since I probably have a limited time to listen to music, I am suddenly grateful for it."

"I've noticed you reading more too."

"Yeah. I'm into this book about Zen now. Do you know what a koan is?"

"Are you serious?"

"It's a kind of riddle—but a riddle that can make your head explode if you think too hard about it."

"What do you mean?"

"They're the kind that don't have real answers. But thinking about them is supposed to bring . . . clarity, I guess."

"I'm lost."

"Okay. Try this on for size. When you can do nothing, what can you do?"

"That's easy."

"Oh, yeah?"

"Sure. When you can't do anything, then you can't do anything. Simple."

"But if you're *doing* nothing, then aren't you really doing *something*?"

"I . . ."

"Don't even try."

"Right."

"There's a great Zen story. A young student went to a Zen master and asked him how he could know Zen. The master told him to go sit on a beach and stare at the sea for ten years. The student protested, saying that that was too long to wait. He asked the master how long it would take if he worked really hard at it. And the master said, 'Oh, then it will take twenty years.' "

"I like that. I'm not sure I understand it—but I like it."

"Join the club."

"You don't understand it?"

"I . . . maybe. I try. Sometimes I . . . you know, catch a glimpse."

"Sounds too confusing for me."

"It's confusing for me too."

"Then why study it?"

"Cause if I didn't, I'd eat instead."

"Tory, you're a reed, for Christ's sake."

"Wanna see my thighs?"

"You're crazy."

"That's what they—well, that's what *some* people say."

"Do you have to meditate when you . . . do—is that the right word?—Zen?"

"It's all part of it, but I've always meditated. I have one I do a lot. Make your mind still like a stone. You should try it."

"Please. Enough people have told me I've got rocks in

my head over the years. I don't need to join in, thank you very much."

"There's another one I found in some book that said to imagine that your body was an empty room with walls of skin. Sometimes that works, but the imagery usually grosses me out and reminds me of that movie *Videodrome*."

"That's disgusting."

"Isn't it, though? I avoid that one."

"Smart girl."

"You saw Carolyn here today, didn't you? I joked with her about working on a Sunday. I said, 'Don't you ever take a day off?' and she said, 'What is this "day off" of which you speak?' She's funny."

"I like her."

"She told me she heard that the D.A. is thinking of calling the doctor who certified me fit to stand trial to the stand."

"Bexley?"

"Yeah. Although I don't know what for. All he can testify about is my competency now. Unless Loren finds a way to get Bexley to admit that I was sane when I . . . you know."

"Do you think he will? Admit that to the D.A.?"

"I don't know. I really don't know."

"Tory, can I ask you something?"

"Sure."

"You're Catholic, right?"

"Yeah. Well . . . let's put it this way: I was baptized."

"Have you prayed over this?"

"No. I used to be a lot more religious than I am now, Chiarra. And my writing reflected it too. Now I'm like a half-assed agnostic—one crisis away from becoming an atheist."

"Oh, don't say that, Tory."

"It's true. I've even had dreams about Jesus, if you can believe that, and when I wake up, I'm even more convinced than ever that I'm alone. Some people—especially Italians—they believe that if you dream about Jesus, or the Virgin Mary, or a saint, it means that they really came to you in your sleep. I know my mother believes that."

"And you don't?"

"I used to. I used to read all sorts of things into my dreams. I dreamt once that Jesus and I were watching workers build his cross. He even spoke to me."

"What did He say?"

"I don't remember exactly, but it was something about him having been through all of it before . . . that he was just one of many christs . . . *christs* with a small *c*."

"Really? How did that make you feel?"

"Like I was watching a science fiction movie. I couldn't shake the image of all these alien Jesuses visiting earth over the centuries. . . . I didn't get it . . . and then I—once again—woke up confused and cynical."

"Don't get mad, all right?"

"Why?"

"I'm going to ask you something, but I don't want you to get mad."

"How can I promise you that when I haven't heard what you're going to ask me?"

"Yeah, I know—but just try not to get mad at me, okay?"

"Okay, I'll try. Fire away."

"Do you think you were able to kill those people because you lost your religion?"

"What—like the R.E.M. song?"

"You know what I mean."

"Yeah, I do. And my answer is maybe, probably, I doubt it, and I don't know."

"Oh. That clears things up for me. Thanks."

"I'm sorry, Chiarra. I don't mean to blow you off like that. It's just that—as pathetic as it sounds—those really are the answers to your question: maybe, probably, I doubt it, and I don't know."

"Don't you have faith, Tory?"

"In what?"

"In *anything*. That life means something. That we go on after we die. That there's a God."

"Well, I always thought I believed that life had meaning—but look at what I did. How could I hold that belief and do what I did? How? Tell me."

"I don't know, Tory."

"Yeah. Me neither. Do you believe, Chiarra?"

"Oh, yes. Always have. Always will."

"You know, deep down, I suspect that I know what you mean. After all, it does make sense to me that there had to have been . . . *something* to start everything off.

Nothing can't come from nothing, right? I sometimes feel that in the pit of my stomach."

"That's not your stomach. That's your soul."

"Oh, yeah? Well, it doesn't show up on an MRI, I can tell you that. And most of the time, I'm fighting a feeling of emptiness . . . that there's *nothing* at all in there."

"You're undergoing a crisis of faith, Tory. Don't worry about it. It'll pass."

"Any way to hurry it up?"

"Not that I know of. But I'm certain that you'll pull out of this nosedive you're in."

"You mean before I crash headfirst into the void?"

"There's nothing in the void. You can't crash into nothing."

"Good point. So does that mean I'll just keep falling?"

"Oh, no. You'll be caught. Believe me."

"I'll try."

"Good. And on that note, my break is over. Thanks for giving me something that will prey on my mind for . . . well, at least for the remainder of my shift!"

"I'm sorry!"

"I'm only kidding. And you still haven't taken your Ambien, Tory."

"Damn. I thought you'd forget."

"I may not remember my cousins' names, but I never forget patient orders."

"Oh, all right. Thanks, Chiarra."

"For what? You don't want the pill, so what are you grateful for?"

"For listening."

44

Court Transcript:

Tory Troy

Defense Counsel Carolyn Payne

District Attorney Brawley Loren

Judge Gerard Becker

Court Personnel

The Visitors' Gallery

The Jury

Dr. Baraku Bexley

"Please raise your right hand and place your left hand on the Bible. Do you solemnly swear or affirm that the testimony you are about to give in this court will be the truth, the whole truth, and nothing but the truth?"

"I do."

"Please state your name for the record."

"Baraku Bexley."

"And would you please tell the court your occupation."

"I am a psychiatrist."

"Are you board certified?"

"Yes."

"Do you have a private practice?"

"Yes."

"Are you on the staff of any local hospitals?"

"Yes. The Hospital of St. Raphael and Yale–New Haven Hospital. Both are in New Haven."

"Do you teach psychiatry?"

"I do. I am on the faculty of the Yale School of Medicine. Clinical psychiatry."

"Thank you. Dr. Bexley, what is your relationship with the defendant?"

"I was appointed by this court to examine the defendant and make a determination as to her fitness to stand trial."

"And what does that mean exactly, Doctor?"

"I interviewed her at length and administered a range of psychological tests to determine if she was able to understand the charges against her and participate in her defense."

"And you determined that she was fit, is that correct?"

"Obviously, Counselor. Or we wouldn't all be here, would we?"

"Yes, of course. Thank you, Doctor. What can you tell us regarding the defendant's state of mind at the time of the murders?"

"That is outside the purview of my work with Ms. Troy."

"I understand that. But as a psychiatric expert, I am asking only for your opinion regarding her mental state when she committed the murders."

"Are you asking me if she was insane, Counselor?"

"No, Doctor. I am asking for your opinion as to her state of mind at the time—sane or insane, whichever you think she was. Do you believe that the defendant, Victoria Abigail Troy, possessed the mental capacity at the time of the murders to realize that what she was doing was wrong?"

"I do."

"Let's be clear, Doctor. As you know, the defendant has pleaded not guilty by reason of insanity. She is claiming a diminished mental capacity extensive enough to prevent her from understanding that her actions were both legally and morally wrong. You are stating here today, on the record, and under penalties of perjury, that you believe she was in full possession of her mental faculties when she killed six people?"

"Yes."

"No further questions, Your Honor."

"Ms. Payne?"

"Thank you, Your Honor. Good day, Dr. Bexley."

"Hello."

"Doctor, you spent several days with Tory, didn't you?"

"Yes. My interviews spanned ten separate days over a three-week period. We spoke many times."

"I see. And during that time, would you say that you got to know Tory fairly well?"

"I believe so. As well as possible under the circumstances."

"The circumstances?"

"She was incarcerated and I was 'on assignment,' so to speak. That is, by its very nature, an artificial situation.

Thus, I 'got to know her' within severely limited parameters."

"I understand. Thank you. Let me ask you this, then, Doctor. Do you think Tory Troy is a good person?"

"Objection, Your Honor. Vague. That question is impossible to answer without agreeing on a definition of *good*."

"Overruled. You may answer the question, Doctor."

"Would you repeat the question, please?"

"Certainly. Do you think Tory Troy is a good person?"

"I do."

"And why is that?"

"During our interviews, I sensed—both professionally as well as on a more intuitive level—no animus or misogyny in her."

"Then, in your opinion, sir, how would you explain her actions at the animal shelter?"

"Anomalous behavior that did not represent part of a *pattern* of behavior that would be expected if it were the result of a psychosis. Displacement activity."

"Displacement activity? And what is that, Doctor?"

"Displacement activity, or displacement behavior, is the redirection of an emotion or an impulse away from its original object—in Tory's case, the euthanasia system—to another, her coworkers."

"And why does this happen, Doctor?"

"A profound stressor."

"Sir?"

"Something triggers the break. We don't know what

triggered Tory's break. Frankly, we don't fully understand what happened to cause her to lash out as she did—to respond to the stressor with actions that resulted in the deaths of her coworkers—but there had to have been something that caused her to abandon her moral codes and act as she did."

"You called this anomalous behavior."

"Yes."

"What would have been, for lack of a better term, *non*-anomalous behavior, assuming the profound stressor occurred in the same manner?"

"Action directed against the original object."

"Could you explain what you mean, please?"

"She could have destroyed the gas chamber, or, perhaps, even set fire to the animal shelter."

"I see. So Tory's behavior wasn't normal, then."

"Well . . ."

"If she acted out in a manner anomalous to what she would have done had she been behaving quote unquote normally, then her behavior was abnormal, isn't that right, Doctor?"

"Yes, but—"

"That'll be all, Doctor."

"Objection, Your Honor. The doctor didn't get a chance to complete his answer."

"Sustained. Please finish what you were about to say, Dr. Bexley."

"Thank you, Your Honor. I was going to say that although Tory's behavior can be considered anomalous, it is only within a very narrow context—that context being the definition of displacement behavior, and the type of behavior that does *not* redirect an emotion. So, anomalous, yes. Inconsistent? Yes. Hostile? Most definitely. But insane? No."

"Thank you, Doctor. You may step down. Court will recess until ten A.M. tomorrow. We are adjourned."

45

Tory Troy
Psychiatric Nurse Chiarra Ziegler

"Hi, Tory."

"Hey, Chiarra."

"What are you reading?"

"Joyce."

"Who's she?"

"She's a he. James Joyce? *Ulysses*? *Finnegans Wake*?"

"Oh, right. Sorry. Yeah, I read him in college. Couldn't make heads or tails of what he was writing about, though. What're you reading?"

"I'm tackling *Ulysses* again."

"Again? How many times have you read it?"

"None. I have never been able to get all the way through it. But now that I've got, ironically, a lot of time on my hands, as well as very little time left, I thought I'd give it another crack."

"Why?"

"Because I've read all the *People* magazines my mother brought me."

"Liar."

"Actually, it ties in with some of that Zen stuff I told you about."

"What do you mean?"

"It's 'Liberation Literature.' A writer named John White came up with the term."

"What does that mean?"

"It's supposed to describe novels and poetry that liberate you. You know—transcend the ego."

"Do you want to be liberated, Tory?"

"I suppose I do."

"Liberated from what? . . . And what happens then—after you're liberated?"

"Those are very good questions, Chiarra. Truly."

"How far into it are you?"

"*Ulysses?*"

"Yeah."

"Chapter Two."

"That far, huh?"

"Very funny. That's misleading, though—I've actually read quite a bit of it piecemeal. And, of course, there's that amazing last line."

"Really? What about it?"

"It's incredibly romantic."

"In *Ulysses?* Are you serious?"

"Oh, yeah. For all its monumental literary significance, the book's last line is pure heat."

"What is it? The last line? Do you know it?"

" '. . . and first I put my arms around him yes and drew him down to me so he could feel my breasts all perfume yes and his heart was going like mad and yes I said yes I will Yes.' "

"That's beautiful. And hot."

"Yeah. Too bad some of the rest of the book isn't as . . . straightforward."

"Well, I'll leave you to your reading, then."

"Chiarra, before you go, can I ask you a question?"

"Of course."

"Have you ever seen one?"

"One what?"

"A lethal-injection execution?"

"Yes."

"Oh, my God, Chiarra. Whose did you see?"

"Should you really be talking about this, Tory?"

"Sure. I'm fine. Tell me. Whose execution did you see?"

"This is probably going to freak you out."

"Why? Is it somebody I've heard of?"

"Timothy McVeigh."

"The Oklahoma City bomber?"

"Yes."

"How the hell did you get to witness McVeigh's execution?"

"Are you sure you want to hear this?"

"Absolutely."

"Okay, then. In January 2001, I started a one-year psychiatry internship at a small community hospital outside Terre Haute, Indiana. At the time, no one was sure when McVeigh's execution would take place. His lawyers were trying all kinds of appeals and legal maneuvers to get his sentence commuted to life imprisonment. Sometime that spring—April, I think—the word came down from the state capitol that all of his appeals had been exhausted and that McVeigh would be executed by lethal injection on June eleventh, 2001."

"I remember reading a lot of stuff that year about his lawyers trying to get him life."

"Yeah, well, none of their attempts succeeded. So the date was set and then they went about approving witnesses."

"I would imagine that the number of requests to be a witness at his execution would be enormous."

"You imagine right. It seemed like every newspaper, TV station, radio station, and Web news site in the world sent in a media request."

"So, with all those people—plus the family members of his victims—how'd you get picked?"

"The Indiana State Corrections Board allowed U.S. universities with psychiatric nursing programs to apply for permission to allow one student to witness the execution. Something like twenty out of the twenty-two U.S. schools with programs applied. Ten schools were then picked randomly, and those ten were each asked to submit one name. My dean submitted mine. The ten names were placed in a sealed box, and the warden picked one name. And that was me."

"Did you want to go?"

"The dean came to me before she submitted my name

and we talked. At first I was a little hesitant, but she told me that the experience would broaden my understanding of several psychiatric issues, including grief, anger, the death penalty—you know, things like that. She also told me that there was a chance I might be able to speak with some of the family members that were there. So I decided to go."

"You have to tell me everything about it."

"Once again, are you sure?"

"Yes. Start with where you sat."

"I was one of the ones who had to watch it on closed-circuit TV. I was with a lot of family members of victims. There were just too many people to fit in the observation room."

"Did any of the family members know who you were?"

"No. Turns out we weren't allowed to talk to each other. They just marched us in and we sat down and waited. The chairs were hard plastic. After a while, my butt started to hurt. We all stared at the blank TV screen for what seemed like an hour, and then they turned it on."

"Did you see him walk into the room?"

"No. When they turned on the TV he was already strapped to the gurney."

"What did he look like?"

"Well, it was kind of an eerie picture. The camera was above his head so the screen was filled with just his face. We didn't see the rest of the room, or anyone else in the room."

"You saw his face?"

"Yeah. He looked scared. His face was white as a sheet, and he looked gaunt. He looked like a lot of terminal patients I've seen."

"Well, that's certainly on-the-nose, don't you think? After all, at that point he *was* a terminal patient, right?"

"I suppose."

"What happened next?"

"His execution was scheduled for seven in the morning. We had all been given a . . . I don't know what you would call it . . . a program to the execution, I guess. We were all given a program. How bizarre is that?"

"Extremely."

"At seven o'clock, he was asked if he had a final statement. That was just a formality, though, since he had already told the warden that he wanted to release a written statement. We all had copies of it."

"What did he say?"

"McVeigh himself didn't say anything. His 'statement' was a poem called 'Invictus.' I think it was written sometime in the late 1800s."

"He released a poem as his final statement?"

"Yeah. I read the whole thing at the time, but all I remember were the last two lines. 'I am the master of my fate. I am the captain of my soul.' "

"He never said anything?"

"Not a word."

"So what happened then?"

"At a little after seven, they gave him the sodium pentothal to knock him out. His eyelids fluttered a little, and then he closed his eyes. For all intents and purposes, that was it for him."

"What do you mean?"

"Pentothal is used as an anesthetic for surgery, and the usual dose for an operation is around one hundred to one hundred fifty milligrams. I think they gave McVeigh five thousand milligrams. That dose alone is fatal, but they continued with the next two drugs."

"What comes next?"

"Tory, are you sure you want to be talking about this?"

"Chiarra, I'm fine. Honestly. What came next?"

"A paralyzing agent."

"Oh."

"Yeah."

"Pavulon?"

"Yes. Pancuronium bromide. In a dose about twenty times what's used for surgeries."

"Okay. Then what?"

"At this point, they couldn't bring him back if they wanted to. The pentothal itself was fatal, and the Pavulon paralyzed his diaphragm and lungs so his body couldn't breathe, even involuntarily. But they proceeded with a fatal dose of the final drug, potassium chloride, which interrupts the electrical signals to the heart and causes cardiac arrest."

"Did he move or make any sounds?"

"Not really. He just lay there. His face twitched a little, and then at seven-fourteen he was declared dead, and the screen went blank."

"What was it like in the room with the other people? Was anybody crying?"

"No. And that's probably because everyone I was with was a family member of an Oklahoma City bombing victim. So there wasn't much sympathy for McVeigh in that room. All of his family members and friends were in the prison viewing room. They deliberately kept them away from the people I was with."

"Considering who you were with, I'm surprised there wasn't cheering or applause in the room."

"You would think they'd all be exuberant, but in fact, everyone was very solemn. Some of the people had expressions on their faces that could only be described as angry. McVeigh might have paid the ultimate price for his crimes, but that didn't bring back their loved ones."

"Is that how I'll be done?"

"Tory!"

"Oh, come on, Chiarra. You know the verdict's going to be guilty and that my sentence will be death by lethal injection. *Everyone* knows it. So tell me. Is that how I'll be done?"

"Yes. The procedure is the same in all of the states that use lethal injection for executions."

"Does it hurt?"

"Tory—"

"Well, does it?"

"We honestly don't know, honey. We don't. What is pain anyway? I once dated a guy who had a wicked skin problem in the winter. His hands itched so bad he would scratch himself until he bled. He tried everything.

Hydrocortisone cream. Prescription ointments. Some of them worked, but they weren't immediate, and they were messy. He told me that sometimes those alcohol-based hand sanitizers would work."

"That Purell stuff?"

"Yeah. But he wouldn't use it the way most people did—you know, squirt a dime-sized drop in your palm and then rub your hands together. He would pump the stuff out onto the tops of his hands and then smooth it over until it completely covered his skin. Then he would blow on it until it dried. It formed like a glove and it gave him some relief."

"He must have hated the winter."

"With a passion. But even though he used the creams and the Purell, he once told me that there were times when he was literally on the verge of going insane from the itching. And that brings me back to your question about pain. Want to hear what he did sometimes to relieve the itch?"

"I'm almost afraid to ask."

"I couldn't believe it when he told me about it, but he made me watch him do it once, and then I was convinced."

"What did he do?"

"He scalded himself."

"Scalded? With hot water?"

"Yes. He said the relief was instantaneous, and that it felt so good, he compared it with an orgasm."

"Oh, come on."

"I'm not kidding. He explained that he had to get the

water running at the perfect temperature. Not hot enough, it would only make the itching worse. Too hot and the relief would turn to pain. He told me that the nerve endings in his skin were so charged from the itching and scratching that he was able to hold his hand under water so hot that he probably would have given himself first-degree burns if his skin were normal. Or possibly even second degree. Somehow the scalding heat short-circuited the itching."

"And you saw him do this?"

"Yes. And I even asked him to let me feel the temperature of the water. I couldn't leave even a finger under there, let alone the top of my hand. And yet he held his hand there, and he told me he could feel the heat sensation permeating his skin until it reached pure relief. He said he had gotten so precise about what worked that even a single degree difference in the water temp would not give him the relief he was looking for."

"Wasn't his hand burned?"

"Nope. Only red. And that went away in a little while, but the relief lasted for hours."

"That sounds dangerous."

"When I met him, he had been doing it for years. And with no harmful results. He told me that he had gotten so good about knowing which water temps worked that he could tell where a person had their water heater set if he had to do it at somebody else's house."

"One man's pain . . ."

". . . is another man's pleasure."

"So what does that have to do with my question?"

"I'm just saying that I don't think what you will feel, if anything, can actually be described as pain. You might feel heat as the drugs run into your body. You may sense some chest pressure or heaviness. But the first drug is given in such a high dose that I find it very hard to believe that you will feel anything at all."

"The pentothal?"

"Right."

"That's the one they give at fifty times the surgery dose, right?"

"Yes."

"Well, I guess I'll find out soon enough, right?"

"Can we talk about something else, please?"

"How about James Joyce?"

"Okay. On second thought, I've got rounds."

"Chicken."

"Bye, Tory."

46

Court Transcript:

Tory Troy

Defense Counsel Carolyn Payne

District Attorney Brawley Loren

Judge Gerard Becker

Court Personnel

The Visitors' Gallery

The Jury

Mrs. Viviana Troy

"Please state your name for the record."

"Viviana Troy."

"Thank you."

"Good morning, Mrs. Troy."

"Good morning."

"Please tell the court your relationship to the defendant."

"I'm her mother."

"When was the last time you spoke to your daughter?"

"Yesterday."

"Are you married, Mrs. Troy?"

"Divorced."

"And what is your ex-husband's name?"

"Crouch Troy."

"Is he Tory's father?"

"Yes."

"How long have you two been divorced?"

"Going on fifteen years."

"So Tory was around thirteen years old when her father left the family home?"

"Yes."

"Could you tell us why you two divorced?"

"Objection. Relevancy, Your Honor?"

"Mr. Loren?"

"I withdraw the question, Your Honor."

"Proceed."

"Mrs. Troy, what can you tell us about your daughter as a child?"

"I don't understand. What do you mean?"

"What was she like as a child? What were her interests? Her hobbies? What did she like in school?"

"She was always a good student. She always got As on all her tests. And she was always reading. I remember her sitting outside under the big elm tree with a book and an apple. And her IQ was very high. She was tested at one forty-five. She was in that club . . . that high IQ club . . . Menses?"

"Do you mean Mensa?"

"Yes! That's it. And she scored high on her SATs too. 1370. Everything fascinated her . . . she loved science, and history, and biology . . . she was always a good student."

"I see. Did she have a pet growing up?"

"Only when she was very little. Henry. A cat. But nothing after Henry died. But she always loved animals."

"Then why didn't she have a cat or a dog?"

"Her father wouldn't allow it."

"How about after he left the house?"

"Yes. Cats."

"To your knowledge, was she ever cruel to animals?"

"Heavens, no! Of course not!"

"You can understand, I'm sure, why we would ask such a question, Mrs. Troy, can't you? After all, she did take a job killing animals for a living."

"Objection. Judge?"

"Mr. Loren, either control yourself or I will charge you with contempt."

"Sorry, Judge. No further questions for this witness."

"Miss Payne?"

"Yes, Your Honor. I have some questions for Mrs. Troy."

"Proceed."

"Good morning, Viviana."

"Good morning, Miss Payne."

"Viviana, during one of our conversations prior to this trial, and again in your testimony here today, you have stated that Tory always loved animals."

"Oh, yes. Even though her father would never let her have a pet when she was little, she always went out of her way to be with animals."

"In what way?"

"Well, she would dog-sit for neighbors if they went away on vacation. Or she would beg her teachers to make class field trips to the Bridgeport Zoo and the East Rock Nature Center. She was very persuasive. They went on several. And then there were the seagulls."

"The seagulls?"

"Yes."

"What about the seagulls?"

"She fed them."

"Where was this, Viviana?"

"Should I tell the story of how she fed the seagulls, Miss Payne?"

"Yes, dear, please do."

"All right. There are these small shopping centers near where we live, and I used to take Tory shopping on Saturday afternoons. Sometimes we went on a weeknight if she didn't have school the next day."

"Go on."

"There was this one center that had a big warehouse type of store. Everything was very cheap . . . uh, inexpensive there. Foil pans, for instance. Stop & Shop sold foil pans for a dollar ninety-nine that the warehouse store had for twenty cents. Twenty cents!"

"Judge?"

"Mr. Loren?"

"Are we now going to be regaled with a complete inventory comparison between Stop & Shop and the warehouse store?"

"Would you please try to keep your answers within the scope of the question, Mrs. Troy?"

"Oh. All right. I'm sorry, Your Honor."

"Please continue."

"In the parking lot of this warehouse store were dozens of seagulls. More so than in any other shopping center."

"And why was that?"

"Because there was also a Burger King in this center, and people, I am sorry to say, would sometimes throw food onto the ground from out of their car. Partially eaten hamburgers. A half box of French fries. You know, that kind of stuff."

"And the seagulls would eat it."

"Yes, ma'am."

"Go on."

"Whenever Tory knew ahead of time that we were going to this warehouse store, she would start collecting whatever food she could for the seagulls. She always took my stale bread—although to be honest, a lot of it wasn't all that stale, but I let her take it anyway. And some of her classmates would give her crackers or cookies from their lunches that they didn't want."

"She saved up food for the seagulls?"

"Yes, ma'am. She kept it in a plastic storage bag on a shelf in her closet."

"Tell us what happened when you two arrived at the shopping center."

"As soon as she stepped out of our car and started walking into the middle of the lot, the birds started gathering at her feet. I'm not saying that they knew her or anything like that, but they did seem to know that people who got out of their car and did not head straight for the store usually had something for them."

"Go on."

"Well, by the time she reached a wide empty spot where there were no cars, and she stopped walking, there must have been fifty birds around her. Just standing there staring up at her."

"Did she then feed them?"

"Oh, yes. She would open her bag and start tossing small pieces of bread onto the ground. The birds would swarm around the food, and they would pick up the pieces and eat them, and then they would turn back toward Tory and stare at her."

"Where were you when this was going on, Viviana?"

"I was standing by the car waiting for her."

"I see. Continue, please."

"After a few minutes of throwing food to them on the ground, she would then start tossing pieces into the air. And the birds would catch the pieces in their mouths! Or is it beaks? It was the most extraordinary thing to watch, Miss Payne! After a few seconds of this, at least twenty or thirty birds were hovering in the air around her. She was standing in the middle of a flock of birds all fluttering in the air! I almost couldn't see her! And she would gently toss a piece to each bird, and the bird would catch it, swallow it, and then continue to flap their wings and hover around her. She would aim the piece at one bird at a time, and the one she threw it to always caught it."

"That must have been an amazing sight to see."

"Oh, it was. It was."

"Viviana, did your ex-husband abuse your daughter? It's all right. You can answer."

"Yes."

"Physically?"

"Yes."

"Sexually?"

"Yes."

"Thank you, dear. No further questions, Your Honor."

"Thank you, Mrs. Troy. You may step down."

47

Tory Troy
Defense Attorney Carolyn Payne

"Hi, Carolyn."

"Hi, Tory. How are you today?"

"Weird."

"Weird? What does that mean?"

"Lately, I've been feeling like I'm floating."

"Floating?"

"Yes. I've been feeling like this almost all the time. I'm not up near the ceiling or anything like that. I'm not *levitating*, or anything like that. I'm just an inch or two off the ground and I feel like I'm bobbing around like a cork in water."

"A cork in water."

"Actually, that's a pretty good way of describing it. I feel like I'm underwater. Even when I'm walking, and I know consciously and empirically that my feet are moving and that I am placing one foot in front of the other, I *still* feel like I'm just floating along through the air."

"Have you told somebody about this? Do you want me to talk to your doctor?"

"No . . . after everything that has happened, nothing seems real to me anymore. I'm immersed in some weird, dreamlike existence where the scene in front of my eyes takes a few seconds to 'catch up' if I turn my head. I once knew a guy—Pete the jeweler—who had Ménière's disease and that was how he described what it made him feel like. In my case, if I'm looking, say, at my bed in my room here in this illustrious institution, and then I turn my head to the right to look at the wall, I still see the bed for a few seconds until it slowly slides to the left and then I see the wall. It's quite the weird experience . . . but not totally unpleasant."

"Tory, you should at least mention this to one of the psych nurses."

"And I keep getting these headaches. They're centered between my eyes, and then they radiate up my forehead and over my scalp. I've completely lost my libido, and much of my appetite too. I feel numb, like I'm made of ice."

"I'm getting alarmed."

"The most unsettling part of this feeling, Carolyn— this overwhelming sense of dreaming while I'm awake— is that I can see and hear the six people I killed."

"Oh, my God."

"I don't mean that they're right in front of me—it's not like they're sitting across from me and I can see and hear them like they were just some ordinary person. It's more like they're on the periphery of my reality. I catch glimpses of them. I hear their disembodied voices. Sometimes I find myself having imaginary conversations with them. Marcy or Teresa will say something that I would have normally responded to if we were all at work together. Now their voices sound all echoey and distant, but I still respond to them. I'm pretty sure they can hear me too."

"Tory, I'm not sure you should be talking to me about this kind of stuff."

"Why not? You're my lawyer."

"Yes, but I don't know how to respond to you when you tell me things like that."

"They didn't cover The Delusional Client in law school?"

"Uh, no, they didn't."

"That's all right, Carolyn. Believe me. You don't have to respond. I'm just grateful that you'll listen to me."

"Okay. If that'll help, go on, then."

"It will, because lately I've also become more frightened. Of what, I'm not really sure."

"Death?"

"Maybe. My fear has actually become *real*, Carolyn. I see it as a black cloak that is wrapped around my body. This cloak has a hood too. No one else can see it but me. Sometimes the cloak is light and kind of floats around me. Other times it's so heavy, I can feel my back slumping. My body still floats, though. The weight of my fear never brings me down to earth. Very weird."

"From what little I remember of my college psych classes, that sounds Jungian."

"Yeah, I guess it does. And?"

"And that's another reason why I think you should be talking to your doctors about this."

"The other night I had the oddest experience. Out of the blue, a question popped into my mind: What if snow were black?"

"How morbid."

"I know! This staggered me. There are certain things we simply take for granted in this world, and white snow is one of them. Along with green grass and blue skies and, to be even *more* morbid, red blood. And as soon as the thought of black snow occurred to me, the imagery manifested itself in my mind, and it was not at all pleasant, Carolyn. I could see black snow falling, and black snow covering everything. I could see people shoveling black snow, and there was no color anywhere."

"What a horrible image, Tory."

"Snow has always been white, Carolyn. White."

"Yes, it has, Tory. And I really think we should wrap it up for today."

"You know, it also occurred to me that I didn't have to stop at black. What if snow were blue? Or green? Or, heaven forbid, red? Can you imagine red snow? The whole world would look like it was on fire."

"I'll see you tomorrow, okay?"

"Red snow, Carolyn. Red snow."

48

Tory Troy
Psychiatric Nurse Chiarra Ziegler

"Hi, Tory."

"Hey, Chiarra."

"How are you feeling?"

"Couldn't be better."

"Really?"

"No."

"Can I get you anything?"

"No, thanks. What's that?"

"What?"

"That pendant. Is it new?"

"Noah gave it to me."

"It's nice."

"Thanks."

"How long have you and Noah been together?"

"Five years."

"Are you engaged?"

"A year."

"When's the wedding?"

"We haven't set a date yet."

"Well, if I'm not around, I hope you'll forgive me for not sending a gift."

"Tory—"

"It's okay, Chiarra. Maybe I'll ask Viviana to send you something."

"Tory, please—"

"Do you like Steely Dan?"

"Yes. Noah too. We have most of their stuff. Why?"

"You know the song 'My Old School'?"

"Sure. What about it?"

"The first line of that song has been running through my mind lately."

"*I remember . . . the thirty-five sweet good-byes . . . ?*"

"Exactly."

"I don't know what to say to that, Tory. I understand what you're saying, but I don't really know if anything I could say would be of any help to you."

"Chiarra, you are a friend, and you *have* been of great help to me, even if you don't think so. I consider you family."

"Oh, my. Well, that is very gratifying to hear. And I want you to know something, Tory. If there's anything I can do for you as this thing progresses—anything— please don't hesitate to ask. Okay?"

"Okay."

"Promise?"

"I promise. You're all right, Chiarra. Everybody else

in this place avoids me like the plague, but you didn't flinch when you were assigned to me. I want you to know how much I appreciate that."

"I've got rounds, which I had better get to before I start crying."

"Baby."

"Don't you know it."

"Okay. I'll see ya, Chiarra."

"Bye, Tory."

49

Court Transcript:

Tory Troy

Defense Counsel Carolyn Payne

District Attorney Brawley Loren

Judge Gerard Becker

Court Personnel

The Visitors' Gallery

The Jury

"Good morning, Ms. Troy."

"Hello, Mr. Lawrence."

"It's Loren."

"Pardon me?"

"My name is *Loren*, not *Lawrence*."

"Of course. My apologies."

"I would now like to ask you some questions about the day of the murders, please."

"Fine."

You look nice, Tory. I always liked when you wore your hair like that.

Jake, leave me alone.

"What time did you arrive at work the morning of the murders?"

"Around eight."

"And can you describe your day up until the time of the murders, please?"

"It was routine."

"What does that mean?"

"It means it was routine. We processed a few animals that had come in late the previous day. We checked them over, fed them, and put them in cages."

"Go on."

"That was the morning, and then we had lunch."

We had cashews that day. Remember, Tory? Instead of a small bag just for myself, I brought in a giant can of Imperial Whole Salted Cashews. They were on sale at Wal-Mart. Two for seven dollars. Remember?

Yes, Marcy, I remember.

You said they were really good and that you liked them better than Planters. Remember, Tory?

Yes, Marcy, I remember.

"Did you have lunch that day at the animal shelter, Ms. Troy?"

"Yes."

"With whom did you eat that day?"

"Ann, Marcy, and Teresa."

"What about Jake, Philip, and Renaldo?"

"Jake always ate alone in his office. Philip had to go to the motor-vehicle department on his lunch to renew his license. Renaldo always skipped lunch. Probably to save money."

Seneca hates you, you know.

Yes, Teresa, I know she hates me.

Can you blame her?

319

No, not really.

"Just out of curiosity, do you remember what you had for lunch that day, Ms. Troy?"

"Cashews."

"Excuse me?"

"I had a handful of cashews. Marcy brought in a big can."

"I see. Nothing else?"

"A diet ginger ale. Do you want to know the brand?"

"Your Honor?"

"Ms. Troy, please."

"Sorry, Judge."

That was snippy, Tory. And rude.

Yes, Ann, I know. I'm sorry.

I always taught my kids to be polite and courteous. I'm glad they weren't here to hear you be sarcastic to that nice man.

Give it a rest, Ann. I said I was sorry.

"No, I do not need to know the brand, Ms. Troy. And it was Schweppes, by the way. The can was part of the evidence taken from the crime scene."

"How efficient."

"What happened after lunch, Ms. Troy?"

"We all went back to work."

"Could you describe for the court your specific duties that afternoon, please?"

"I did some paperwork until around two."

"What happened at two?"

"A family came in looking for a dog."

"A family?"

"Yes. Mother, father, two kids. The kids were a boy and a girl. The boy was around seven. The girl was, I think, twelve."

"Go on."

"Marcy called me when they told her they were looking to adopt an animal."

"Adopt?"

"Yes, that's what we call it when someone takes an animal into their home."

"Doesn't adopt usually refer to a child?"

"Not in animal shelters."

"So you talk about people adopting animals, is that correct?"

"Yes. Do you have a problem with that?"

"No. Of course not. And please allow *me* to ask the questions, Ms. Troy?"

"Right."

"So a family came in looking to adopt an animal."

"Yes."

"Please continue."

"So I introduced myself and then sat with them for a few minutes and explained how it worked. That they would have to make a donation to the shelter, and that they would have to agree to get the animal vaccinated and neutered."

"Is that standard procedure?"

"Yes."

"Go on."

"I also explained to them that any of the dogs I would be showing them for possible adoption had been temperament-tested and that we felt confident they would do very well in a family environment."

"Temperament-tested?"

"Yes."

"And what is that, please?"

"We test the dogs for three things. First, their reaction to having their teeth looked at; second, how they act when a rawhide toy is taken away from them; and, third, what they do when their eating is interrupted."

"Why those three things, Ms. Troy?"

"Because they are the three most common experiences a dog will have to go through as a pet. The teeth thing is to see how he or she will react to a veterinarian examination. The rawhide is to simulate what might happen during play. And the food test is to see what he'll do if a child tries to pull him away from his food or play with him while he's eating."

"I see. Are these tests common in all animal shelters?"

"I can't speak for all animal shelters, but I know they are routinely carried out at many shelters."

"At no-kill shelters too?"

"I suppose."

"Thank you. Please continue telling us about the family that wanted to adopt a dog."

My kids have a dog in Manacor, Tory. A little yellow beagle. Her name is Evita.

Yes, I know, Renaldo. You told me they probably would not have been able to bring her with them if they came here. I remember.

*Now they all alone, Tory. They no have a daddy any-
more.*

Yes, I know, Renaldo. I'm sorry.

"So after they agreed to everything and said they understood what I had explained to them, I took them in the
back where we keep the animals."

"How many animals were in the shelter this day, Ms.
Troy?"

"I don't remember."

"Go on."

"As is usually the case, the kids went nuts as soon as
they walked into the kennel area. They started running
from cage to cage, talking to the animals, calling each
other to come and look at different animals. This was
typical. And of course, the dogs were all barking and
standing up on their hind legs. It really was quite a sight.
And quite a racket. A lot of the newer dogs even stopped
owner-searching when the kids were there."

"Owner-searching?"

"A lot of newer dogs surrendered to a shelter go
through a period of owner-searching, when they do
nothing but, well, search for their owners. It takes time
for them to acclimate to the shelter. It's very sad to see."

"I see. And what were the parents doing during all this
commotion?"

"They just stood there. They both had huge smiles on
their faces."

"Why was that?"

"Because they were happy that their kids were so excited about getting a companion animal."

"Is *companion animal* the preferred term over *pet* these days, Ms. Troy?"

"Yes, it is."

"Did this family pick out a pe—sorry—companion animal?"

"Yes."

They took the miniature collie, right? I liked that dog from the moment we took him in.

Yes, Phil, they took the collie. He was a beautiful animal.

He was scheduled to be euthanized that afternoon, wasn't he?

Yes, his week was up.

Lucky for him, then, right?

Yes, lucky for him.

"Which animal did they select, Ms. Troy?"

"A miniature collie."

I'm praying for you, Tory.

Give it a rest, Phil.

I'm serious. You are in my prayers.

You are such a goddamned hypocrite.

Hey! No blaspheming, please. And what is that supposed to mean anyway?

Do you think I forgot the Home Depot incident? Did you thank God when you pocketed the money the girl gave you by mistake, Philip? Did you?

"What happened then, Ms. Troy?"

"I filled out the paperwork, gave them a receipt and an instruction sheet, and walked them out to their car."

"I see. What did you do next, Ms. Troy?"

"I did the workup sheet for that day's euthanasia agenda."

"How many animals were scheduled for that day, Ms. Troy?"

"I don't remember."

"Perhaps this will help refresh your memory?"

"Where did you get that? That's the workup sheet."

"How we acquired it is not relevant, Ms. Troy. Could you just look it over and tell us what it says, please?"

"If you already knew how many were euthanized that day, why did you ask me?"

"Judge?"

"Ms. Troy, simply answer Mr. Loren's questions, please. This is not a debate."

"Could you look it over, please, Ms. Troy?"

"I'm looking it over. So?"

"Could you tell the court how many animals were scheduled for euthanasia that afternoon?"

"Nine."

"Four dogs and five cats. Is that correct?"

"Yes."

"Could you please tell the court how you euthanize animals, Ms. Troy."

"No."

"Excuse me?"

"I am not going to describe the procedure. I just won't do it."

"Judge?"

"Ms. Troy?"

"I'm sorry, Judge. I just can't do it."

"Your Honor?"

"Yes, Ms. Payne?"

"Sidebar?"

"Make it quick."

"Your Honor, my client is on trial for six felony murders, not for euthanizing animals. Is it really necessary to subject the jury to a graphic description of how animals are killed at animal shelters? She will have to describe how she killed her coworkers. Isn't that enough? I have a feeling my honorable colleague is grandstanding, Your Honor."

"Carolyn, I resent that!"

"Oh, come on, Brawley. You know you're going for shock value. So get over it, will you?"

"Counselors! Address your comments to me and only me, please? Ms. Payne, did Ms. Troy describe the animal euthanasia process in her competency interviews with Dr. Bexley?"

"In detail, Judge."

"Mr. Loren, would you accept entering into evidence the transcript of the particular session in which the defendant described the process to Dr. Bexley?"

"The jury will have access to this material, Judge?"

"Of course."

"Then I agree. I simply want the details of what she does—sorry—what she *did* for a living to be part of the trial record."

"Ms. Payne?"

"Agreed."

"Step back. Ladies and gentlemen of the jury, at this

point the Prosecution is entering into evidence the transcript of a competency interview with the defendant conducted by Dr. Baraku Bexley in which Ms. Troy describes the animal euthanasia process. This material will be available to you for review in the jury room during your deliberations. Proceed, Mr. Loren."

What do you think that was about, Tory?

I don't know, Marcy. Why don't you ask them?

Ha-ha, very funny.

"Did you euthanize the animals that afternoon, Ms. Troy?"

"No."

"Why not?"

"The gas chamber was occupied."

"It was filled with the bodies of your six victims, isn't that correct, Ms. Troy?"

"Yes."

"Please tell the court how you killed your coworkers that afternoon, Ms. Troy."

"Do I have to?"

"I'm afraid so, Ms. Troy. Begin by telling us how, and in what order, you subdued them."

"I poked them all in the back of the neck with a syringe of Pavulon. Pancuronium bromide."

"What does Pavulon do, Ms. Troy?"

"It's a paralyzing drug."

"It is used in lethal-injection executions, is it not?"

"Yes."

You poked me hard, Tory. It felt like the worst bee sting I ever had.

Yes, I know, Teresa.

"Can you tell us a little about this drug, please?"

"What would you like to know?"

"Whatever you can share with us, please."

"Well, Pavulon is used in surgeries to paralyze the lungs and diaphragm and stop breathing."

"In what doses?"

"Between twenty and fifty micrograms per pound of body weight."

"And what is a microgram?"

"A millionth of a gram."

"So, a hundred twenty-five-pound person—say, someone like Marcy or Teresa—if I'm doing my math correctly, would have received around five or six milligrams of the drug before surgery. Is that correct?"

"Very good, Mr. Loren! You must have been excellent in math in school."

"Thank you, Ms. Troy, but can we stick to the line of questioning, please? Am I correct?"

"Yes."

"Do you know how many milligrams are used for lethal injections?"

"Yes."

"And that is?"

"One hundred milligrams."

"I see. And could you tell the court how many milligrams you used for each of your victims?"

"I don't remember."

"It was close to ten milligrams, Ms. Troy."

"Is that a question?"

"And how long does Pavulon take to work, Ms. Troy?"

"Up to three minutes."

"That's with the conventional use of the drug. But isn't it true that it can also take effect almost immediately?"

"Yes."

"Isn't it true that if a drug is injected directly into a vein or artery, the effect is almost immediate?"

"Yes."

"The autopsy reports state that your six victims were each injected into the posterior internal jugular vein, which resulted in the drug rushing into the pulmonary veins and immediately circulating throughout the bloodstream. Is that correct?"

"Yes."

"Was this intentional?"

"Yes."

"Ms. Troy, before you began working at the animal shelter, you were a sales representative for a pharmaceutical company. Is that correct?"

"Yes."

"Why did you leave that position?"

"I didn't leave it. I was laid off."

"Why?"

"They didn't need me anymore. The company set up a Web site for ordering drugs, and doctors and hospitals started taking care of their pharmaceutical needs on their own."

"I see. I'd like to ask you a direct question now, Ms. Troy."

"These haven't been direct?"

"Did you steal several syringes of Pavulon from the drug company before you were laid off?"

"I won't answer that."

"Very well. I think that answer tells us enough. Getting back to the afternoon of the crimes, do you recall in what order you injected your coworkers?"

"Yes."

"Could you tell us, please?"

"Jake, Teresa, Marcy, Renaldo, Ann, and Phil."

"So after they were all incapacitated by the Pavulon, what did you do next?"

"I dragged them into the gas chamber."

"And then?"

"I closed and sealed the door."

"And then?"

"I turned on the gas."

"And then?"

"I stood there."

"You just stood there as the lethal gas was being pumped into the chamber into which you had just dragged your six coworkers?"

"Yes."

"How long did you just 'stand there,' Ms. Troy?"

"I don't know."

"Was it longer than fifteen minutes?"

"Probably."

"What did you do next?"

"I vented the chamber."

"And then?"

"I opened the door."

"And what did you see, Ms. Troy?"

"They were all dead."

"Your six coworkers—Jake, Teresa, Marcy, Renaldo, Ann, and Phil—were all dead. Correct?"

"Yes."

"Could you describe what you saw, please?"

"What do you mean?"

"Could you tell the court how they were situated?"

Yeah, Tory, tell them how we were situated. Tell them what you saw. Tell them how I had my arms around Ann. And tell them how Teresa was curled up in a fetal position by herself in the corner. And tell them how Renaldo was sitting with his back against the rear wall with his eyes wide open. And tell them how Philip and Marcy were in each other's arms with their faces pressed together. Tell them all about that, Tory. Go ahead, I dare you.

Fuck you, Jake.

"Ms. Troy?"

"Yes?"

"Could you please answer the question?"

"About how they were situated?"

"Yes."

"I don't remember."

"Oh, come now, Ms. Troy. I'm sure you can recall what you saw."

"Objection. The witness said she did not remember, Your Honor."

"Move on, Mr. Loren."

"No, it's okay, Judge. I guess I do remember. I'll tell him what he wants to know."

"Very well. Proceed."

But that's not what you saw, is it, Tory?

Shut up, Jake.

"Could you tell us how they were situated, Ms. Troy?"

"They were all crowded together on the floor."

"Yes, they were, weren't they? They were all crowded together—lying next to and on top of each other—just the way you dragged them into the chamber, weren't they, Ms. Troy?"

"Yes."

"And what did you do then?"

"I just stood there looking at them. Then Tommy showed up."

"Thank you. No further questions, Your Honor. The Prosecution rests."

"Ms. Payne? Questions?"

"Yes, Your Honor."

"Proceed."

"Tory, do you believe in the euthanasia of animals?"

"I accept it."

"Why?"

"Because there are worse things than death for many of these animals."

"Such as?"

"Starving, suffering, and being alone and unloved."

332

"Could you tell us how many shelter animals are adopted?"

"Seven out of ten are euthanized."

"Why did you kill your coworkers, Tory?"

"I don't know."

"You possess great love for animals, don't you, Tory?"

"Yes, I do. Although I'm not sure that *love* is the right word."

"And why is that? What word would *you* use to describe your feelings for animals?"

"Respect."

"Respect?"

"Yes."

"What happened inside you that Friday, Tory?"

"Friday is euthanasia day. It always rains on Friday."

"It doesn't always rain on Fridays, Tory."

"Yes, it does. It was raining that Friday. I remember. The animals cry when I close the door. And it was raining."

"Tory, are you all right?"

"The animals cry when I close the door."

"No further questions. The Defense rests."

"You may step down, Ms. Troy."

Well, you're all done, Tory. In more ways than one.

You're right, Jake. I really think you're right about that.

"Mr. Loren? Closing argument?"

"Yes, sir. I'm ready."

"Go ahead, then."

"Thank you, Your Honor. Ladies and gentlemen. I

have a law degree. I read books. And I like to think I can conversationally hold my own in the arena of ideas and intelligent discourse. I also have great respect for the truth. And I believe that facts are facts and that facts often, if not always, reveal the truth. Victoria Abigail Troy is guilty of six counts of premeditated murder. Now, you may be asking yourself, how does he know with such certainty that the murders were premeditated? Simple. The Pavulon syringes. Victoria Abigail Troy deliberately carried six syringes of pancuronium bromide with her to work that rainy Friday. What does premeditation tell us, ladies and gentlemen? It tells us that her plea of not guilty by reason of insanity is laughable at best, and a legal and moral travesty at its worst. Did Victoria Abigail Troy kill her six coworkers? Jake, Ann, Marcy, Philip, Renaldo, and Teresa? Yes. Did Victoria Abigail Troy think about committing these murders beforehand? Yes. Was Victoria Abigail Troy insane at the time she committed these horrible crimes? Unequivocally no. So where are we now, ladies and gentlemen? You've heard the witnesses. You are aware of the evidence. You know of her crimes. All you need to do now is retire to the jury room, agree on a guilty verdict, and also agree to recommend the death penalty for the defendant. The facts are plain. And the facts reveal the truth. Thank you."

"Thank you, Mr. Loren. Ms. Payne?"

"Yes, Your Honor, thank you. Ladies and gentlemen, in 1979, the Irish rock group the Boomtown Rats had an enormous, worldwide hit with their song, 'I Don't Like Mondays.' You may know this song. They play it on FM rock stations all the time. Now, why am I talking to you about a twenty-three-year-old rock song? Because of the story behind the song. On January twenty-ninth, 1979, a sixteen-year-old San Diego, California, girl who lived across the street from an elementary school took the rifle her daddy had given her for Christmas, walked to a window, and opened fire on the schoolyard. She managed to kill the principal and the head custodian. She also wounded eight children and a police officer. When the police made contact with her and asked her why she was doing this terrible thing, she responded, 'I don't like Mondays.' Imagine. Something as simple as a dislike for Mondays caused this teenage girl to snap. If nothing but a Monday could trigger a murder rampage in a young girl, is it so far-fetched that the emotional trauma of Tory doing what she had to do as part of her job could trigger what she did? Was the young playground shooter temporarily insane at the time she committed these murders? We all certainly have our ideas about that, but the question is moot. The girl pled guilty and is currently in a federal penitentiary serving a twenty-five-years-to-life sentence. Tory Troy similarly snapped, ladies and gentlemen, but in her case, her abandonment of everything she knew about right and wrong was due to something far more vile than a Monday. She simply couldn't take the mass slaughter anymore . . . the massacring of scores of innocent animals . . . every Friday . . . for almost a year. Put yourself in her position, ladies and gentlemen. Would you be able to handle going to work and executing dogs and cats—some of whom were no more than

335

puppies and kittens? Would you be able to cope with such a horrible duty? Each of you must look inside yourself and answer those questions honestly. And if the answer is 'no,' or even 'I don't know,' then it is your profound duty to return with a verdict of not guilty by reason of insanity. Thank you."

"Ladies and gentlemen of the jury: testimony is now complete. You are now charged with determining a verdict and, if the verdict is guilty, making a sentencing recommendation. My bailiffs will provide you with a verdict checklist, which will delineate the specific issues you must decide upon during your deliberations. As you know, you will not be sequestered, and deliberations will conclude each day at five P.M. until a verdict is reached. Once the jury-room door is locked, however, you will not be able to leave. A guard will be posted outside the door and will tend to your needs, both pertaining to this trial and personally. She will be the one who will serve as your liaison with me. You will not be served food during the deliberations day. A variety of beverages will be available all day. You will break one hour for lunch. You may dine at any of the many restaurants in the area. You may dine only with a fellow juror, or alone. At this point, I ask you all to adjourn to the jury room. This court is in recess."

50

The Jury

"This room smells."

"No it doesn't."

"We're not supposed to use our names, right? Only our juror numbers, right?"

"Yes, that's right."

"Well, then, hello, all. I am Juror Number Nine. I'm an accountant."

"Interesting job."

"Excuse me? We haven't met."

"I said, 'Interesting job.'"

"Are you being sarcastic?"

"Who, me? Hell, no. Working with columns of numbers all day long must be fascinating work."

"And what is it you do for a living, if I may ask?"

"I spot-solder circuit boards at Raytheon."

"On an assembly line? Doing the same thing over and over all day long? Talk about calling the kettle black."

"Can we can the crap, please? We need to pick a foreperson. I am Juror Number Six. I'm a stockbroker."

"Can we play music in here? You know, like a radio or a CD? I'm Juror Number Twelve. I'm a pharmacist."

"No TVs or radios are allowed. It says so right in your 'Being a Juror' pamphlet. And I am Juror Number Three. I'm a stay-at-home mom."

"You actually read that thing?"

"Yes."

"You don't work?"

"I work at home."

"But you don't earn a paycheck?"

"No."

"Enough chitchat, please? Can we pick our foreperson? I'd like to get out of here before Christmas. I'm Number Eleven. I'm a reporter for the New Haven *Messenger*."

"Do you want the job? I'm Number Seven. I work on the assembly line at Pratt and Whitney."

"I'll take it if everyone agrees."

"I have no problem with him being foreperson. I'm Number Two. I'm a hospice nurse."

"Does anyone object to Juror Number Eleven being the foreperson? No? All right, then. Juror Number Eleven, you are our foreperson and fearless leader."

"Yeah, that's funny. I suppose the first thing we should do is assign seats at the table, right?"

"Every courtroom movie I've ever seen has the

foreperson at the head of the table, and then the jurors seated in numerical order starting on his left."

"Like in *Twelve Angry Men*, right?"

"Exactly."

"I liked the remake better than the original. Tony Soprano was in it. This was before *The Sopranos*, though."

"People? Please? Can we limit all—or at least most—of our conversations to matters related to the trial? Please? Okay, let's take our seats. I suppose the first thing we should do is take an initial vote to see where we stand."

"That makes sense. I'm Juror Number Five, by the way. I go to college. And I work at the Olive Garden."

"I love their bread sticks."

"Jurors . . . please?"

"Hello, it's nice to meet you. I'm Juror Number Ten. I'm a teacher. We should talk later."

"Okay, okay . . . enough chitchat, please? Can we take a preliminary vote now?"

"How do you want to do this?"

"Well, if we agree it should be a secret ballot, I can cut up a sheet of legal paper into twelve pieces. Each of you can then write *guilty* or *not guilty* on your ballot, and I'll collect them."

"That sounds all right."

"Unless you all want to do a public vote now instead of a secret one?"

"Frankly, I think—oh, I'm Juror Number One, by the way. I'm a thoracic surgeon—"

339

"Even a doctor couldn't get out of jury duty?"

"Frankly, I think we should vote by a show of hands. Since we're all in here until we come to a unanimous verdict, I think we should know right off the bat where everybody stands."

"That makes sense to me. I'm Juror Number Four. I stay at home and take care of my kids."

"Another one that doesn't work."

"That's enough. How do you all feel about a show of hands instead of a secret ballot? Do we all agree to do it that way?"

"Sure. Let's get it over with. Who knows? Maybe we'll think she's either guilty or not guilty right off the bat and we can get the fu—sorry—get the hell out of here. I'm Juror Number Eight, and I work as a landscaper."

"Okay, then. Let's do it. All who think the defendant should be found guilty, raise your hand. One, two, three, four, five, six, seven, eight, nine, ten, eleven. All who think the defendant should be found not guilty, raise your hand. One. The first vote is eleven guilty, one not guilty."

"Juror Number . . . what's your number?"

"Three."

"Juror Number Three. You voted not guilty? Are you crazy? She admitted doing it!"

"Yes, but the not-guilty verdict is by reason of insanity."

"So?"

"So I think she was insane when she did it."

"Bullshit."

"Language, please?"

"She was as sane as you or I, and she knew exactly what she was doing. That 'reason of insanity' thing is nothing but a lawyer trick to get her off."

"I don't agree."

"And we're off."

"Juror Number Three, what would it take to convince you that the defendant is guilty? What would convince you to change your vote?"

"I don't know."

"This is pathetic. And I don't want to be here."

"Oh, yeah? Doesn't it fill you with pride to know you're doing your civic duty?"

"My only civic duty is to earn a living so I can pay my taxes and not live off the state."

"Excuse me, gentlemen? The more off-topic conversations we have, the longer we will be locked in this room."

"Which smells."

"So, right now we are eleven to one in favor of guilty."

"What happens if she won't change her mind?"

"Technically, we'd be deadlocked. Hung. But there is no way the judge is going to accept that right off the bat."

"What do you mean?"

"I mean he'd send us back in here and tell us to try again. Judges hate hung juries. He'd have to declare a mistrial and she'd have to be tried all over again."

"I just don't think she was in her right mind when she did what she did."

"Crap."

"Hey! Aren't I entitled to my own opinion about this?"

"Of course you are. I'll ask you all to maintain civility, please. Maybe you can explain to us why you think she should be acquitted?"

"You know, I remember once reading in a novel about the 'irresistible impulse' test."

"What's that?"

"It means that a person should get a not-guilty verdict if her actions were the result of her being unable to defy an 'irresistible impulse.' There was an example in the book about a cop at a person's elbow."

"What does that mean?"

"It means that to qualify as an irresistible-impulse crime, you have to ask yourself if Troy would have done the exact same thing if a cop had been standing right next to her. I think she would have."

"Yes, but I think that a person should not be held responsible for his or her actions *only* if their insanity prevented them from making a moral decision."

"So?"

"*That's* why I'm voting guilty! Don't you see? She killed those people because she believed it *was* the moral thing to do!"

"But murder is immoral . . ."

"She knew exactly what she was doing! You're trying to say she was unable to distinguish between moral and immoral. I'm saying she committed an immoral act believing it was moral."

"But it *wasn't* moral. So doesn't that mean she couldn't tell the difference?"

"In her mind, she *decided* the difference. It was a conscious act. That's *not* crazy in my book."

"Juror Number Three, can I ask you a question?"

"Of course."

"Are you a Beatles fan?"

"Sort of."

"Do you think the guy who killed John Lennon should have been executed?"

"I don't know."

"Well, he wasn't. He's in Attica. And someday he may get out. Do you think that's right?"

"Actually, no, I don't."

"Can I ask one more question?"

"Go ahead."

"Did you know that the guy who tried to kill President Reagan is trying to get permission to leave the mental institution on unsupervised trips?"

"Yes, I knew that. But wouldn't the Secret Service watch him?"

"Yes, they would, but in the eyes of the legal system, he would be sane enough to go traipsing around Washington with his parents. And he was found not guilty by reason of insanity. Do you think that's right?"

"I . . ."

"Do you think that's right?"

"No."

"Stop berating her."

"I'm not berating her. I'm trying to make her understand why her thinking is wrong. Troy killed those people. Six families are now completely devastated. Some of her dead coworkers were young—a couple were barely out of their teens. And how about the family of that immigrant now left all alone in . . . whatever country he came from?"

"Spain, I think."

"He worked his ass off to save money to bring his family to America, and she executed him. There is no way I'm voting to send her to a mental institution for the rest of her life where she'll lie in bed high on tranquilizers and watch TV all day."

"That's no way to live."

"Hey, honey. Pick a hand. In this one is a bed, Valium, and cable. Not to mention three squares a day. In this one is a syringe filled with enough poison to wipe out the entire cast of *The Practice*. I know which one *I'd* pick. I think she's guilty, and I think she should die. Period. End of sentence."

"Do you all think she knew what she was doing?"

"Of course she knew what she was doing."

"But don't you have to be insane to do something like that?"

"You want to know something, honey? I'm not a shrink, and I don't think it's my job to make those kinds of decisions. I ask myself two questions. The first is, did the defendant kill six people? The answer is yes. She fucking admitted it! And before Mr. Foreman can charge me a quarter, I'll say I am sorry for the profanity. The second question I ask myself is, should she be punished for her crimes? Once again, I answer yes. See how easy it is?"

"But this is a person's life we're deciding on."

"Oh, spare us the melancholy, please? She executed six people. What if they were all members of your family?"

"Oh, don't say such a thing!"

"Why not? Hits home then, right? You're too caught up with legal technicalities, and I also think you're afraid to take responsibility for deciding someone should die. I'm not going to ask any of you women to respond to this, but I'll say one thing. If any of you have had an abortion, then you have nothing to say about not wanting to vote guilty, or not wanting to impose the death penalty."

"Since all the other women here have already voted guilty, you're addressing that to me, aren't you? You want to know if I've had an abortion? If I have had one, and I'm voting not guilty, then you can call me a hypocrite, right?"

"I was talking to everyone. The women, I mean."

"Yeah, right."

"Do you have children?"

"None of your business."

"Oh, come on. Don't be like that."

"Yes, I have children."

"How many?"

"Three."

"Boys? Girls?"

"I have two girls and a boy."

"Ages?"

"The girls are both sixteen. Twins. My son is twenty-two."

"The girls are in school?"

"Yes."

"And your son?"

"He has his own business."

"At his age?"

"He started it right out of high school."

"What does he do, if you don't mind my asking?"

"He has his own catering business."

"Oh, yeah? Can we give him a call? I'm getting kind of hungry."

"What kind of catering business?"

"Vegan."

"No animal foods of any kind?"

"None."

"Are you a vegetarian?"

"Yes, but I don't see what that has to do with anything."

"Okay."

"What does that mean?"

"I find it interesting that a vegetarian mother with a vegan son would like to give a pass to a murderer who killed in the defense of animals."

"That is not—"

"Let me ask you another question."

"Do you deliberately try to be obnoxious? Or does it just come naturally to you?"

"What if your son—what's his name?"

"Peter."

"What if Peter worked part-time at the Waterbridge Animal Shelter and just happened to be working one particular Friday afternoon?"

"I guess subtlety is not your strong suit either."

"Let's take it one step further. What if it were your twin sixteen-year-old daughters who volunteered at the Waterbridge Animal Shelter, and *they* were working one particular Friday afternoon?"

"Stop talking to me, please."

"Mr. Foreman?"

"Lighten up, Juror . . . whatever your number is."

"Well, what are we going to do now? Eleven to one and I can't talk to her about it?"

"Of course you can. Just don't get personal. And don't be confrontational. And don't be arrogant or rude."

"Forget it. I'm done. We can sit in this room 'til fucking doomsday as far as I'm concerned."

"And don't be vulgar."

"Aye-aye, Commandant."

"And don't be disrespectful."

"Fuck you."

"Hey!"

"Okay, okay, everybody calm down. Is there anything any of you would like to discuss before I call for a second vote?"

"Yeah, how about last week's episode of *Friends*?"

"Anybody?"

"Excuse me?"

"Yes?"

"Can I ask a question?"

"Of course."

"I was just wondering how many of us here have pets. I'm still voting guilty, but I was just curious."

"Hands? Anyone with pets? Wow. Ten. Why don't we go around the table?"

"Cat."

"Cats. Three."

"Dog."

"Dog."

"I have twin golden retrievers."

"Goldfish."

"Dog."

"Hamster."

"Ferret."

"Cats. A mother and five kittens. Anyone looking for a kitten?"

"I thought ferrets were illegal."

"They're not."

"I'm trying to find homes for all the kittens."

"Maybe you should talk to the defendant—she works at an animal shelter, right?"

"Ha-ha-ha. Very unfunny."

"I'm considering getting a kitten . . ."

"Great. We'll talk when this is over."

"Okay."

"Anyone else?"

"Mr. Foreman?"

"Yes, Juror Number Three?"

"I've changed my mind."

"Would you like to take another vote, Juror Number Three?"

"Yes."

"Okay. Once again. All who think the defendant should be found guilty, raise your hand. All right. All who think the defendant should be found not guilty, raise your hand. The verdict is unanimous. Guilty as charged."

"Well, that was a surprising turnabout."

"Don't talk to me, please."

"Do we have to come up with a sentencing recommendation now?"

"Yes."

"What are our choices?"

"Life in prison without parole. Death by lethal injection."

"I think we should vote on that too."

"That's fine with me. Does everyone agree to vote on a sentencing recommendation? Okay. Here we go. All those in favor of life in prison without parole, raise your hand. One."

"That figures."

"Hey. Cool it."

"Why should I? First she's against finding her guilty, and now she doesn't want to execute her. Well, at least she's consistent—in her own twisted way."

"I resent that."

"Too bad."

"Would you like to tell us all why you don't think she should be executed, Juror Number Three?"

"Isn't . . . isn't . . ."

"Isn't what? Speak up, willya?"

"Isn't life in prison without the chance of ever getting out enough?"

"Enough what?"

"Enough punishment?"

"I think you know how any of us would answer that question."

"Yes. I suppose I do."

"Well, then, you should also know that no one is going to change their mind—again—and that all you'll be doing is dragging out the time we have to spend in this room."

"Which smells."

"You might as well accept it. She killed six people, we've found her guilty, and eleven of us feel she should be executed."

"Fine. I give up. Do what you want."

"Okay. Let's take another vote. All those in favor of death by lethal injection, raise your hand. By unanimous vote, we the jury find the defendant guilty as charged, and we will make a sentencing recommendation to the judge of death by lethal injection. Ladies and gentlemen, our business here is concluded. Thank you for your service."

"I'll tell the bailiff."

51

Court Transcript:

Tory Troy

Defense Counsel Carolyn Payne

District Attorney Brawley Loren

Judge Gerard Becker

Court Personnel

The Visitors' Gallery

The Jury

"Ladies and gentlemen of the jury. Have you reached a verdict?"

"We have, Your Honor."

"Proceed."

"We, the jury, in the matter of Victoria Abigail Troy, find the defendant guilty in each of the six cases of felony murder with which she is charged."

"Attorney Payne, would you like the jury polled?"

"Not necessary, Judge."

"Mr. Loren?"

"No, Your Honor."

"The verdict is hereby accepted. Jury Foreperson, do you have a sentencing recommendation?"

"We do, Your Honor."

"And what is it?"

"Considering the gravity of the defendant's crimes, we have decided, after careful consideration and in unanimous agreement, to recommend to the court that she receive the death penalty."

"So noted. The court thanks you for your conscientiousness in arriving at a reasoned, thoughtful, and very prompt determination, and the court expresses its appreciation for your service. The jury is hereby discharged. Ms. Payne? Motion to appeal?"

"No, Your Honor. The defendant waives her right to an appeal."

"You are aware that all capital sentences are automatically appealed, Ms. Payne?"

"Yes, Your Honor, unless the defendant waives that right. And she does, Judge."

"Ms. Troy, do you waive your right to an appeal?"

"Yes, Your Honor."

"May I ask why?"

"You may ask, Your Honor, but I choose not to answer the question. All due respect, sir."

"Are you aware that you are sealing your death warrant, ma'am?"

"Yes, sir, I am."

"Very well. The defendant will be remanded to the security wing of the Woodward Knolls Psychiatric Institute until she is transferred to the prison facility where the sentence will be carried out. This court is adjourned."

52

Tory Troy
Viviana Troy

"You shouldn't have come to see me, Mom."

"I had to."

"You're going to get upset, which is going to make *me* upset."

"No, I'll be fine."

"Are you sure?"

"Yes."

"Actually, I was going to write you a letter about a few things. There are some details I want you to know for . . . after."

"Oh, my."

"See what I mean?"

"No. I'm sorry. I'm okay."

"We can go over it now . . . if you're up to it. . . ."

"Okay. What do I have to do? Should I write this down?"

"That's probably a good idea."

"All right."

"First, everything that's mine is yours. Everything. I'm not going to tell you how to pay my remaining bills, or what to do with my clothes. That's completely up to you."

"Oh, Tory."

"Please don't cry, Mom? This is hard enough for me."

"All right. I'm sorry."

"There's only one special thing I want you to do for me."

"Anything."

"Inside my jewelry box is a small cloisonné box. It's got a painting of a medieval lute player on it. Inside this box is the starter pearl necklace you began for me when I was born. We never finished it. It's got, I think, twelve pearls on it now, and they taper from a couple of large ones in the center to smaller ones at the end. It's on a gold chain and it's about sixteen inches long. What I'd like you to do is have one big pearl strung onto it right in the center, and then give it to Carolyn Payne, my attorney. You can give it to her as it is now, I suppose, but if you'll add the single pearl for me, it would mean a lot to me."

"All right. I will. This is so sad."

"Yes, I know, Mom, but it has to be done."

"I know . . . I know."

"There's only one more thing. My funeral."

"No."

"Mom—"

"No. I will not talk about your funeral."

"You don't have to. What I was going to say is that I don't want one."

"What do you mean?"

"I don't want a ceremony. Or calling hours. I want to be cremated, and I want you to scatter my ashes."

"I can't do that."

"Of course you can."

"No."

"Yes."

"Where do you want them . . . I can't believe I'm asking you this . . . where do you want the ashes . . . your ashes scattered, Tory?"

"You'll have to drive out here."

"To Old Saybrook?"

"Yes."

"That's all right. I'm used to the ride by now."

"You should take someone with you."

"I will."

"There's a tiny private beach at the end of . . . I think it's Donnelly Road. . . . You just take a right off Route One and drive until you hit the water."

"I'll find it."

"There's a long rock promontory jutting out into the water. You can walk out on this quite a ways into Long Island Sound. When it's high tide, the water comes up onto its sides, but the top is never covered."

"All right."

"Years ago . . . remember my friend Gail Ravine?"

"No."

"It doesn't matter. The two of us took a ride out there

one day and walked out onto this rock. Almost to the end. When we were out there, I picked up a rock about the size of my head and threw it into the water. I remember trying to throw it as high into the air as I could. And I still remember the loud *kerplunk* sound it made when it hit the water."

"When was this, Tory? You never told me about going to Old Saybrook."

"I was in high school. Senior year, I think. There are a lot of things I never told you about, Mom."

"Okay."

"Well, that rock is still there, in the water. And it will be there for ages. It'll probably never move from the spot where it landed. I think about that rock a lot."

"What about the ashes?"

"I want you to scatter them in the water near where I threw that rock."

"How will I know exactly where it is?"

"You don't have to know exactly where it is, Mom. All you have to do is walk out onto the promontory as far as you can go—be careful!—and then turn and face the direction where the sun will set. Then just scatter my ashes into the water."

"I don't know if I can do that, Tory."

"Sure you can . . . sure you can. And you don't have to do it right away. You can wait, say, a year if you want to. You'll know when the time is right."

"How will I know?"

"You'll just know, Mom. Trust me. And promise me you'll do it."

"All right. I promise."

"Thanks."

"Well, that's it. That's everything I wanted to tell you. Can you stay a little longer?"

"I can stay."

"Good. We'll have coffee."

"Yes. We'll have coffee."

"I love you, Mom."

"I know, Tory. I know. And I love you too. More than you will ever know."

"I . . ."

"You don't have to say anything. Let's just have coffee."

"Okay. Okay."

"It's all right, Tory."

"I know."

53

Tory Troy
Father David North

"How nice of you to come, Father!"

"Of course."

"How's everything at St. Fran's?"

"Everything's fine, Tory. The church needs a new roof, and the organ needs a reed job, but all in all, the parish is okay."

"That's good. Can I ask you a question?"

"Of course."

"What do you think, *Père?* Am I going to hell?"

"God sends souls to hell only as a last resort, Tory. You can be joined with Him if you only repent and make a sincere Act of Contrition."

"I've done that."

"Well, then, as soon as your life here is ended, you will be called home, and then spend all of eternity in God's love."

"Do you really believe that, Father?"

"With all my heart."

"Really? The whole 'salvation through crucifixion' thing?"

"Yes, Tory. The whole 'salvation through crucifixion' thing, as you so piously put it."

"I suppose I can be honest now and admit that Catholicism just never made any sense to me."

"What about it doesn't make sense to you?"

"Well, the whole notion that God would demand a horrible blood sacrifice—and from his son, no less—to atone for 'sins' committed by creatures he created."

"That's a bit simplistic, Tory. There's more to the dogma of redemption than that."

"Maybe I wasn't paying close enough attention in grammar school, then, but I still have to say it just doesn't make sense to me."

"It's one of the basic tenets of Catholicism, Tory. That, the Virgin Birth, and the Resurrection."

"Yes, I know. But—and don't get mad at me—I think Jesus was one of *many* christs who have come to earth."

"One of many? Oh, no, my dear. He was the only one, and He is the only way to salvation."

"An awful lot of Hindus and Buddhists would argue with you on that point, *Padre*."

"I know. But that doesn't change ultimate truth."

"How can you be so sure it is, in fact, *ultimate truth*, Father?"

"Faith."

"Sorry, but that's a whole lot to accept solely on faith, Father."

"My dear, dear Tory. Isn't that the whole point?"

359

54

Corrections Officer Miranda Wiater
Corrections Officer Jesus Moralés

"Testing line three."

"Line three."

"Flushing saline."

"Saline flow confirmed."

"Voiding line three."

"Line three voiding confirmed. Three lines tested and confirmed."

"Ready for the chamber tests?"

"Let's check inventory first."

"Okay."

"Sodium thiopental?"

"Fifty thousand milligrams in stock. Not expired."

"Pancuronium bromide?"

"One thousand milligrams in stock. Not expired."

"Potassium chloride?"

"One hundred grams. Not expired."

"Okay. We're all set in here. Let's go check the chamber, and then we're done. I'll file the readiness report this afternoon, and then the only thing left on the agenda is her six P.M. execution."

"I hate it when they're this young."

"I know."

"Have you seen her?"

"Yeah. She sort of looks like Bridget Fonda. Or maybe Jennifer Aniston. A combination of Bridget Fonda and Jennifer Aniston. I saw her mother too. She looks like Stockard Channing. And her lawyer looks like Téa Leoni."

"You like to describe everybody by what actor or actress they look like, don't you?"

"You've got to admit it works, doesn't it?"

"I suppose. How would you describe me?"

"Seriously?"

"Yes."

"A short Julia Roberts."

"Really?"

"Yes."

"She's pretty."

"I know."

"Well, thanks for that, Jesus. Are you on tonight?"

"Escort. You driving?"

"Yeah. I'll be the one who turns the key."

"Part of the job, right?"

"Part of the job. Okay. Here we go. General condition of gurney?"

"Good."

"Cleanliness of gurney?"

"Clean."

"Condition of sheets?"

"Clean."

"Arm restraints?"

"In good condition. In working order."

"Leg restraints?"

"Ditto."

"Torso straps?"

"Same."

"IV couplers?"

"Tight and clean."

"Line ports?"

"Secure."

"Floor?"

"Clean. Linoleum worn in several spots."

"Windows?"

"Clean."

"Vertical blinds?"

"Clean and functioning."

"Microphone?"

"In position and functional."

"Clock?"

"Working and on time."

"Telephone?"

"Working."

"That's it, then."

"How about the post details?"

"Jerry's on them. He already confirmed the disposition funeral parlor."

"Okay. Anything else you need me for? I'm off in ten minutes."

"No, we're done. Thanks, Jesus."

"Call me if you need me."

55

Tory Troy
Dr. Baraku Bexley

"I admit I was surprised to hear from you, Tory."

"Really? Why's that?"

" I wasn't sure how you felt about my declaring you fit to stand trial—or testifying for the prosecution, for that matter . . . albeit reluctantly."

"Oh, I was fine with that. Let's face it. We both knew that my standing trial was a foregone conclusion."

"Perhaps. But why did you want to see me now?"

"My days are numbered, Doc. You don't have to respond to that. They are. I've accepted it. So I thought I'd have a last chat with you as an acquaintance rather than a patient."

"I'm flattered."

"Really? Thank you. But did you notice that I used the word *acquaintance* instead of friend?"

"Yes, I noticed. So?"

"That's because I did not want to be presumptuous about our relationship. I'll tell you this, though. If I had used the word *friend* and it didn't offend you, then I would be very pleased and grateful."

"I have very warm feelings for you, Tory. Always have."

"Do you? I've always wondered what you really thought of me, Dr. Bexley. I knew you thought I was sane enough to stand trial. But I've also wondered what you thought of me personally. Do you like me? Did you mind spending all that time with me? Do you think I'm a despicable person for what I did? Do you ever think of me? I think of you often."

"Do you want answers to those questions, Tory?"

"Absolutely not."

"Ignorance is bliss?"

"I suppose."

"Then why *did* you ask to see me?"

"Just to talk, I guess."

"About what?"

"I . . ."

"Animals, perhaps?"

"Always the shrink, right, Doc?"

"Comes with the diploma."

"I talked about animals on the stand."

"I know. I was there. Anything else on your mind?"

"I don't know. Yeah, I guess. I suppose we can talk about it."

"What's that?"

"It recently occurred to me that it's quite possible that the real purpose of animals is to humanize people."

"How so?"

"They bring down barriers."

"Yes, that's true."

"Did you ever see how people act when they run into somebody—like in the park—with a dog?"

"Yes."

"They start chatting with the person like they've known them for years."

"Yes, I've seen that happen. Actually, I've done it myself."

"So have I. This happens sometimes with babies too, but people are more reserved when they talk to strangers about their babies. They're careful as to how personal they get. How 'loose' they get."

"You're right."

"But with animals, people crouch down, they talk to them, they put their faces right up to the animal's face . . . they let down all barriers, it seems."

"And what do you think this means?"

"What does it mean?"

"Yes, in the scheme of things. This insight must have struck some kind of chord in you for you to not only remember it but to bring it up."

"Not to mention asking to see you."

"Not to mention asking to see me."

"I don't really know, Doc. But it just seems . . . unseemly to me that we take for granted that we *own* animals."

"You know what Scripture says about this, don't you?"

"Enlighten me."

"Genesis. *And God said, Let us make man in our image . . . and let them have dominion over the fish of the sea, and over the fowl of the air, and over the cattle. . . . Dominion.* That's a pretty strong word."

"I'm impressed."

"Don't be. It's one of the few passages I've somehow managed to remember over the years."

"But don't you find that passage . . . arrogant?"

"I don't want to discuss Scriptural apologetics, Tory. I want to know why you felt so strongly about this that you asked to see me."

"It's not why I asked to see you."

"All right. Go on."

"You're part Jewish, aren't you, Doc?"

"Yes."

"Your grandfather died at Auschwitz, right?"

"Yes."

"I know your father was Tanzanian, so that means that your mother's family had to have been Jewish, right?"

"Yes."

"So you must have some Jewish friends, right?"

"Yes, I do have some Jewish friends. And some Jewish extended-family members. Why do you ask? Why the sudden interest in my genealogy?"

"Do you know what the Kaddish is?"

"Of course. The Jewish Mourner's Prayer for the

Dead. It's recited over the body of the deceased at the interment."

"I want one."

"You're not Jewish."

"And better yet, I don't even want a funeral."

"Then what are you talking about?"

"I've left instructions for my mother for . . . after I'm gone."

"And?"

"And I asked her to scatter my ashes in the ocean."

"I see."

"And if at all possible, I'd like her to recite the Kaddish before she scatters them."

"Ahhh . . ."

"And that's why I'm asking for your help, Doc. Can you provide my mother with a Kaddish?"

"Do you believe in God, Tory?"

"As an entity? . . . You know, like a person?"

"However *you* conceive of the concept."

"Did you know that Galileo—I think it was Galileo . . . it might have been da Vinci—was an atheist until he began to study the human eye?"

"I didn't know that."

"And then—reasonably, in my opinion—he asked the question: How could this have evolved from nothing? He saw that there was intelligence to the design of the eye. It was so meticulously structured and obviously 'thought out.'"

"Yes. I agree."

"And it happened by chance? As did the rest of the human body and all of nature, for that matter? By chance? It makes no sense whatsoever to me that we live—there's the operative word, by the way: *live*—in a mindless, chaotic universe."

"Many do *not* believe that, Tory. Many people see the structure and order as a sign of God's handiwork."

"Can you blame them? I mean, there is just too much . . . *sense* . . . to everything . . . I . . . Am I making any sense at all?"

"Yes. You are. I always think about what Albert Einstein, who no one would deny was a scientist, said about creation."

"What was that?"

"He looked out at the stars and asked, 'How could such a magnificent symphony not have a conductor?' Or something like that. I take it one step further, though, Tory, and ask the question, 'How could such a magnificent symphony not have a *composer*?' "

"I like that."

"So you'd like a Kaddish recited at your . . . disposition."

"Yes."

"The Kaddish is usually recited in Aramaic. And it is usually recited for eleven months and a day after the death of a loved one."

"Really? Aramaic might pose a bit of a problem for Viviana Troy. There are none in English?"

"Oh, yes, there are many translations of the prayer."

"And the eleven-month thing is probably not going to happen either."

"Well, I'm sure a single recitation will serve what you want just as well."

"I think so too. Can you help me, Doc?"

"Of course. I will find a Kaddish—in English—for your mother to recite."

"Thanks. I really appreciate it."

"It's all right. Is there anything else you'd like to talk about before I go? I'm at your disposal."

"No, that's pretty much it. . . . I guess this is good-bye, Dr. Bexley, right?"

"Who really knows, Tory? It would seem to be, but sometimes things don't always happen the way we expect them to."

"I think death is a door, Doc. I truly do."

"Perhaps. And perhaps that door will yet remain closed to you, or perhaps it will open wide. We never really can know for sure what the next moment will bring, Tory."

"Okay . . . but that door seems to be swinging wide open for me right now."

"We never truly know what the next moment will bring, Tory."

Ward Nine

Tory's last meal before leaving Old Saybrook for death row is brought to her in her room on a tray. One vegetarian patty. White rice. Peas and carrots. A roll. Butter in a small plastic container. Ketchup in a foil packet. A small packet each of salt and pepper. One eight-ounce can of Schweppes ginger ale. One container of vanilla pudding. One apple.

She eats none of it. She sits on her bed in pale violet pajamas, her chin on her knees, twirling her hair with her little finger, and staring at the TV—the TV that she never once turned on her whole time here. Finally, very late, after the ambient light filtered through the closed vertical blinds fades to total darkness, she drifts off to a fitful, restless sleep.

The Last Dialogue

"Who are you?"

"Hi, Tory."

"Who are you?"

"Look around you, Tory. What do you see?"

"I know this place."

"Of course you do."

"But how can I be here?"

"Where, Tory? How can you be where?"

"Underwater."

"That's right. You're underwater. What do you see?"

"That rock . . ."

"Yes?"

"That rock over there."

"Go on."

"I threw that rock into the water."

"Yes, you did."

"It's still here."

"That's right. It's exactly where you hurled it a long time ago."

"But how can I be . . . am I really underwater?"

"What do you think?"

"I . . . this is crazy."

"Okay. It's crazy. What now?"

"What do you mean?"

"What happens next, Tory?"

"Why are you asking me?"

"Because you're Tory!"

"Yes. I'm Tory."

"You are Victoria Abigail Troy. Daughter of Viviana Troy. Estranged daughter of Crouch Troy. Animal euthanasia technician."

"Who are you? Tell me."

"College graduate. Unpublished writer. Friend to many. Bearer of Tic Tacs. iPod enthusiast. Lapsed Catholic. Half-assed agnostic. Slim of build. Watcher of documentaries. Libra."

"Who are you?"

"I think you know."

"I don't."

"Oh, yes, you do."

"No."

"What do you see, Tory?"

"It doesn't matter what I *think* I see. I'm obviously dreaming. I'm lying in my bed in the Woodward Knolls Psychiatric Institute in Old Saybrook, Connecticut, in my pale violet pajamas, and I'm having a strange dream."

"Oh, yeah?"

"I'm not?"

"I didn't say you weren't. What do you see when you look at me?"

"I *can't* see you. In fact, I don't know how I'm hearing you. Everything is silent."

"That's right."

"I'm cold."

"Maybe you have low blood pressure. Or hypo-glycemia."

"I'm cold."

"No, you're not. You only think you are."

"What place is this?"

"Don't you recognize it?"

"It looks familiar . . ."

"Think hard, Tory."

"It's the house . . . the animal-shelter house."

"Ding-ding-ding! Correct!"

"But it doesn't look the same."

"What's different? What do you see?"

"It's empty . . . the walls are leaning in toward me . . . there are very weird shadows everywhere . . . I'm scared."

"No, you're not. You only think you are."

"I can't see anything outside the windows. Just black."

"Look again."

"Do I have to?"

"No. Of course not. Look again."

"There is something . . . I see shapes at the windows . . ."

"Look again, Tory."

"Oh, Jesus . . . there are faces at the windows."

"That's right, honey. Faces. Any of them look familiar?"

"I don't want to be here."

"It's a little late for that, my dear. What do you see, Tory?"

"I see . . ."

"Yes?"

"I see the dead."

"That's right. You see Marcy, and Jake, and Teresa, and all the others, right? They're the people you worked with, aren't they, Tory? They're the people you killed."

"Leave me alone."

"Did you know that razor wire was invented by the Germans during World War Two?"

"What?"

"Barbed wire was okay for cattle, but it was too easy for people to circumvent."

"What are you talking about?"

"The razors on razor wire look like crows with their wings spread open. Razor wire tops all the fences surrounding the Northern Correctional Institution."

"I don't understand."

"In Somers, Connecticut. The NCI is the home of Connecticut's death row. But you already knew that, didn't you, Tory? Would you like to hear some music?"

"What the hell are you talking about?"

"Perhaps a song?"

"I'm going insane."

"How about a poem? Perhaps something by Michael Wigglesworth?"

"I don't hear you."

"Of course you do."

"No."

"Wigglesworth was quite the raconteur. Except that every story he told usually involved someone being savaged for their sins."

"Stop."

"In 1662 he wrote a cheerful ditty called 'The Day of Doom.' Know it?"

"Why are you doing this to me?"

"It's all about hell and sin and the blaring of the trump and the return of Christ the King to hurl all the thieves and fornicators—and *murderers*—into the lake of fire."

"Fuck you."

"Do you like Steely Dan, Tory? 'My Old School'?"

"Leave me alone."

"How about Barry Manilow? Nat King Cole? Jerry Vale? Paula Cole? Sinatra? Nirvana?"

"One, two, three, four. Can you imagine an imaginary menagerie manager imagining managing an imaginary menagerie?"

"That won't do it, Tory."

"Cows graze in groves on grass which grows in grooves in groves."

"Or that either, dear."

"Do what?"

"Push the mental reset button. Reboot your brain. Reformat your psyche. Restart your gray matter. Relaunch your lucidity. You're in this for the duration, darling. Tongue twisters certainly won't get you out of it."

"No."

"Oh, yes. Most assuredly yes."

"I said no."

"Declawing is really a surgical amputation procedure. Did you know that?"

"Yes, I knew that. But it's sometimes necessary."

"Oh, really?"

"Yes."

"The empirical formula for pancuronium bromide is $C_{35}H_{60}Br_2N_2O_4$."

"Stop."

"Have you seen some of the new research on the psychic abilities of animals?"

"I'm not listening."

"Oh, yes, you are. I know that for a fact, Victorious."

"It's Victoria."

"Same thing."

"No, it's not."

"The British military awards a bronze cross to those who have performed acts of great courage and valor."

"So?"

"It's called a Victoria Cross."

"How nice for them."

"By the way, that's the real name of the Nile, you know."

"*What* is the real name of the Nile? You are exhausting me."

"Some sections of the Nile are called the Victoria Nile."

"That's not true."

"It certainly is. It's because old man ribber flows from Lake Victoria in Uganda into the Mediterranean."

"Why are you telling me these things?"

"That question should be punctuated with both a question mark and an exclamation point."

"What in the name of God are you talking about?"

"Just now—when you shouted, 'Why are you telling me these things?'—you were so emotional that I felt that a question mark wasn't enough. It needed more."

"Please stop."

"Did you know that there actually is a punctuation mark that combines a question mark and an exclamation point? It's called an interrobang. No one uses it, though."

"I don't feel well."

"Headache? TMJ? Brain tumor? Hangnail? Angina? Menstrual bloat? Shingles? Nausea? Leprosy?"

"I can't take any more of this."

"Really? That's too bad, dear, because we're only just getting started."

"I want to wake up. I'm going to throw up."

"No, you're not. You only think you are. Tell me, what do you see, Tory?"

"What is this room?"

"You know."

"I don't."

"You do. Look around. What do you see?"

"It's so bright."

"What do you see? There? In the corner."

"That's a . . . that can't be . . ."

"But it is, Tory. Tell me what you see."

"It's a pill bottle."

"That's right. But there's something unusual about that pill bottle, isn't there?"

"Yes."

"What is it?"

"It's the size of a goddamned refrigerator."

"That's right. It's a pill bottle the size of a goddamned refrigerator. And what's written on the side of the bottle, Tory?"

"The number six hundred fifty."

"That's right. And what significance is that number to you, Tory?"

"It's the number of milligrams."

"Milligrams of what?"

"Hydrocodone."

"That's right. In that bottle the size of a goddamned refrigerator is six hundred fifty milligrams of the hydrocodone you stashed away and considered using to kill yourself, isn't it, Tory?"

"Yes."

"Although if the pills inside the bottle are proportionately as large as the bottle, then perhaps the dosage is much higher per tablet. Someone should do the math."

"Now it's gone."

"Look around the room, Tory."

"No."

"Yes. Look around the room. What do you see?"

"I see a window. Covered by vertical blinds."

"That's right. By the way, those blinds are from Brilliant Blinds & Wallpaper in Tempe, Arizona, and that color is eggshell. It's made of a new material that doesn't collect dust. Very easy to clean. That color is very soothing, don't you think? Perfect for any soon-to-be corpse."

"This is driving me crazy. I feel like my head is about to explode."

"Well, try to keep your head from exploding just yet, okay?"

"What do you want from me?"

"There's someone here who wants to talk to you, Tory."

"Who?"

"She's an old friend."

"I don't have any friends."

"Sure you do, Tory. You've got Marcy . . . and Ann . . . and Renaldo . . . and even Jake."

"I'm not listening."

"Yeah, you keep saying that, but we both know it's bullshit, so why don't you just stop, okay?"

"Who wants to talk to me?"

"She's standing right behind you. I'll shut up for a while while you two old friends catch up."

"Hi, Tory."

"Who are you?"

"You don't recognize me?"

"No."

"No . . . of course you don't. You've never actually seen me in person."

"Who are you?"

"Maybe this'll help."

"Jesus Christ! Where did that baby come from? Wait . . . you're Sarah."

"That's right, Tory. And this is Annie Bananny."

"She's beautiful."

"Yes, I know. And I have you to thank for that."

"Me?"

"Of course. You created her. And me, for that matter. And I'm very grateful you didn't kill her. Granted, what you put me through was horrible, but all's well that ends well, I guess. Thanks for that."

"Why are you here?"

"To help you."

"But you're not real."

"I'm not?"

"This is a dream."

"Is it?"

"Yes. I'm sure of it."

"Well, then, if you're *sure* of it, then maybe it is. But then again, maybe it isn't. Maybe you only think it is."

"I'm so confused."

"I understand, Tory. I truly do. But there's no turning back now. You've got to see this thing through. All the way."

"What thing? What do I have to see all the way through?"

"You know."

"My death? My execution?"

"Perhaps. Perhaps not."

"What was it like, Sarah?"

"What was what like, Tory?"

"What you went through . . ."

"You mean with Annie?"

"Yes. What was it like believing that someone you loved had died?"

"Don't you know?"

"No."

"How could you not? *You* were the one who made *me* believe it. You were my God."

"Your God?"

"My creator. And I'm here to help you see this thing through, Tory."

"How?"

"That's completely up to you, Tory."

"What do you mean?"

"You're in charge."

"How the hell am *I* in charge? I feel like I have no control whatsoever."

"The mystery of love is greater than the mystery of death, Tory."

"Oh, yeah? It is?"

"So I've been told."

"By who, Sarah? Who told you that?"

"You did, Tory."

"What does it mean?"

"Exactly what it says. We can understand death. That's easy. You yourself believe it's a door, right?"

"How did you know that?"

"Oh, a little birdie told me."

"Very funny, Sarah."

"It was Caleb's bird, actually. The one at the end of your story that jumped on his shoulder after his mother died."

"Even funnier."

"Death is knowable, Tory, if only for its . . . inevitability. Its *presence*. Love, on the other hand, is a whole 'nuther ball game, it would seem."

"I'll take your word for it."

"No, Tory. It's not my word. It's yours."

"Right. I forgot. I'm your God."

"Yes, you are. All right. That's it. I'm finished. I'm leaving now."

"You are? Do you know what happens next?"

"Yes."

"Will you tell me before you leave?"

"No. Now, look at me."

"I am looking at you."

"What do you see, Tory?"

"I see . . . no, it can't be . . . but, then again, this is a dream, so I suppose . . ."

"What do you see when you look at me, Tory?"

"I . . . I see myself."

"That's right. Bye, Tory."

"So, did you enjoy visiting with one of your creations, Tory?"

"You again. Yes, I suppose."

"Look around the room, Tory. What do you see now?"

"That's me . . . lying on a table."

"Yes, it is."

"I don't want to be here."

"Sorry. No choice."

"I don't want to be here."

"Yes. I heard you the first time. But this is where you belong, my dear. This is most definitely where you belong."

"No."

"What do you see, Tory?"

"I told you. I see myself lying on a table."

"Go on."

"There's a sheet over me."

"That's right."

"Am I dead?"

"Oh, no. Haven't you ever watched *ER*, Tory?"

"What has that got to do with anything?"

"The sheet only comes up to your neck, right?"

"Yes . . . but . . ."

"The sheet is pulled over the face when the person's dead."

"So that means I'm alive on that table?"

"For now. What else do you see?"

"My arm is stretched out."

"It most certainly is. Can you see what's going on with that arm, Tory?"

"There's a tube in it."

"That's right. That tube is your passport to eternity, Tory. Once certain solutions begin flowing through that tube, it's hasta la vista, Tory."

"That noise . . ."

"What about it?"

"What is it?"

"You know what it is."

"I don't."

"Of course you do, Tory. You just won't admit it."

"No."

"Yes."

"No!"

"Say it."

"Why?"

"Because I said so."

"No."

"Tory . . ."

"All right, you pain in the ass! I hear dogs barking. Lots of dogs."

"Ding-ding-ding! Correct! Very good, Tory! And what do we have for Tory before we move on to the bonus round, Johnny? What's that? A body bag and a lifetime supply of Triscuits? How about that! But there're only six Triscuits here. But of course! That's all Tory will need for the minuscule slices of life remaining for her to live!"

"Very funny."

"Keep your eyes on those blinds."

"Why?"

"Just watch."

"The blinds are sliding open."

"That's right. Care to place a small wager on what you're going to see on the other side of that window? Behind the eggshell-colored vertical blinds?"

"No."

"Aren't you curious?"

"I don't even want to be here. These games you're playing with me are horrible."

"Games? You think I'm playing games with you? This isn't a game, Victorious Abigail. Believe me. Games have winners and losers. There are no winners here."

"Sometimes games end in a draw."

"Not today, darling."

"What does that mean?"

"It means what you think it means. There most assuredly will be a loser in our game today. And it won't be me."

"It'll be me, right?"

"Yes. And me."

"But you just said it wouldn't be you."

"Yes, I did, didn't I? But I'm you, Tory. And you've known that all along."

"What the hell is going on here? And what the hell are you talking about?"

"Never you mind, honey. Just keep your eyes on the bouncing ball—er, sliding blinds."

"I'm sick."

"No, you're not. You only think you are."

"Are those blinds opening? They don't look like they're even moving."

"Oh, yes. They're opening. They're opening very slowly . . . in tiny, tiny increments . . . little movements that reveal a minuscule slice of the window behind it . . . slowly . . . millimeters at a time. At this rate, it might take an eternity for the blinds to fully open."

"This is insane."

"No, that's not the word to describe it, Tory."

"Then what is the word? How would *you* describe all this craziness? How would you describe all this weird stuff coming from someone I can't even see?"

"Watch the blinds, Tory."

"No. I'm through with this. I'm not listening to you anymore. And why *am* I even listening to you? And talking to you? This is my dream and I should be in charge, not you."

"Ha-ha-ha. That's hilarious, Victorious."

"If you're me, then I'm in charge."

"What do you see through the window, Tory?"

"There are so many of them."

"Yes, Tory."

"Are these the animals I . . . ?"

"What do you think?"

"I'm afraid."

"Of what? The truth? Should I do that Jack Nicholson scene from *A Few Good Men* for you? *You can't handle the truth!*"

"Why are you doing this to me?"

"It's time to wrap things up, dear."

"What exactly does that mean?"

"Remember the song 'Good Night' on *The White Album*?"

"Yeah. Ringo sings it. John wrote it."

"That's right. Well, the first line says it all."

"*Now it's time to say good night?*"

"Right. And it is."

"Have I ever told you how much I loathe euphemisms?"

"That's not surprising. After all, you're a writer. Clear, plain language is always the writer's goal, isn't it?"

"Yes. So would you be so kind as to speak in clear, plain language, please?"

"You're irked by the *good night* reference?"

"Yes. Say what you mean."

"Okay. Fine. I will. Now it's time to die, Tory. Now it's time to die."

"No . . ."

"Oh, yes. Look at where you are now, dear."

"I'm on the table . . . there's a tube . . . oh, Jesus . . ."

"What can you see, Tory?"

"All I can see is the ceiling . . . I'm on my back . . . all I can see is the ceiling . . ."

"Turn your head, Tory. Look at the window. What do you see?"

"The animals are gone . . . I should say that prayer that old lady gave Sarah . . . I should say it . . . but I can't remember a word of it . . . I don't remember . . ."

"You're rambling, sweetheart. It's better to just be quiet and let it happen."

"No . . . I don't want to die . . . I . . ."

"Welcome back, my friends, to the show that never ends."

"I'm lying here . . . and you're singing Emerson, Lake and Palmer to me?"

"Sure. Why not?"

"That's cruel."

"I suppose it is. What do you see now behind the window, Tory?"

"I feel sick."

"No, you don't. You only think you do."

"I'm afraid."

"Look at the window, Tory. Tell me what you see."

"I see . . . you."

"That's right. And who am I, Tory? Go ahead. Say it."

"You're . . . you're . . . you're *me*."

"Yes."

"I want to wake up."

"Now what do you see, Tory?"

"I see . . ."

"Yes?"

"It's . . ."

"Go on."

"It's full of . . ."

"Hold it right there. Don't you dare even think you're going to tell me it's full of stars. Arthur C. Clarke and Stanley Kubrick are the only ones allowed to use that phrase. Do you understand?"

"But . . ."

"No buts. What do you see?"

"I'm afraid."

"You should be. What do you see?"

"The window's gone."

"Indeed it is. What do you see now, Tory?"

"I see myself."

"That's right. Tell me what you see."

"I'm looking down . . . I see myself lying on the table below me . . . there's an unbearable heat rushing through my body . . . I . . . I . . ."

I watch myself from above . . .

Euthanasia Day

The gas chamber is silent. Tory knows that the lethal carbon monoxide has done its job. Now comes the removal, the disposal, and the cleaning of the chamber.

She pulls on heavy yellow rubber gloves, dons a face mask, and steels herself for the task before her. This is getting harder, she thinks. Much harder.

Jake never leaves his office when Tory is emptying the chamber, and none of the front office staff comes anywhere near the back of the building.

This part of her job sometimes summons to mind stray lines from Eliot's "The Waste Land": "He who was living is now dead/We who were living are now dying/With a little patience."

Tory pauses a moment, her gloved hands hanging by

her side, her silent headphones embracing her neck. *With a little patience.* She feels something welling up inside her, but she can't identify the feeling. Is it sadness? Anger? Panic? Fear? She doesn't know, but she does know she has never felt like this. Yes, there have been moments when she has felt *all* of those emotions, in brief flashes that stabbed at her consciousness—but today is different.

And then, a sudden kaleidoscope of images and sounds floods her mind . . . the dogs and cats that have passed through the shelter over the past many months . . . the inside of the death chamber . . . the families walking through the kennel area, the children looking for the absolutely perfect pet . . . the heartbreakingly pleading expressions in the eyes of the caged animals as they mentally beg these strangers to take them home—*away from this place* . . . the mundane chatter of the office staff, oblivious to the reality of what is happening at the back of the building . . . her image of herself sitting on the couch in her mother's living room on any Friday night over these past few months, hugging a pillow, her legs curled beneath her, utterly unable to eat a thing until, at the earliest, Saturday night . . . the looming shadows the old house throws when the sun hits it a certain way . . . and then, once again, the animals . . . the animals . . .

Tory reaches out and grabs the door handle of the gas chamber.

She closes her eyes a moment and takes a breath. Then she opens her eyes . . . and then she opens the door.

And then Tory sees . . . she sees . . .

I watch myself from above . . . with newly luminous eyes . . .

"Jake! JAKE!! Call 911! It's Tory! I don't think she's breathing!"

The Hospital of St. Raphael

"She's so young."

"A heart attack at twenty-eight? Yeah, I'd say so. Why are you late?"

"Traffic's a bear. The Columbus Day Parade. They close Chapel Street. She came in by ambulance?"

"Yeah, but they had to shock her in the field."

"She worked at an animal shelter?"

"Let's up her Lasix a little . . . her morphine too."

"Yeah, Waterbridge."

"And she just collapsed?"

"Yeah. One of her coworkers found her lying on the floor in front of the shelter's gas chamber."

"Christ. And you've found no evidence of heart disease—no sclerotic buildup?"

"None. She's as healthy as you might expect her to be for somebody her age."

"Toxic gas?"

"No. They say the door won't open unless the gas is completely vented."

"Then what the hell happened?"

"I don't know. But they said one of the animals didn't die."

"What do you mean?"

"The guy who manages the place—Jay somebody—he said that when they found her on the floor, there was a kitten sitting next to her."

"You mean from the gas chamber—one of the animals they euthanized?"

"Yeah. The cat didn't die."

"Oh, my God! Do you think that did it? Caused her to go into cardiac arrest?"

"Who knows? I've heard it can happen."

"She's so young, though. And does seem to be in good shape."

"She should bounce back pretty quick then. All things considered."

"Yeah. Wanna go for coffee?"

"You read my mind."

October 21, 2002

Jacob Slezak, Manager
Waterbridge Animal Shelter
167 Gilman Place
New Haven CT 06510

Dear Jake,
This letter is to inform you that I, Victoria Troy,
do hereby resign my position at the Waterbridge
Animal Shelter, effective immediately.

Sincerely,
Victoria A. Troy

362 Elizabeth Anne Road • New Haven, CT 06512
(203) 790-1953 • torytroy@snet.net

EPILOGUE

Saturday, November 2, 2002
All Souls' Day

The young woman sits, chin on knees, staring out at the water.

The rock on which she sits is dark gray and cold, with tendrils of seaweed and patches of lichen clinging to it.

She does not move as she gazes at the horizon.

She does not notice the chill November air; she does not smell the brine; she does not listen to the sluicing of the waves.

But her eyes see more now.

The heart attack did not kill her, although it did spur her to quit a job she thought she had been able to handle.

She relives that day over and over; sometimes in the night when the trees move and the branches scratch the panes of her bedroom windows; sometimes in the afternoon, when driving to the store or bending to empty out the dryer; sometimes in early morning, when her new kitten, sleeping beside her, wakes up and climbs onto her chest to signal it's time to eat.

She relives the moment she opened the heavy door and saw the bodies of the dead animals—all of them lying on their sides, their eyes closed. . .

She relives the moment she heard the sad, frail sound of a tiny white-and-black kitten crying.

She relives the moment she looked down and saw it— sitting between two dead dogs, its tail wrapped around its body in fear, looking up at her, its wide eyes pleading.

And then Tory relives—*what?* She still doesn't know what she experienced. She still doesn't fully understand what happened to her in that dark time when she was . . . someplace else. So she focuses instead on the transformation it caused, though she can't forget the . . . the details . . . the people she didn't know, the voices she had never heard before, the bizarre, free-floating scenarios, the fears, the sadness . . .

The *details*.

She doesn't remember Marcy finding her, unconscious on the floor in front of the chamber, her heart literally shocked into silence, the kitten mewing beside her.

She remembers awakening in the hospital, but she doesn't remember the shouts before that, or the EMTs, or the ambulance, or the tears of her coworkers and her mother.

Later, she thought about what had happened, about what she lived through in those unreal . . . what? seconds? minutes? ages? when her heart wasn't beating. She thought about the horror of what she had done, her talks with Dr. Bexley, the trial, and the verdict. And yes, she thought about watching her prone body from above as she received the lethal injection . . . and how, for a millisecond, she saw herself lying below on the floor in front of the euthanasia chamber. She remembered sensing her soul separating from her body and traveling into a realm of light, the kaleidoscope of images and voices that rushed through her consciousness—a ball of light that appeared behind her newly luminous eyes until all of time stood still. And then she thought about awakening in the hospital and the sight of her mother's terrified face when she opened her eyes.

Tory stares at the horizon, not seeing the ponderous drift of a hull-down tanker, the whitecaps, or the soaring arcs of the Caspian terns with their shiny black crests. Instead, her eyes see more: the glorious light, the boundless sky, the dark maria of a diurnal moon.

There is a rock in these waters and her mind turns to it often. It will be there for eons, there where she once hurled it, the water washing over it with every tidal swing.

Tory feels a stirring against her chest and looks down. Bexley is awake, curled in the baby carrier, and he wants to be fed. Now.

She scratches him behind his ear, smiling at the purr coming from deep inside the little body, and rises to her feet.

Her hair is a little longer now. As a chill wind ruffles it, she wonders momentarily if she should get it cut.

She stares out at the water one last time, the vivid colors of refracted light on the waves looking surreal to her.

Her clear green eyes squint against the wind as she turns away from this bright, cold place.

As she walks along the rocky promontory toward the beach, she sees a small white dog pawing at a discarded hamburger wrapper in the sand, his hunger and desperation obvious even from a distance.

As soon as her feet reach the sand, she heads straight for him, grinning at Bexley's retreat into the recesses of the baby carrier.

When the dog spots her, he cowers and begins to growl, frightened and threatened, but unwilling to surrender the meager scrap in the wrapper. She stops a few feet away from him. He looks at her with a mixture of puzzlement and fear, but does not flee.

She reaches into a side pocket of her jacket and pulls out a Ziploc bag filled with fresh ground beef. Some days she carries bird seed, some days tuna for stray cats. Today it's meat. She opens the bag, upends it, and dumps the contents onto the hard sand.

The dog's eyes widen, but he still doesn't move.

Tory puts the empty bag back in her pocket and begins walking toward the parking lot, knowing the dog won't go near the meat as long as she is standing near it. She glances back and sees him move slowly, tentatively, toward it. When he gets close enough, he sniffs it, then begins to devour it. The waves roll up onto the sand. The dog ignores them.

When she reaches her car, she looks back one last time. Multicolored sparks of sunlight reflected off the water dance in her eyes, and she smiles.

ACKNOWLEDGMENTS

I would like to thank my literary agent and dear friend, John White, for his help and advice. John played an enormous part in getting this book into your hands.

I would also like to thank my editor, Ann Harris. Fortune smiled upon me when I was blessed with Ann as the conductor of this symphony. Her wisdom and guidance were invaluable. My appreciation also goes to all the fine folks at Bantam Dell, especially Irwyn Applebaum, Matthew Martin, Nita Taublib, Judy Young, and Meghan Keenan.

I thank Laura Ross at Black Dog & Leventhal and Salvatore V. Didato, Ph.D., for allowing me (Dr. Bexley, actually) to use several personality tests from Dr. Didato's book *The Big Book of Personality Tests* (Black Dog & Leventhal, 2003). Thank you both for helping Dr. Bexley better understand Tory.

I also appreciate the support of family, friends, and colleagues who cheered me on: Carter Spignesi, Steve and Marge Rapuano, Frank Mandato, Mike Lewis, Dolores Fantarella, Dr. Michael Luchini, Dr. Edward Goglia and my friends at Ridgehill Animal Hospital, Alyse "Ally McSpero" Spero-Geremia, Mary Toler, Charlie Fried, Jim Cole, George Beahm, Stan Wiater, Tyson Blue, Dave Hinchberger, Jay Halpern, Andy Rausch, Ann LaFarge, Colin Andrews, Paul, Andy, Chris, Bill, and Mike at the East Haven P.O., Laura Ross, Marilyn Allen, my good friend Adrienne, and the inestimable Bill Savo.

And lastly, I thank my wife Pam, my mother Lee, and my sister Janet—extraordinary women all.

Stephen Spignesi
New Haven, Conn.
All Souls' Day, 2004

ABOUT THE AUTHOR

STEPHEN SPIGNESI is the author of more than three dozen nonfiction books. *Dialogues* is his first novel. He lives in Connecticut with his wife, Pam, and their cat, Carter. He can be reached via his Web site, www.stephenspignesi.com.